Jessica Huntley

# THE DARKNESS THAT CAME BEFORE

## Book 3 of The Darkness Series

# About Jessica Huntley

Jessica Huntley is an ex-British soldier and Personal Trainer turned author of addictive psychological thriller books. She has spent almost three years writing and is now the author of eleven books, including two trilogies, two standalone thrillers, an anthology, a co-written horror project and a novella.

She writes books for thriller readers who like their stories dark and twisty with complex, yet memorable characters, who often suffer from relatable mental health disorders. When she isn't writing, Jessica is either keeping fit, copywriting, walking her dog or looking after her young son.

Sign up to my email list to receive news about upcoming book releases and download a FREE thriller novella by visiting my website: www.jessicahuntleyauthor.com

# Other books by Jessica Huntley

### The Darkness Series

The Darkness Within Ourselves
The Darkness That Binds Us
The Darkness That Came Before

### My ... Self Series

My Bad Self: A Prequel Novella
My Dark Self
My True Self
My Real Self

### Standalone Thrillers

Jinx
How to Commit the Perfect Murder in Ten Easy Steps

### Writing in collaboration with other authors

The Summoning
HorrorScope: A Zodiac Anthology – Vol 1

# Acknowledgements

A huge thanks must go to my loyal readers, who have been with me since I published my debut novel, Book 1 in The Darkness Series, The Darkness Within Ourselvs. You wanted more from that book and I'm so glad you convinced me to write two more!

Thank you, as always, to my editor, Jennifer Kay Davies who continues to edit my books with great detail, care and attention.

Thank you to my wonderful author friends (you know who you are) who always have my back and support me through the hard times when writing gets very lonely.

Thank you to my amazing Beta Readers, Hayley Anderton, Kimberley (@theariteslibrary) and Autumn (@musictinkerbelle). Your insightful and helpful notes helped me iron out some inconsistencies and ensured the story was wrapped up how I imagined.

# Connect with Me

Find and connect with me online via the following platforms.

Sign up to my email list via my website to be notified of future books and receive a twice-monthly author newsletter and also receive a **FREE thriller novella called My Bad Self.**

www.jessicahuntleyauthor.com

Follow me on Facebook: Jessica Huntley - Author - @jessica.reading.writing

Follow me on Instagram:  @jessica_reading_writing

Follow me on Twitter:  @jess_read_write

Follow me on TikTok: @jessica_reading_writing

Follow me on Goodreads: jessica_reading_writing

*This book is dedicated to the real Lee Man*
*who hid his own darkness from the world.*
*I'm sorry we never realised*
*until it was too late.*

*And I'm sorry I never let you read the books*
*I wrote when we were kids.*

*This one is for you.*

**To: StephenPMallow@londontimes.co.uk**
**From: anon.anon@hotmail.co.uk**
**Date: Friday, January 12, 2024, 09:15:33 GMT**
**Subject: Another body found in Cherry Hollow**

*Dear Mr Mallow,*

*You may be interested to hear that another body has been found in Cherry Hollow, the town in the Lake District you visited in May 2022. This news has not yet been released to the media, so you are the first to know.*

*The body was found yesterday in a small cave at the bottom of Beaker Ravine, a place I understand you're familiar with. It has been down there a long time, probably close to forty years or maybe more. It's too soon to tell who the remains belong to, but I thought you'd appreciate the heads up.*

*I understand you have a fascination with the town, and I know you got scared the last time you were there, but it's time you came back, Mr Mallow, and finished what you started.*

*The Creature has returned – or maybe it never left – and it's haunting the town.*

*I'm telling you because I read your article, the one you published after you visited the first time. You want to find out the truth as much as I do.*

*Someone in this town isn't telling the truth. I'm fed up with the lies.*

*You're welcome.*

*From,*

*Anonymous*

***********************************************************

To: anon.anon@hotmail.co.uk
From: StephenPMallow@londontimes.co.uk
Date: Friday, January 12, 2024, 09:18:46 GMT
Subject: RE: Another body found in Cherry Hollow

*Dear Anonymous,*

*Who the hell are you?*

*Kind regards,*
*Stephen P. Mallow*
*Journalist for the London Times*

***********************************************************

To: StephenPMallow@londontimes.co.uk
From: anon.anon@hotmail.co.uk
Date: Friday, January 12, 2024, 09:25:16 GMT
Subject: RE: Another body found in Cherry Hollow

*Dear Mr Mallow,*

*Anonymous means I don't want to tell you my name.*

*From,*
*Anonymous*

********************************************************

To: anon.anon@hotmail.co.uk
From: StephenPMallow@londontimes.co.uk
Date: Friday, January 12, 2024, 09:28:22 GMT
Subject: RE: Another body found in Cherry Hollow

*Dear Anonymous,*

*Ah, you're a smart guy (or girl). Okay, I get it. But I'm afraid you're asking the wrong man. There is nothing on this earth that will convince me to return to Cherry Hollow. You're wasting your time. I'll happily provide the email address of one of my colleagues who will be more than happy to assist you.*

*Kind regards,*
*Stephen P. Mallow*
*Journalist for the London Times*

**********************************************************

**To: StephenPMallow@londontimes.co.uk**
**From: anon.anon@hotmail.co.uk**
**Date: Friday, January 12, 2024, 09:35:02 GMT**
**Subject: RE: Another body found in Cherry Hollow**

*Dear Mr Mallow,*

*It must be you. Please.*

> *Come to Cherry Hollow.*
> *I need help with this investigation.*
> *I can't do it by myself.*
> *I don't trust anyone.*

*From,*

*Anonymous*

**********************************************************

**To: anon.anon@hotmail.co.uk**
**From: StephenPMallow@londontimes.co.uk**
**Date: Friday, January 12, 2024, 09:37:22 GMT**
**Subject: RE: Another body found in Cherry Hollow**

*Dear Anonymous,*

*Have we met before? Who are you? I don't understand why it must be me. Surely, that's what the police are for. They can help you.*

*Kind regards,*
*Stephen P. Mallow*
*Journalist for the London Times*

******************************************************

**To: StephenPMallow@londontimes.co.uk**
**From: anon.anon@hotmail.co.uk**
**Date: Friday, January 12, 2024, 09:48:58 GMT**
**Subject: RE: Another body found in Cherry Hollow**

*Dear Mr Mallow,*

*No, we haven't met. I don't trust the police. It must be you. Because if you saw The Creature or are so scared of what happened when you came here last time, then it means you have your own darkness to face. Just like I do. I believe you can help me. I believe you can uncover the truth about Cherry Hollow and The Creature once and for all.*

*There is nothing I can say or give you in compensation, but ... sometimes we have to face up to the darkness and what we've done, don't you agree?*

*Cherry Hollow needs your help.*

*I need your help.*

*Please. Come.*

*From,*

*Anonymous*

*************************************************************

To: anon.anon@hotmail.co.uk
From: StephenPMallow@londontimes.co.uk
Date: Friday, January 12, 2024, 10:02:25 GMT
Subject: RE: Another body found in Cherry Hollow

*Dear Anonymous,*

*I'm sorry, but the answer is still no. I wish you luck.*

*Kind regards,*
*Stephen P. Mallow*
*Journalist for the London Times*

********************************************************

To: StephenPMallow@londontimes.co.uk
From: notdelivered@hotmail.co.uk
Date: Friday, January 12, 2024, 10:02:59 GMT
Subject: RE: Another body found in Cherry Hollow

*Message not delivered. The email address you provided no longer exists.*

********************************************************

To: KevinWhite@londontimes.co.uk
From: StephenPMallow@londontimes.co.uk
Date: Friday, January 12, 2024, 10:05:01 GMT
Subject: A story in Cherry Hollow...

*Hey Kevin,*

*Any issues with me taking a few days to go back to Cherry Hollow? I'm thinking of heading up there maybe next week. There's a possible situation that may make for another decent story. I'll type up a quick story to print for the 15th of January to drum up some interest in the meantime.*

*What do you think?*

*Kind regards,*
*Stephen P. Mallow*
*Journalist for the London Times*

********************************************************

**To: StephenPMallow@londontimes.co.uk**
**From: KevinWhite@londontimes.co.uk**
**Date: Friday, January 12, 2024, 10:10:32 GMT**
**Subject: RE: A story in Cherry Hollow...**

*Stephen,*

*That freaky town that's haunted in the Lake District by some weird creature? Sure. Go for it. Make sure your life insurance is in place before you go.*
  *Good luck. Keep me updated.*

*Kind regards,*
*Kevin White*
*Editor in Chief at the London Times*

# Prologue

### *5 July 1980*

He wasn't thinking clearly, nor was he fully aware of his surroundings. Something – he didn't know what – had pulled him to this spot by an invisible rope. He couldn't understand what was happening. Darkness clouded his mind, stopping his brain from making the decision to turn and walk back home, back to safety.

With every footstep, the darkness had intensified. And the rope had pulled him tighter, urging him forward. The rope was a vice, constricting his chest. The only way to feel relief had been to keep moving, putting one foot in front of the other.

It wasn't until he'd emerged from the thick wood and reached the edge of the steep cliff that he felt as if he were back in control of his body. The fog and darkness in his head lifted, almost as if he'd been in a trance or hypnotic state.

*Where the hell am I?*

He looked down at his feet, noticing his shorts were torn at the hem, his legs dirty and scratched. But there was no pain, no stinging from the long nettles he'd walked through and no burning from the small scratches made by the thorns that had clung to his skin and clothing.

He was standing by a deep chasm: Beaker Ravine.

He vaguely knew of it but had never visited before. It wasn't a well-known location. In fact, most of the locals in Cherry Hollow barely knew it existed. He'd only heard about it from old Mrs Price when he visited to cut her grass every week after her husband suddenly passed away. She told him the ravine was a magical place, and she'd spent many a day in her childhood playing at the top of it, attempting to throw rocks across the vast chasm to the other side.

The sun had tucked itself behind a dark cloud and the wind had picked up, causing his long fringe to dance across his forehead and stick to his damp eyelashes. He shouldn't be here, but he couldn't bear to stay at home a moment longer. He wanted to be out with his friends, but he was alone. All alone. And had been for weeks. It felt as if the earth had shifted under his feet recently, and he couldn't find his balance. Without his friends, he didn't know what to do.

That was when he saw the tree, teetering on the edge of the ravine like a prospective jumper.

Over the past two weeks, the area had received an abundance of heavy rainfall. So much, the ground was saturated, unable to soak up a single fluid ounce more. The river below was engorged, the sheer force of water carving new paths at the bottom.

The large tree by the ravine was dangerously close to collapsing. The huge amount of rain had soaked the roots, weakening them, and causing them to crack.

It was only a matter of time before rot settled in and the tree gave up the fight, surrendering itself to gravity. That was how he felt – like he wanted to give up, end it all and accept his fate.

He stepped closer to the tree.

Another strong gust whipped across the chasm, catching him off guard.

The tree groaned as the wind caught its branches and leaves, acting like a sail. He watched as the tree, which had more than likely stood proud for hundreds of years, finally succumbed to age and gravity.

It let out an almighty roar. The roots snapped like kindling, crying out in pain as they split apart.

He stood with his mouth open as the tree fell sideways across the ravine, coming to a rest with a thud that caused the ground to tremble as if an earthquake had struck. It spanned the entire gap, like a makeshift wooden bridge.

He didn't move a muscle. Had the tree waited for him to arrive before falling?

No. That was ridiculous. There was no way that was possible, and yet ... it was entirely possible because he'd only been standing there less than a minute before it had collapsed.

Was it a mere coincidence?

Or was the falling of this tree a symbol of something more ...

The start of something ...

Something dark ...

# Chapter One

## Stephen

### *22 January 2024 – 14:05 p.m.*

The heater in his beat-up blue Vauxhall was on the brink of giving up completely when he pulled into the tiny car park of The Cherry Tree, the local hotel in the picturesque town of Cherry Hollow. Burning metal, or whatever it was, wafted through the air vents, blowing straight onto his face. It didn't matter now. He had arrived at his destination, luckily having not suffocated during his journey.

He'd visited the town once before, a couple of years ago, but had forgotten how far it was to drive from London to the Lake District. Including a pit stop for fuel, food and to empty his bladder, it had taken just shy of six hours. And when the temperature outside barely hit one degree, it made for a less-than-pleasant journey. He could barely feel his feet or his fingers. In fact, he'd had to put his gloves on for the final two hours just so he could drive the car safely. Changing up and down gears around the narrow country roads had been somewhat difficult with numb hands. And then, when the heater spluttered and chucked out warm air that smelled like a bonfire, he'd known the rest of his journey would be hell. Indeed, it had been.

Stephen pulled into a parking space, able to take his pick because his was the only car there. He looked through the dirty windscreen at the hotel. Despite the town being relatively small and quaint, The Cherry Tree was a decent place to stay. It couldn't be booked via Booking.com or any other travel site. He had to book directly through their website, which could benefit from an upgrade. It surprised him the place wasn't more popular with tourists, although he may have had something to do with that, having written an article about the town last year that had been more than a little damaging to the town's economy and reputation.

But that wasn't his fault. He'd only written the truth. It was his job after all. Well, sometimes he liked to stretch the truth ever so slightly. There was no harm in that.

And that was why he was back, even though he swore he'd never return after the harrowing events of his last trip. If it hadn't been for the strange, anonymous email he'd received, he wouldn't have been here at all, or even considered coming back.

His last visit still haunted him, and it was why his suitcase contained more than double his usual dose of benzodiazepines, effective in treating anxiety. His doctor had prescribed them when he'd complained of not being able to sleep and his nyctophobia had returned with a vengeance. He'd not always been afraid of the dark. It had only come about after a traumatic childhood experience, but since visiting Cherry Hollow in 2022, it had spiralled out of control and now, the only way of getting through the night was by being loaded up on medication with a strong night light beside his bed. He'd also packed the night light.

His legs creaked and groaned as he hauled himself out of the car. He stretched his back and twisted to the side until he heard a satisfying crack.

A woman walked along the pavement at the bottom of the car park carrying a couple of shopping bags. Her grey hair poked out from under an oversized bobble hat, and she was bundled up in a thick coat, complete with a scarf and matching gloves. Her eyes drifted up to him and he waved overenthusiastically, but the gesture caused her to increase her speed and avert her eyes. Within seconds, she was gone.

Stephen frowned. The last time he'd been here, the town had been a lot friendlier. Well, not *friendly* per se, but they'd been happy to talk to him about the area and the local people. However, as soon as he questioned them about the events of nearly twenty-six years ago, they'd clammed up.

But he wasn't here to talk about Kieran Jones and the fact his murder had been covered up by his four best friends.

He was here about the body that had supposedly been found dating back to the early 1980s, a full eighteen years before Kieran Jones had been killed.

The lights flickered in reception when he shoved the door open using his right shoulder. The door had stuck last time too, but now, thanks to the damp and cold weather, it had got a lot worse. At least the place was warm. He stamped his feet on the welcome mat for two reasons: to get the excess water and dirt off his boots that he'd tramped in from the car park and to force some feeling back into his toes.

No one was behind the front desk, so he took the opportunity to look around, checking for any changes. The small bar area was off to the left, the lit fire giving off a warming, ambient glow. His favourite leather armchair was still there, which he remembered from last time. He made a mental note to get himself a whiskey tonight and settle down in front of the fire with a good book. Ah, damn, he hadn't brought a book to read. Hopefully, it didn't matter because by tonight he'd have some information to read about the body that was found over two weeks ago.

But that was the strange thing. There was nothing, other than his own article which hadn't been published yet, about a body being found in this town. So, either the police hadn't reported it to the mainstream media yet, or they were pretending like it hadn't been found. Kevin, his boss at the London Times, hadn't wanted to publish the article until he had solid proof there even was a body, as an anonymous email wasn't enough to go on.

It wasn't normal. Why did Cherry Hollow keep so many secrets when it came to how many dead bodies it had in its closet ... metaphorically speaking?

He looked up at the sound of approaching footsteps.

'Ah, Mr Mallow. Welcome. It's so lovely to see you again,' said a chirpy female voice.

A woman he recognised from his last visit entered from a doorway behind the desk, smiling from ear to ear. Her simple uniform of black trousers and a white shirt, slightly open at the collar and with a name tag over her left breast that read *Rachel*, emphasised her slight figure. Her blonde hair was pulled into a neat ponytail and her young, fresh face was free from too much make-up.

'Yes, hello,' said Stephen, stepping up to the desk and setting his suitcase down.

'Did you have a pleasant journey here?' asked Rachel, typing a few words into the computer.

'Not really. It's cold as fuck out there.' Rachel looked up at his use of language. 'Sorry,' he added. 'The car heater broke, and I think my hands and feet might be suffering from the beginnings of frostbite.'

'You're welcome to warm up by the fire while I take your case to your room.'

'Oh, no, thank you, but that won't be necessary. Is it definitely room 11 you've put me in?'

Rachel nodded as she looked back at the computer screen. 'I think so ... Oh, I'm sorry, but no. We can't put you in that room as there's no hot water. I think it's something to do with the pipes freezing. Jordan Evans, the local handyman, left recently, so it's taking longer to fix than usual. I've put you in room 10 instead, which is slightly bigger and has a much better view across the valley. I hope that's okay.'

A cold shiver ran up his spine.

No, no, no, no ...

He shook his head vigorously, making himself dizzy. 'No, I'm sorry, but I have to have room 11.'

Rachel looked up as a blush crept over her cheeks. 'I'm sorry, Mr Mallow, but there's no hot water in that room, and we don't have any separate shower facilities for you to use.'

'I don't care. I want room 11.' He sounded abrupt, but he didn't care. He watched as Rachel's face turned a deep shade of red. 'I'm sorry … I didn't mean to be rude. It's just … please put me in room 11. I don't care about the hot water.'

Rachel opened her mouth, probably about to argue her case further, but then nodded and typed on the computer. 'Very well, Mr Mallow. The plumber from the next town over should be arriving sometime tomorrow.'

'That's fine. I plan on being out most of the day anyway.'

Rachel finished typing and looked up, her colour finally returning to normal. 'I hope you have a lovely stay at The Cherry Tree. Are you sure you don't need help carrying your bag up the stairs? Room 11 is on the top floor.'

'I'll manage, thanks. Um, actually, while I'm here, you don't happen to know who I need to speak to about the body that was found a couple of weeks ago, do you?'

Rachel sucked in a breath and held it. Her eyes darted from side to side, looking like a deer caught in headlights. Clearly, she wasn't expecting to be questioned.

'Sorry, I should probably clarify a bit. You remember I'm a journalist? I'm here to find out what happened and write a story.'

Instead of turning red, Rachel turned pale as she said, 'You're not writing more about … T-The Creature, are you? The townspeople weren't happy the last time you were here. I'm not sure digging into the past is entirely necessary. Sometimes it's best to let the past stay in the past … you know what I mean?' Her eyes widened and she shuddered, wrapping her arms around her body like a shield.

'I realise the past can be difficult to talk about, but this town has been bottling it up for decades, and now a forty-odd-year-old corpse has been found. Why hasn't anyone reported the person missing? I've checked the newspaper archives from that time, and there's nothing about a missing person in this town. The only one that pops up is Kieran Jones, and we all know how that turned out. Plus, why hasn't the mainstream media been informed about this body?'

Rachel lowered her head, avoiding his eye contact. 'I'm sorry, Mr Mallow, but I don't know anything about it.'

'You said Jordan Evans has left town now, yes?'

Her head perked up. 'Yes, only a few weeks ago.'

'What about Brooke Willows?'

'Yes, her too.'

Stephen bit his lip, thinking. 'Is there anyone in this town who lived here forty years ago?'

Rachel scratched her neck. 'Yes, I think so. Detective Williams has lived here all his life. Possibly one or two other older residents, but I can't remember their names. The police station is situated just outside the town. If you follow the main road left out of the car park, you'll eventually drive right by it.'

Stephen nodded as he picked up his case. 'Thank you for your help.'

'Would you like to book in at the hotel restaurant tonight?' asked Rachel, handing him the key to his room. It had a large wooden number 11 attached to it.

'Yes, please.'

'Is eight o'clock okay?'

'Perfect.'

'See you then, Mr Mallow. I hope you enjoy the rest of your day.'

Stephen climbed the steep stairs to the top floor and followed the narrow hallway around to the right, through a set of double doors. He stopped outside door number 11 and set his case down. The key slid effortlessly into the lock and the door swung open with a groan.

His eyes found the light switch and, before he stepped a foot into the room, he reached in and flicked the lights on and off seventeen times in quick succession.

Once finished, he picked up his bag and stepped into the room, feeling the build-up of pressure in his chest dissipate and float away. He was much more relaxed when things stayed the same.

Sometimes, he thought his OCD was under control. But other times, like just now downstairs, it threatened to run away with him.

Being in this town again was already putting him on edge. What was it about this place that filled people with a dark dread? Or was it just him? The Creature had certainly turned this town from quaint and happy to disturbed and terrifying, but was there something more to it?

The reason he'd fled the town so quickly last year was because of what he'd witnessed at Beaker Ravine, the place where the nightmares seemed to originate.

Whatever it was … it was time to face his own darkness and find out the truth. Just like whoever it was who'd sent the email had said. Come to think of it, how had that person known about his past? Or had they merely taken a wild guess?

It was true though. He was fascinated with this town. Not just the town itself, but the mysteries and lies nestled in the middle of it. On the outside, it looked like the perfect place to visit on a summer holiday, but in reality, there was something much more sinister here.

Did he believe in dark creatures, hauntings, and ghosts? No.

But he did believe the human mind was a fragile and complicated thing, and somehow this town had created its very own monster. Demon. Creature. Whatever they wanted to call it. It was real to them and that's all that mattered.

He was certain when the truth came out, it would make one hell of a story.

# Chapter Two
## Olivia
### *22 January 2024 – 14:30 p.m.*

Olivia fumbled with the keys through her gloved hands as she unlocked the front door to her house. She stepped inside and involuntarily shivered as the warmth enveloped her. Frank liked the heating on all year round, despite the cost-of-living crisis, but in January the boiler seemed to be working overtime to heat the large house, although she did turn the heating down in most of the rooms because her husband rarely left his bedroom now, so there was little point in heating rooms that weren't occupied. She only used her bedroom, the kitchen and the lounge. She refused to allow him to freeze during his final weeks on this earth. He always seemed to be cold, even wearing a wool hat in bed, which wasn't surprising considering his illness had transformed his once muscular body to mere skin and bone, but it meant Olivia had to strip her layers of outer clothing quickly before she started sweating as soon as she stepped through the front door.

Her friend would be here any minute and she was only just getting back from the shops, having been waylaid by Hayley, the owner of The Bean Café, who had asked after Frank. Hayley, despite her previous coldness towards Brooke, Olivia's oldest daughter, continued to visit Olivia each week, usually on a Tuesday, and she almost always brought fresh cookies from the café. But now Olivia was running late. She knew she should have taken the car to the shops, but it was icy outside, and she hated driving when the roads were slippery. She preferred to walk everywhere these days. It kept her joints mobile, even though her dodgy ankle played up during the colder months. Despite having broken it many years before, the hospital had never set it quite right. But she was grateful she could still get about. Besides, the walk had done her good and there was now a healthy flush to her cheeks. However, that may have been from carrying the heavy shopping bags. Next time, she'd take her trolley, even though it made her feel like her grandmother. God rest her soul.

Olivia hung up her thick coat, hat and scarf and then stuffed her gloves into the coat pockets so she didn't lose them, before carrying the bags into the kitchen. She hefted them onto the counter, but before she put anything away, she hurried up the stairs and popped her head around the door to Frank's bedroom.

His eyes were closed, and his arms rested across his chest, a book underneath them. She watched his chest rise and fall in time with the beeping on the machine next to him. The oxygen mask was resting by the side of his head should he need it. He wasn't due his next set of medication for another hour and, later tonight, she needed to give him a sponge bath, as she hadn't managed to get around to doing it yesterday.

Olivia crept into the room and gently placed a kiss on her husband's forehead, then removed the book from his grasp, sliding the tatty bookmark in between the pages where it had laid open, so he didn't lose his spot. His lips twitched. She squeezed his hand to let him know she was home, but he was still asleep, so she made sure the monitor was working properly before returning downstairs to unpack the shopping.

'Is it all of these plants you need ripping out, Olivia?' asked Emma from the flowerbed at the end of the garden.

Olivia looked up from where she was kneeling on her gardening pad, leaning over another flowerbed nearby. 'Yes, please, Emma. It all needs to come out.'

The garden was in a dire state and had been ever since Frank had fallen ill almost eight months ago. She'd had to let the weeds grow, the flowerbeds overrun and the grass take over. She couldn't afford a gardener on top of everything else.

Olivia planned on starting from scratch with the garden to make it more manageable for her as she got older. She was fifty-nine, and although she was fit enough to carry two shopping bags back from town and up the steep hill to her house, she knew she wouldn't be able to keep up with the gardening, housekeeping and errand running as well as she did now for much longer. She only had to look at her husband lying in bed, dying from an invisible illness rotting away his insides, to know that life and health were fleeting.

'I'm on it,' replied Emma.

Olivia smiled. She and Emma Smithson had become close friends over the past few months. Emma had moved to Cherry Hollow at the end of October last year, but already their friendship had flourished. Unfortunately, it wasn't because of their mutual enjoyment of chatting over tea and cake. It was due to much more sinister and devastating circumstances.

Emma's wife, Linda, had tragically died in a house fire on Halloween night, only a week after moving in. Emma had been alone in her grief, or so she'd thought. Having only lived in the town a week, she hadn't made any firm friends, but Olivia had welcomed her and her teenage son, Alex, into her home while Emma had got back on her feet. Now, their friendship was cemented. Emma had been through her share of loss and heartbreak, and Olivia had had her share of it too, especially with Frank now so close to departing this life.

Emma and her son now lived in Jordan Evans' old family home, which he'd sold to them at a decent price before moving out of town with his girlfriend, Olivia's daughter, Brooke. She and Jordan now lived in a beautiful country house in the New Forest. Olivia hadn't been able to leave Frank and visit them yet, but soon … soon it wouldn't be an issue.

Cancer would take him eventually.

Of course, that's what the doctors told her was sapping his life away, but Olivia knew it wasn't the whole reason. Cancer was just the name given to the sickness within, but deep down inside was something much darker that had been growing for a long time. They both knew it, but neither spoke about it.

Olivia looked over at her friend. She was proud of Emma for how far she'd come in battling her dark demons. Emma had suffered from severe post-traumatic stress disorder after losing her seven-year-old daughter, Phoebe, two years ago. Upon arriving in Cherry Hollow, Emma had believed her daughter was still alive and had spoken and interacted with her daily, much to the shock and dismay of her wife and son.

But, when Linda died, Emma broke free from her darkness and appeared to make a miraculous recovery. She was now seeing the local therapist, Dr Allan, about the loss of her daughter, her wife and her ex-husband who had taken his own life soon after Phoebe's death. She had a long way to go, but Olivia believed she was improving each time she saw her, which was several times a week. Usually, Emma came to help with gardening twice a week, and they also met at the Saturday coffee morning at the community centre, a place where most of the women in town could catch up with the local gossip.

Olivia couldn't leave the house for too long due to caring for her husband, but Emma was happy to come and visit. Plus, working in the garden, despite the cold temperature at the moment, was doing them both a world of good, even though Olivia's knees and back ached at the end of the day, something she supposed she had to get used to as the years went by.

'Right, I think that's the last of it,' said Emma as she dumped a tangle of weeds and grass onto the compost heap. 'It's looking so much better.'

'I couldn't have done it without you,' said Olivia, getting to her feet and dusting off the dirt from her gardening gloves.

'Well, I was never the gardening type. It was always Linda who—' Emma looked down at the ground and pushed a small stone into the turf.

Olivia smiled at her friend.

Emma cleared her throat. 'Sorry, sometimes I forget.'

'You shouldn't apologise, Emma. And you shouldn't try and forget about Linda, nor avoid talking about her if she crops up in conversation.'

Emma sniffed loudly. 'I know, but … I regret what I said to her. The last words she heard from my mouth were that I'd never forgive her. I shouted at her. I was angry. The guilt is eating me alive. That's what it feels like.'

Olivia nodded along as Emma continued to talk. Emma often went through phases where she'd tell Olivia in-depth details about what had happened. Yes, she spoke to Dr Allan, but Olivia was her friend, and she was more than willing to listen.

Olivia once had friends like that, a long time ago.

'I know Linda didn't physically push Phoebe into the road, but … I still hold her responsible for what happened. Does that make me a bad person? Dr Allan says no, but I don't believe him.'

Olivia took a deep breath. 'Emma, I think what happened to your daughter was an unimaginable tragedy. Your wife covered up the truth for two years, lied to you and made your son lie to you as well. It doesn't make you a bad person for holding it against her. It makes you human. You loved your daughter very much. Trust me when I say that holding onto a lie like that can really do a lot of damage. I'm sure Linda thought she was doing what was right for you at the time.'

Emma looked up, blinking through thick tears which streaked her grubby face. She'd wiped a dirty hand across her cheek at some point. 'I did love Phoebe so, so much. I still do. I miss her. I even miss the memory of her, the one I spoke to even though she wasn't real.' Emma chuckled. 'Oh my God, I sound completely crazy. Thank goodness I'm seeing a therapist, right!'

Olivia chuckled back, glad Emma could see the lighter side, but she knew, deep down, the darkness had always been there within Emma, and probably always would be. There was no escaping it. Her own daughter, Brooke, and her boyfriend, Jordan, were living proof of that. They each suffered for twenty years after what had happened in 1998 when they'd barely been teenagers ...

Olivia decided a change of topic was in order. 'I saw someone in town earlier today. Stephen Mallow.'

Emma straightened up. 'Why do I recognise that name?'

'He was the journalist who came from London back in 2022. You wouldn't know him to look at him because you didn't live here at the time, but he caused quite a stir.'

Emma nodded. 'Oh, yes. I remember Alex telling me about the article he'd written.' Olivia saw a shadow pass over Emma's face, as if she were remembering something bad. 'Why's he back? Did you speak to him?'

'No, I only saw him briefly. He had just arrived at The Cherry Tree.'

'Do you think he's here about the body that was found?'

Olivia's heart missed a beat. 'Quite possibly, but how did he find out about it? The local police haven't released the news to the media yet.'

Emma squeezed her lips together, her eyebrows furrowed. 'Someone must have told him.'

A shrill ringing came from inside the house.

'Ooh, that's my phone. Excuse me a moment,' said Olivia, pulling her gloves off and heading towards the house, relieved at the reprieve from such a depressing topic of conversation. She'd found out about the body from Emma a couple of weeks ago and had barely slept since.

'I'll finish these borders,' said Emma.

Olivia kicked off her boots and slid the doors shut to stop the heat from escaping. She had built up a sweat in the garden with all the work she'd been doing, and now with the invisible cloud of heat hitting her, she had no choice but to take off her hat and coat as she picked up the phone. She hoped it hadn't woken Frank.

'Hello?'

'Hi, Mum.'

Olivia's heart swelled with joy. 'Brooke, darling, how lovely to hear from you. Is everything okay?'

'Yes, of course. Why wouldn't it be?'

Olivia felt silly. She had to stop imagining the worst happening all the time. Brooke was free from this place now. She'd escaped the darkness and this town and was enjoying life creating a home of her own somewhere new and exciting.

'Sorry, darling,' she said. 'How are you? How is Jordan?'

'He's good. He's enjoying his new job. Even though he's not running his own business anymore, he's enjoying the freedom of a normal salaried plumbing job. Obviously, he's still recovering from surgery, but he's getting stronger every day. At least he's home at reasonable times of the day now.'

'That's wonderful. And you? How's your job going?' Olivia knew her daughter dreamed of being a make-up artist in London, and for a brief time she had lived her dream after leaving the town five years ago, but now she was with Jordan, her dreams involved decorating their new home and going for long, country walks with their dog, Morgan. But she'd got herself a job at a small beauty salon doing make-up for weddings.

'It's going fine. I've had to take some time off recently though. I've not been very well. Haven't been able to keep anything down.'

Olivia's heart lurched and she instinctively reached for something to lean against, which happened to be the kitchen counter. 'Oh, Brooke, are you okay?'

'I'm fine, Mum. In fact, the doctors say it's only a nine-month thing.'

Olivia stopped breathing.

Then she screamed, jumping up and down as tears rolled down her cheeks.

# Chapter Three

## Alex

### *22 January 2024 – 15:30 p.m.*

He cupped his hand around the tip of the cigarette and lit the end using his dad's old lighter. As he breathed in the first lungful of smoke (always the best), he allowed the flame to linger. He watched it dance at the top of the small silver lighter like a tiny inferno ready to explode.

His mind drifted to Halloween last year; to the moment he'd set alight his house, burning his step-mum to death while she lay unconscious in bed after attempting to take her own life merely days before. At least she'd felt no pain. How could she with the amount of sleeping tablets he dissolved in her glass of water, which she'd downed in one? He'd been kind really.

He hoped Linda was in a better place … But what if she wasn't?

Alex didn't believe in heaven or hell, but wherever she was, it was better than being here and taking up his mum's time, lying to her and causing her stress.

He was so proud of his mum for how far she'd come in such a short space of time, although she did seem to be spending a lot of time with Mrs Willows and her new therapist, Dr … Whatshisname. Something beginning with A. Why couldn't she talk to him about her feelings instead? Her own flesh and blood. Why did she have to talk about her problems to adults? Was it because she thought she was protecting him? He didn't need protecting. He was the one who was protecting her and always had done. That's why he killed his dad by pushing him off a bridge when he'd been too drunk to even know his own name. The police had said it was death by suicide. That's why he killed Linda by drugging her and burning her alive. He hadn't killed Phoebe though. Linda had. It had been the catalyst that had started it all, bringing about more pain and destruction than he could ever have imagined.

But it was better now ... Sort of ...

Granted, his mum seemed more together, but whenever she looked at him, he saw something in her eyes that made his stomach do a loop. Fear. Mistrust. Sadness. It could have been anything. If only she'd fucking talk to him then maybe he could understand why she looked at him that way.

He flicked the lid closed, extinguishing the tiny flame. He liked to fiddle with it every so often. Striking the wheel, watching the flame burn and then snuffing it out made him feel ... powerful. After all, he was nearly seventeen and had already taken two lives, snuffed them out like the lighter's flame. Too easy.

He inhaled another lungful and held the smoke in. Then coughed his guts up.

'Why do you insist on smoking if it makes you cough so much?' asked Harriet. 'E-cigarettes are much healthier, you know.'

Alex spat on the ground and levelled his breathing before taking another drag. 'E-cigarettes are for wimps.'

'Whatever.' Harriet stuck the e-cigarette in her mouth and held it between her teeth while she rubbed her hands together. 'Urrgg, it's bloody freezing. See, another good thing about e-cigarettes is that you can smoke them *inside*.'

'No one's stopping you from going back inside,' replied Alex.

'Yeah, but the school won't let us smoke them inside, will they?'

'Look, we promised Alex the First we'd wait for him to finish detention.'

'Fine.' Harriet put away her e-cigarette and crossed her arms over her chest, tucking her hands under her armpits.

They leaned against the low wall in silence for a few moments. Alex glanced over at his girlfriend, although he used the term very loosely when it came to her, but he, Harriet and Alex the First were a team and, although the other two were practically psychopaths after what they'd done to that poor girl, they were the only friends he had, which was exceptionally pathetic in his eyes.

Alex had learned that between them they had bullied and played a very inappropriate joke on twelve-year-old Bethany Walker, the girl who used to live in his old house before his mum bought it and before he'd burned it down. Bethany's mum, Amber, had suffered from severe sleep paralysis, insomnia and hallucinations and she'd imagined a dark entity called The Creature was after her and her daughter. Bethany had found out about it, written a poem at school and Harriet and Alex the First had stolen it. They'd then spread a rumour about The Creature haunting Cherry Hollow, about it coming after you, and that if you went to Beaker Ravine, it would make you jump to your death. That's what had happened to Amber a year ago (even though it was later revealed she'd been killed by two of the town's residents), but ever since then, the people of Cherry Hollow were convinced a strange, dark creature was lurking about in the shadows.

The thing was … it wasn't all nonsense.

People believed The Creature was real. Therefore, its power had grown and spread and was now a festering cancer upon the town.

That's why a journalist had visited in 2022 and interviewed people. He'd written an article, which had catapulted the town's reputation, but not in a good way. That's why the townspeople avoided Beaker Ravine, but Alex didn't.

And, thanks to him, that's why another body had been found there just over two weeks ago.

'I went to visit my mum in prison yesterday,' said Harriet, stamping her feet.

Alex puffed on the end of his cigarette. 'Oh yeah, how'd that go?'

'Okay, I guess. She's still awaiting trial, but she and Trisha Sharp are sharing a cell, so at least she's not lonely.'

'That's good,' replied Alex. It was hard to feign interest in something he didn't care about. Harriet's mum, Lucy Forrester, and her best friend, Trisha Sharp, had been arrested and sentenced for burning down Jordan Evans' business on Halloween last year as well as killing Amber Walker by knocking her off the tree that spanned Beaker Ravine. They'd also been arrested for burning down Alex's house with Linda inside because there was no evidence to suggest they hadn't done it, other than their word.

Only Alex knew the truth.

He didn't feel bad about it either.

They were locked up in Ashmoore Prison, situated about an hour away. Apparently, Harriet visited her mum every month.

'I believe her, you know,' added Harriet.

'Huh?'

'Mum says she and Trisha didn't burn down your house and kill your step-mum.'

Alex shrugged. 'I guess the courts will decide.'

'But why would they? I mean, they had nothing against your family.'

Alex stared at her. 'No offence, Harriet, but your mum and Trisha were crazy. They covered up the fact they accidentally killed Amber Walker, and then burned down Jordan's business to drive him out of town. Well, congratulations, it seems they succeeded. What's to say they didn't kill my step-mum too?'

Harriet pulled her hat further over her ears. 'Well, I believe my mum. I don't care what you think. You liked Jordan and Brooke, didn't you?'

Alex snorted and turned his face away from Harriet's inquisitive stare. It was true. He did miss Jordan and Brooke. They were the only people who'd treated him like an adult and not a stupid kid. He was almost seventeen, not a baby. Jordan had even offered him a job, but now that was shot to shit because Jordan had lost everything and moved away.

'They were okay,' he said.

Harriet sighed and was quiet for a moment, then straightened up and pointed in front of her. 'Hey, isn't that the journalist from last year?'

Alex whipped his head around and saw a beat-up old car drive past, heading out of town. 'How the hell should I know? I never saw him.'

Harriet squinted against the glare of the low winter sun. The car had driven away now, disappearing over the brow of the hill. 'I could have sworn that was him. What's he doing back here?'

'Probably has something to do with the body we found last week.'

'Right.' Harriet shuddered. 'Don't remind me.'

### 11 January 2024

*Lake Peace was the most tranquil place on earth, like something out of a fantasy movie. Beautiful, quiet and still. Harriet and Alex the First had taken Alex there for the first time. He'd heard about the lake, but since it was the middle of winter, hadn't felt the urge to visit a large body of freezing water. But Harriet convinced him when she said they could walk upstream along the river and get to the bottom of Beaker Ravine, underneath the fallen tree where three of the Fated Five had lost their lives. Apparently, a secret cave was carved into the side of the ravine where kids back in the 80s and 90s had hung out and smoked weed. That's what Harriet's mum had told her, but Alex had come to learn most of what that woman said was complete rubbish. However, it was an intriguing enough premise to venture out in search of the elusive cave.*

*The Fated Five was the collective name given to Kieran Jones, Tyler Jenkins, Jordan Evans, Brooke Willows and Amber Walker; the original five who had started everything back in 1998 when four of them covered up the accidental death of Kieran. Over the years that followed, the four survivors had been plagued by various mental health disorders due to their overwhelming guilt about what they'd done. Eventually, twenty years later, Tyler confessed to killing Kieran and took the heat for them all, letting Amber, Jordan and Brooke off the hook. But Amber hadn't seen it that way and had become increasingly anxious, convinced The Creature, the make-believe entity she'd hallucinated, was still after her and her daughter, Bethany. Then, a year ago, Amber had been killed by Trisha and Lucy because they wanted the remaining members of the Fated Five out of Cherry Hollow so the town could return to normal.*

*It hadn't worked out exactly how they'd planned. They were locked up in prison, for one thing.*

*But at least things seemed to have calmed down and everyone was getting back to their normal, boring lives, which was why Alex had decided to befriend Harriet and Alex the First and attempt to salvage his teenage years by acting like one and exploring the bottom of a ravine where people had died. It was what a normal teenager would do.*

*The river from the lake started out quite wide, but a small path ran alongside it that the trio followed for half a mile before the river narrowed and became shallower. It was a one-and-a-half-mile hike along the river to the bottom of the ravine. They were bundled up in coats, hats and scarves, which they discarded one by one when the terrain became uneven and tricky to navigate, catapulting their heart rates through the roof.*

*'Fucking hell, I hope this trek is worth it,' said Alex, stopping to take a breath. He undid the zip on his coat and flapped his t-shirt underneath to allow some cool air to circulate before wiping his forehead with his scarf.*

*'No one's been down here for a long time, so the path has degraded,' said Alex the First.*

*'You're telling me.'*

*Alex the First smirked. 'Not really a country boy, are you?'*

*Alex glared at him. Alex the First was a nickname they'd adopted when Alex arrived on the scene last year. He was known as Alex the Second. Alex the First was the son of Trisha Sharp, one of the women arrested and sentenced for arson last year. It was a strange thing being friends with the offspring of the women who were behind bars for his step-mum's death. But they made it work, mostly by not bringing it up at all. Sometimes Alex wondered why he even bothered with them.*

'Next time, we're bringing water and food,' said Alex.

'I have some Coke in my bag,' said Harriet as she pulled off her backpack. She rummaged around and found the half-empty bottle, handing it to Alex who took a couple of sips before passing it back to her. She drank and then handed it to Alex the First, who did the same.

Momentarily refreshed, they continued following the river which slowly started shrinking in size, but thanks to the copious amount of rain they'd had recently it was still deep enough to come up to the top of their boots in places. Alex had heard in the height of summer, the riverbed dried up, which was why the people who'd fallen from above had died instantly with nothing to cushion their fall.

As the sides of the ravine began to steepen, Alex craned his neck upwards to see the top. The only way out of this ravine was back the way they'd come.

'Didn't there used to be a path down the side of the ravine from where the tree is?' asked Alex.

'Yeah, there was, but there are so many landslides after lots of rain and stuff that the path eventually got destroyed. I mean, you could attempt to climb up and down the side, but I wouldn't recommend it unless you have a death wish,' replied Alex the First.

'How much further is it?'

'Not far. I can see the fallen tree just up there. Look.' Harriet pointed into the distance where a large, fallen tree spanned the top of the ravine. Alex had been at the top last year *and had even walked across the tree to the other side. At the time, he thought he'd seen his dead sister standing and waving at him, which had freaked him out. She hadn't been there ... obviously. Because she'd been killed two years earlier by a speeding car, which had knocked her down after she ran away from Linda who had frightened her by shouting.*

*Harriet told him that's what the ravine did to people: made them see things that weren't there. That was the power of The Creature and the darkness that seemed to engulf the town.*

*Alex stopped underneath the tree, avoiding the river as best he could, but he could already feel his socks getting damp. He looked up, imagining falling from such a height. Then he stared down at the ground, imagining a body disintegrating into pieces upon impact. He glanced around where he was standing, almost expecting to see body parts strewn about, but the bodies had long since gone. The crime scene tape had been taken down. And the riverbed had swallowed up any remaining evidence or trace that anyone had fallen to their deaths.*

*Harriet shuddered again. 'It's one thing looking down from the top, but it's another thing actually being down here where people ... you know ... died.' She whispered the word as if it was illegal.*

*Alex the First kicked a nearby stone into the water.*

*'Where's this secret cave then?' asked Alex, looking around.*

'I have no idea,' replied Harriet. 'I've never been down here. I've only heard about the cave. But Mum told me it was underneath the tree.'

'It probably doesn't even exist,' said Alex the First. 'It's probably been washed away or covered up by a landslide by now.'

'Only one way to find out,' said Alex, putting his woollen hat back on.

Now they'd stopped hiking, the chill factor had increased, the icy wind seeping through his clothes, cooling his sweaty skin. He zipped up his jacket.

'I'll look over here.' He wandered away from the other two without waiting for a response. He heard them murmuring, but he didn't care what they were talking about. It was probably something about him.

He navigated the uneven, rocky ground as best he could and, when he reached the steep left side of the ravine, he turned and followed it up a bit further, away from the fallen tree. It was an eerie sensation walking in the footsteps of the kids who'd been there before. He thought back to what Jordan had told him, that he and his friends had helped their friend Tyler cover up the death of Kieran and buried his body down here. And how that moment had caused a chain reaction for the next twenty years of their lives, twisting and changing them into mere shadows of their former selves, tormented by their own darkness and guilt.

In a way, the same thing had happened to Alex. That's how Jordan had explained it. He'd lost his sister, his mum had spiralled into a dark depression, and his step-mum had told him to lie to his mum about her involvement in Phoebe's death. Having to carry heavy stuff like that around for so long had eaten him alive, so he could only imagine how hard it must have been for Jordan, Brooke and the others. No wonder Tyler had taken his own life.

Alex tripped over a rock and swore, almost face-planting the ground. When he recovered, he looked up and spotted a pile of rocks in front of him. Yes, there were rocks all around him, but these seemed out of place, as if they weren't supposed to be there.

He crept closer.

The rocks were piled in a large heap at the bottom of what appeared to be a landslide. Mud, rocks and debris from above had been washed down by the rains and deposited the rocks there, but at one edge of the rock pile was a dark opening.

The closer he got, the more he was convinced there was a hole behind the rock pile.

And, when he moved a few rocks out of the way, the hole revealed itself to be the mouth of a small, dark cave.

Alex grinned and opened his mouth to call for the others, but as he did, a dark shadow darted across the mouth of the cave.

He leapt back and landed hard on his back.

The shadow hovered in place for a few seconds and then dispersed.

Alex took a deep breath, winded after such a shock and landing hard.

'Hey, guys. I think I've found it.'

# Chapter Four

## Graham

### *22 January 2024 – 15:00 p.m.*

His head and neck hurt again: a sharpness at the top of his spine and across his shoulders, which then crept up and over his skull, settling into a dull ache around his puffy, dry eyes. He just wanted to close them and keep them closed. Seeing darkness through his eyelids was the only way of numbing the pain. It wouldn't go away.

Detective Chief Inspector Graham Williams sighed as he reached into his desk drawer and pulled out a packet of painkillers. It was empty. Again. He tossed the packet into the bin and groaned. The guy at the pharmacy was going to think he was some sort of painkiller addict at this rate. He found a new packet, popped two pills into his palm and knocked them back dry, grimacing as the chalky taste hit the back of his throat.

It was this case.

No. It was this *town*.

Another body had been found.

Another death needed to be solved.

What was it with Cherry Hollow? It was supposed to be one of those quaint chocolate box towns in the middle of nowhere where people visited to unwind and destress from their busy lives. Instead, it had turned into the murder capital of the Lake District.

He should have moved out of the area years ago when he'd had the chance. He'd been dating a woman called Claire back in 2002 and she asked him to move in with her. She'd lived in Ambleside, which wasn't miles away, but it was far enough that he wouldn't have to hear the name *Cherry Hollow* again unless he wanted to. But the locals had a saying: *Cherry Hollow is a place where if you leave to live elsewhere, you never return, and if an outsider moves in, they never leave.*

There certainly was some truth to the statement. He couldn't think of anyone who'd moved out of town and then come back to reside other than Brooke Willows, but she hadn't returned to live. She'd come back to help Jordan Evans solve a murder and then, after it had been solved, they'd both moved away. Good on them. They deserved a fresh start. In fact, mild envy lingered under the surface. He wished he could press the reset button on the last few years. Hell, he would've pressed the reset button on his whole damn life if he could.

If only he could go back to that day when he was fifteen …

Had it all started then, or had his life taken a downward spiral when the disappearance of Kieran Jones rocked the town over twenty-five years ago? He'd been a fresh-faced sergeant at the time, and had been giddy with excitement when the kid had gone missing because it was the first big case of his career. Before that, nothing had ever happened in Cherry Hollow, bar maybe a missing dog or a few minor burglaries and a couple of unexplained deaths that had turned out to be nothing.

Then Kieran had gone missing and turned the town into a grieving mess of doubt, sorrow and confusion. That case had never been solved until twenty years later when a blue watch was found at the bottom of Beaker Ravine by some random kids who'd gone down there to explore. He'd been a DCI then too, newly promoted. During the twenty years the case remained unsolved, he always felt as if he'd let the town down because he'd never been able to solve it, never been able to help bring peace and closure to Kieran's parents.

But then Tyler Jenkins had confessed to murdering the boy when he was a teenager, burning the remains and scattering them across the hills.

Since then, all hell had broken loose.

Suicides.

Accidental deaths.

Murder cover-ups.

Two arson assaults on the same night, culminating in yet another death.

And now this …

Another body at that fucking ravine, found by another bunch of kids, buried in a cave.

But the body outdated even Kieran's disappearance and murder.

The pathologist's report had dated the body at over forty years old …

What did that mean? Could it have anything to do with—

'Boss … we're ready for you.'

Graham flinched as the voice of Detective Constable Carter came through the intercom on his desk. The woman had a voice like a banshee at times, especially when his head ached the way it did.

He rubbed his stubbly chin with his left hand. Thanks to the discovery of the body and the ongoing investigation, he had little time to do menial things like shaving or eating a healthy meal. He'd been ordering takeout from the shop in town for the past three days and had barely slept in his own bed, sometimes crashing at his desk and waking up with a sliver of drool dangling from his mouth early the next morning. But bless DC Carter, she at least made him coffee when he needed it, even though he often forgot to drink it and it would turn cold sitting on his desk on a pile of paperwork.

Graham groaned as he stood up. His fifty-nine-year-old body was beginning to feel its age. He couldn't wait to retire. One thing was for certain: he wouldn't be retiring and settling down in Cherry Hollow. Once he'd retired, he would leave this town and never think of it again, but not yet. Not until he'd solved this last case. He needed closure on the past. And he could feel the weight of the world pressing down on his shoulders.

The buzz in the briefing room was electric, despite the small number of people in attendance. He only had a small team of two DCs: Carter and Baker, but there were other people connected via a secure video link whom he needed to brief as well, including the pathologist lab and the DCI of the larger police station in

Keswick who'd offered his assistance with the case. Graham had sworn everyone to secrecy. The news had not yet reached the mainstream media and he wanted it to stay that way for as long as possible. The last thing Cherry Hollow needed was another death and another influx of negative attention caused by enthusiastic and attention-seeking journalists who only wanted to further their careers by getting the biggest scoop of the decade.

Just like that twat, Stephen Mallow, back in 2022 who'd come sniffing around, poking his nose into everyone's business, and writing the most ridiculous article he'd ever laid his eyes on. Graham didn't believe in The Creature. Unless he saw it with his own eyes, the only thing he'd believe was that people liked to make up stories and blow things out of proportion to make something seem more interesting. The town had suffered through its fair share of trauma, grief, and mental health issues, but it didn't mean some huge, angry creature was roaming the streets, tormenting children in their beds.

Graham held his hand up and the room fell silent, all eyes on him as he stood in front of the briefing board, which had recently been named 'The Cherry Hollow Death Board'. Someone (he guessed DC Baker due to the crude drawing of a skull and crossbones next to it) had written it in black, swirly writing. They'd only recently removed the details of Amber Walker and Linda Smithson. Now, a new set of information and notes graced the board, which amounted to very little.

'As you all know, a body was found in the small cave at the bottom of Beaker Ravine on the eleventh of January by three teenagers: Alex Sharp, Alex Smithson and Harriet Forrester. The body was removed on the twelfth of January and transported to the pathologist lab in Keswick where it underwent an autopsy.

'The cause of death was blunt force trauma to the head. The body appears to have been down there for around forty years, meaning the person was killed in the mid-80s or maybe earlier. We are still waiting for the DNA sample to be tested and returned.

'We have checked the missing person's reports from around that time, but no matches have been found. We will now be conducting investigations and interviews with the people of Cherry Hollow to see if anyone has any information. Hopefully, someone will know something.' Graham finished talking and cleared his throat. 'Any questions?'

DC Baker, a young and enthusiastic member of his team, raised his hand. For a moment, Graham felt as if he were taking assembly at school. 'Does this have anything to do with all the other deaths that have happened in Cherry Hollow over the past twenty-five years? Kieran Jones. Tyler Jenkins. Amber Walker. Linda Smithson.'

Graham shook his head, already expecting the question. 'At the moment, there's nothing to suggest the deaths are linked, but we cannot rule it out completely.'

Another hand shot up, this one from DC Carter, her blue eyes shining in the bright lights of the briefing room. 'Shouldn't we warn people about going to Beaker Ravine? It seems to be a death trap. I know there's a sign, but kids keep going there.'

Graham attempted to hide a frustrated sigh. 'Yes, the area of Beaker Ravine has been cordoned off once again and a new sign has replaced the old one. No one is allowed anywhere near that ravine. If anyone is found there, then they are to be brought in for questioning. I am sick and tired of people dying in my town, and all of them have ended up at the bottom of that godforsaken hole.' He cleared his throat and rubbed his chin, aware he'd probably over-stepped his mark. Sometimes it was difficult to keep a lid on his emotions. 'Any other questions?'

'Why are you not announcing this on the national news?' It was a question from DCI Phelps, the detective in charge at the Keswick branch who was watching via video link, the computer screen set up just to the side of where Graham was standing.

Again, Graham had been expecting this question. 'You may remember a journalist coming to town a couple of years ago and the damage his article did to the mental and emotional well-being of this town. By putting this new discovery on the national news, we'd be inviting journalists, conspiracy theorists and unwelcome visitors.'

DCI Phelps frowned. 'That may be true, but by *not* announcing the discovery of the body you're limiting your investigation to Cherry Hollow itself. There may be former residents who have moved out of the town who may know something. How will they learn about the body otherwise? I can think of two people already who have moved away who may know more … Jordan Evans and Brooke Willows, for instance.'

Graham fought the urge to grind his teeth. 'Jordan Evans and Brooke Willows wouldn't have even been born back in the early 80s. I think we can safely rule them out.'

It seemed DCI Phelps wasn't ready to give up just yet. 'But they were the last ones down in that ravine, weren't they? When they were burying Kieran Jones' body.'

Graham shook his head. 'No, they were cleared of all charges. Tyler Jenkins was the one who killed, buried and then dug up Kieran's body and burned it. I have his full confession on tape.'

'Yes, but that's not what the people of Cherry Hollow believe happened, is it, DCI Williams?'

An awkward silence enveloped the room. Graham glanced at his two DCs who were trying their best to stare anywhere but at him.

He took a deep breath. 'I don't care what the people of Cherry Hollow believe, DCI Phelps. This is my town and I believe they are innocent. Rumours have no place in a murder investigation. Unless a specific piece of information is found or they come forward of their own accord, then I will not be pursuing Jordan Evans and Brooke Willows for questioning. They are to be left out of this.'

DCI Phelps turned red and nodded. 'Very well, DCI Williams. However, I would strongly recommend you announce this discovery on the national news tomorrow. I can arrange all the details. It will help raise awareness because there have been several families who have moved from the town since the mid-80s, so they may know something, as I mentioned previously.'

The tension in the air still hovered like a bad smell. Graham had dealt with DCI Phelps and his wrath on more than one occasion. Despite them being the same rank, DCI Phelps seemed to think he was superior due to running a larger station and having more years under his belt as a DCI (only two).

He wasn't finished because he continued before Graham could get a word out. 'I think your investigation should focus on finding out the truth about this body rather than trying to keep the national press out of town. Hopefully, it might flush out the information you need. I'm sure all your officers can follow a direct order to not disclose any information to any journalists or news channels without your permission.' DCI Phelps glared at the two DCs through the monitor who both nodded their heads, sending side glances to their boss for some form of direction or acknowledgement.

Graham looked around the room. There was no getting away from it this time. He had to admit defeat. 'Very well. Set up the press release for tomorrow at noon. Here.'

DCI Phelps grinned, seemingly pleased he'd won this round.

*Just you wait.*

Graham cleared his throat. 'I believe you all know your assignments. Any questions, you know where I am. Another quick briefing will be held at 0800 tomorrow morning, by which time we may have the DNA results back from the lab. I expect you all to be in attendance for the press release too.'

Graham stayed in the briefing room after he'd dismissed everyone. He spoke to the pathologist who'd completed the autopsy, asking her further questions about her report, but in the end it merely repeated what he already knew, which was next to nothing.

A few minutes later, DC Carter knocked and stuck her head around the door. 'Um, sorry boss, but there's someone here who wants to speak to you.'

'Who?'

'It's that journalist from last year, Stephen Mallow. He says he isn't leaving until he's spoken to you.' DC Carter blushed.

Graham let out a long sigh. 'And here comes the blood-sucking parasites looking for any juicy piece of ... Wait a minute, how the hell did Stephen Fucking Mallow find out about this body? We've only just decided to announce it to the media ...' DC Carter shrugged her response. 'Thank you, DC Carter, I'll be there in a minute.'

'He's in your office, boss. You want me to offer him a brew?'

'Hell no, he won't be staying long enough to drink one.'

Graham remembered when he used to be a pleasant man, back before he'd lost faith in his community and discovered he was living and working in a town full of liars and killers.

# Chapter Five

## Stephen

### *22 January 2024 – 15:30 p.m.*

The chair was rigid and uncomfortable. It was stationed in front of a large mahogany desk he knew belonged to Detective Chief Inspector Williams for two reasons: one, his name was on the small nameplate at the front of the desk, and two, he'd been here before. The chair was new though. The last one he'd sat in had padding. He wondered what had happened to it.

He decided to pass the time by counting the pictures hanging on the wall behind the desk.

Fifteen.

There were fifteen pictures from left to right, lined up in date order (he guessed due to the hair on the detective's head getting greyer in each photo and the lines around his eyes growing deeper and more prominent). The frames of the pictures didn't match, nor were they level; that frustrated Stephen more than it would anyone else. Clearly, the detective had no regard for precision and uniformity, which seemed odd considering he was a cop.

A tingling crept over Stephen's body, something that always happened when his OCD wanted to kick in. He had to keep it under control, but it was hard, especially when there were fifteen fucking frames on the wall and not one of them was level …

Stephen distracted himself by studying the photos.

Most of them were of the detective and a colleague or two in uniform. A couple were of him shaking hands with other greying officers, probably receiving an award or maybe a promotion. Another was of him holding up a large fish (he assumed the man liked to fish in his spare time).

But one photo, the very first one, wasn't related to him as an officer at all. It was a photo of several kids, teenagers he imagined (maybe aged fifteen or sixteen), and the photo itself looked to have been taken back in the 80s or even earlier, he couldn't quite tell. The quality of the print wasn't good enough to make out details on faces, but he guessed one of the boys must have been the detective, otherwise, why would he have it hung up?

But it was crooked.

The picture.

It was more crooked than any of them.

Stephen bit down on his tongue, drawing pain and blood.

He couldn't deal with that. He couldn't sit there and stare at a lop-sided picture on a wall.

Mind made up, he rose to his feet and walked behind the desk. Starting from the right and working backwards, he straightened every frame on the wall until he got to the first one; the one of the teenagers. Stephen leaned in close to try and recognise the faces, but none were familiar. He assumed the detective must be one of the three boys in the photo, but clearly the years hadn't been kind to him because there was no resemblance to any of them.

Maybe Stephen was wrong. Maybe this wasn't a photo of Detective Williams as a kid, so who were these five teenagers?

'What are you doing behind my desk?'

Stephen spun around. He hadn't heard the door open. 'Apologies, Detective. Your pictures were all wonky.'

The detective gave him a frown. 'Did you straighten all of my pictures?'

'Yes.'

'Hmmm.'

Stephen walked over to the detective and extended his hand. 'Good to see you again.'

Detective Williams shook his hand but didn't look like he returned his compliment. 'Mr Mallow, didn't you cause enough trouble the last time you were here?'

'Trust me, Detective, if it were up to me, I wouldn't be here. But I received an anonymous email saying another body had been found, this one dating back to the early 80s and ... well ... let's just say, I was curious.'

Detective Williams raised his eyebrows but said nothing as he walked slowly to his own chair behind the desk. That one was high-backed, leather and looked much more comfortable than the wooden one Stephen had sat on. 'An anonymous email, you say?'

'Yep. Here, take a look.' Stephen fished his phone from his pocket, scrolled a few times and then handed the phone to the detective who took it and furrowed his brow while his eyes scanned the screen.

'And you have no idea who sent it? No idea at all?'

Stephen shrugged, taking the phone back. 'I'm assuming it's someone from this town, but no, I have no idea. I didn't exactly make friends the last time I was here, but clearly someone wants me to help with this murder. I assume it wasn't you?'

The detective scoffed. 'You'd be the last person I'd ask for help, Mr Mallow.'

Stephen brushed off the insult. He was used to them.

Detective Williams raised his chin. 'Besides, what makes you think it's a murder?'

'A body hidden in a cave for forty-odd years … It doesn't exactly point to natural causes now, does it? My question is … why is this police department keeping it from the mainstream media? Why have no missing person reports been filed from that time … Yes, I checked. And why does no one outside this town know about this body yet?'

The detective took a deep breath. 'I thought you just had one question …' They held firm stares for several beats before the detective nodded. 'Fine. Okay, well, I hate to disappoint you, Mr Mallow, but I cannot confirm or deny anything right now. As luck would have it, I'm announcing it officially tomorrow, so you'll have your wish. Once the media get hold of this story, it will no doubt blow out of control.'

'I can help keep a lid on things,' said Stephen, taking a step forward. 'Let me write this story. Give me full access to everything and I swear, I'll help dampen the blow.'

Detective Williams threw his head back and let out a loud laugh. 'Not a chance in hell am I letting a journalist have full access to this investigation. I'll say this once and only once, Mr Mallow. Do not traipse across town interviewing unsuspecting residents. You are welcome to stay for the press conference tomorrow and ask your questions there, but after that, you need to leave.'

Stephen thought about that for a moment. 'Does this have anything to do with The Creature?'

Detective Williams barely reacted bar a blink. 'Did you even listen to what I just said?'

'Yes, but I'm choosing to ignore you, Detective.' Stephen grinned. He sat down on the uncomfortable chair again. 'My job is to get to the bottom of this story. I don't care if you don't like me. I have a right to be here. I'm not breaking any laws.' He watched the man in front of him fight the urge to shout. A vein had appeared on the detective's forehead that was in danger of exploding if he didn't take a much-needed breath. 'Who are they?' asked Stephen, nodding towards the now-straight photo behind the detective's head, the one of the five teenagers smiling.

The detective craned his neck over his shoulder, glanced at the photo and turned away, the scowl on his face now replaced by sadness. 'No one of importance.' Detective Williams placed his elbows on his desk and leaned towards him. 'Mr Mallow, can I ask you a personal question?'

Stephen raised his eyebrows. 'By all means, please do.'

'What is your *real* interest in this town? As far as I can tell you don't have any family connections. You're merely a journalist from London, so what the hell are you doing all the way up in the Lake District?'

'That's not as personal a question as I was expecting, but okay. I have a curiosity for the unbelievable and weird, and this town, thanks to The Creature, ticks both of those boxes, plus a few more, wouldn't you say?'

Detective Williams narrowed his eyes. 'The Creature is nothing more than a woman's hallucination brought on by sleep paralysis and insomnia which then manifested itself onto her daughter, who then wrote about it and the rumour was spread around the town. The Creature isn't a real being, Mr Mallow, you realise that, right? I don't believe in the supernatural, nor do I believe in ghosts or demons.'

Stephen shrugged. 'I'm not saying it's any of those things, Detective.'

'Then what *are* you saying?'

Stephen took a deep breath, held it for a few seconds and exhaled loudly. He stood up as he spoke, pacing back and forth in front of the desk. He felt the detective's eyes on him the whole time.

'I believe The Creature lives in all of us in some form or another. It's a ... shall we say ... *metaphorical being* who torments those who have done wrong, forcing them to admit the truth so they can save themselves. I don't believe The Creature is as evil as everyone makes it out to be. It only wants the truth. It wants people to face up to their pasts and admit they've done wrong.'

'I don't believe in metaphorical beings either,' came the abrupt reply.

'Well, maybe *you* don't, but a lot of people in this town *do*. And that is the whole point.'

'Okay, so if The Creature isn't as bad as you think … why the hell did you run out of this town a couple of years ago and never come back? What scared you so badly?'

Stephen stopped pacing, realising the detective wasn't as dumb as he first thought. The man paid attention. Stephen opened his mouth, but the words got stuck in his throat.

'That's what I thought,' said Detective Williams.

Stephen sighed. 'It's complicated.'

'I'll bet.'

Stephen stopped at the light switch by the door. He stared at it as he continued. 'The Creature is a representation of a person's mental health. But what I'm saying is that not all mental health is bad, but it can be if you keep your lies hidden. The Creature is a manifestation of someone's troubled past, and it seems to present itself as a form of severe mental health disorder. For example, Jordan Evans and Brooke Willows—'

'Here we go …' The detective's tone dripped with sarcasm.

'—Jordan used to be an angry and aggressive man, didn't he?'

'Yes, he was locked up at least once and I personally arrested him several times over the years.'

'And Brooke ... She was trapped inside her family home for twenty years, right? A severe form of agoraphobia.'

'Yes.'

'Okay, so ... when Tyler Jenkins admitted he was the one who killed Kieran Jones and took the blame, what happened to them?'

Detective Williams stared at him without blinking. 'They appeared to make a recovery.'

'Right. Exactly. Tyler took the blame for the murder of Kieran, but remember Amber Walker ... She couldn't live with her guilt, could she? She still saw The Creature.'

Detective Williams rose to his feet. 'I'm going to stop you there, Mr Mallow. Everything you're saying is pure conjecture. There's no solid proof. It's all been made up and twisted over the years. Amber Walker started the rumour about The Creature, and then her daughter wrote a poem, and it got passed around at school. The rumour continued to grow and now people are freaking out. That's all this is.'

'Are you saying you've never seen anything weird around here? You've never felt a cold, tingling sensation creep up your spine? You've never done anything in your life you regret, you've lied about or covered up? Can you, Detective Williams, honestly say you've never experienced a darkness inside yourself at one time or another?'

He watched as the detective's face turned pale. He knew he didn't need to say anything else, but he did have one last nail to hammer in.

'Detective, I'm not sure if you've considered this, but I think the body that's been found recently, the one dating back to the 80s, is related to all the other deaths somehow. I think it's what started it all.'

Detective Williams snorted. The colour came back to his face. 'Do you have any proof of that, Mr Mallow?'

'No, not yet.'

'So, what you're saying is it's merely a hunch you have?'

'For now.'

Detective Williams cleared his throat. 'Mr Mallow, might I remind you I'm the detective around here and my team are more than capable of conducting this investigation without your help. You can believe whatever you want about creatures and mental health and darkness. I don't want any part of it, and I don't want you spreading this shit around my town.'

'I understand, and I promise I won't get in your way.'

'If I find out you've been questioning anyone, or you in any way get involved, I shall personally arrest you for sticking your nose into places where it doesn't belong.'

Stephen smiled. 'Detective Williams, I'm afraid you can't arrest me for something like that. Unless I break the law, which I won't, you can't arrest me for walking around town and talking to people. It's in my job description.'

Detective Williams pointed a finger at him. 'I'm keeping my eye on you.'

'And I you, Detective. Oh, one more thing … are you one of those kids in the photo up there? If so, whatever happened to that happy, smiling teenager? You all look like a proper little gang.'

Stephen watched as Detective Williams clamped his jaw shut. He took that as his cue to leave. He flicked the lights on and off seventeen times and then left the room, leaving a bewildered-looking detective behind.

# Chapter Six

## Olivia

### *25 May 1980*

*Fifteen-year-old Olivia Grace sneezed for the fourth time as grass pollen tickled her nose. Hay fever struck every year usually around this time, causing her nose to itch and her eyes to water, and as spring turned to summer, it was only going to get worse. She rubbed her eyes again, despite knowing the action would make them sting further.*

*Olivia knew she should stop lying in the long grass, but she loved being in the fresh air now the weather was getting warmer. Plus, she couldn't stay indoors all day just because she could barely see out of her streaming eyes. Ensuring the pockets were full of tissues, she'd brought a light jacket but hadn't needed it yet, so she tied it around her waist, which she thought made it look smaller anyway. Her pale-yellow dress came to just above her knees and her white sandals were already covered in dirt.*

*Jack Evans was lying on his back next to her with his eyes closed. She reckoned he was faking being asleep, but he looked so peaceful, so she left him alone and watched as his chest rose and fell slowly. He was a handsome boy, and strong too. Already, his chest and arms were filling out and he looked more like a grown man every day. No longer the baby of the group. He could have easily passed for eighteen, especially since his chin had started erupting with tiny hairs, which, of course, everyone made fun of.*

Frank Willows and Mary King were sitting a few feet away and talking between themselves, keeping their heads close together and their voices low. Mary kept reaching over and stroking Frank's arm and laughing. Olivia's stomach did a flip. She didn't like it when her friend flirted with Frank. Mary knew Olivia liked him, yet she did it anyway.

Frank was the most perfect boy Olivia could have imagined. He was polite, attractive and a genuinely nice person. He didn't have a bad word to say about anyone. His dark blonde hair flapped in the breeze. It was overdue a cut, but Olivia liked it when it was slightly too long. She loved the way it covered his eyes. It made her want to reach out and brush it away from his face. She'd been in love with Frank for as long as she could remember, but had never acted on it. How could she when he could have his pick of any of the girls in town? Olivia was happy to be his friend.

Mary King was very pretty; too pretty. Despite Olivia's bright blonde hair and blue eyes, she felt plain next to Mary who seemed to light up every room with her bubbly personality. Plus, she'd developed in the chest area two years ago, and all the boys had been paying her much more attention ever since.

Olivia looked down at her flat chest. She thought she should have been developing by now, but her mother told her to be patient, it would happen eventually, and that she should enjoy being a child for as long as possible before hormones took over and changed her into a young woman.

It seemed hormones had already taken over Mary King, and the boys.

*Olivia stood, rubbed her eyes and smoothed out her dress, giving Frank and Mary one last glance before taking off her sandals and walking to the water's edge. Lake Peace was beautiful this time of year and lots of people from all over the local area visited throughout the spring and summer months. There was even an area of grass where people could camp overnight if they wished.*

*She dipped her toes into the cool water and wiggled them around. Mary let out a loud laugh behind her. Olivia tried to think of something else. She looked into the clear blue sky and watched as a bird circled above, calling to its mate.*

*'Liv, you want to come for a hike?'*

*Olivia turned at the sound of Frank's voice, which was smooth and deep. It seemed he was developing those hormones too. Everyone was growing up without her. 'Sure,' she replied as she returned to put on her sandals.*

*'It's a shame Lee Man isn't here,' said Frank.*

*'You know he hates to be called that,' replied Olivia with a giggle.*

*'Well, he's not here to defend himself, is he?' Frank winked at her, and Olivia let out another childish giggle, then thought better of it and put on a more serious face. She didn't want him to think of her as a little girl, even though she practically still looked like one.*

*'Where is he again?' asked Mary, coming to stand next to Frank, a little too close for Olivia's liking.*

'He and his family have gone on holiday somewhere on a canal boat,' said Olivia. 'He's back tomorrow, I believe.'

Mary nodded, then laughed as she glanced at Jack, still lying with his eyes shut on the grass. 'Shall we wake him or leave him?'

Frank made the decision and kicked Jack's feet with his boot. Jack sat bolt upright. 'Huh? What? What's going on?'

'You fell asleep,' replied Frank with a laugh.

'No, I didn't,' said Jack as he scrambled to his feet and dusted the grass off the back of his shirt and trousers.

Mary and Olivia laughed together. 'We're going for a hike,' said Mary, pointing towards the river that flowed away from the lake. 'Up there.'

'Up the river?' asked Olivia. 'Is that even safe?'

'We'll find out, won't we?'

Olivia watched as Mary headed in the direction of the river. She wasn't so sure about the hike now. As far as she knew, no one had been upriver before because there was a steep ravine further up and no way out other than to turn back or continue, but she didn't know where it came out on the other side, or how far it stretched into the distance.

Frank held out his hand towards her. 'Shall we?'

Olivia flushed as she took his hand, feeling elated that she was touching him.

Jack followed behind and began to complain his feet hurt within five minutes.

## *22 January 2024 – 16:00 p.m.*

Olivia flinched when the phone rang, the daydream dissolving before her eyes. She was in the middle of chopping potatoes for the casserole she was making for dinner. The knife in her right hand nicked her middle finger as she flinched. She sucked the blood off and then wiped her hands on the dishtowel tucked into her apron while hurrying to the phone. She still had a landline, something Emma often teased her about, but she was set in her ways and had no need for a mobile phone because she barely went anywhere to use it.

'Hello?'

'Hello, Mrs Willows. It's Detective Williams.'

Olivia's heart leapt again as she gulped in a mouth full of air, attempting to steady her racing heart. 'Oh, hello, um, Detective. What can I do for you?' The last time she'd spoken to the detective was last year when she'd had to provide a short statement regarding her friend Emma and her wife Linda when their house had burned down. Before that, she'd barely had any involvement with the police in this town, something she was quite proud of.

'I, er … was wondering how Frank, um … Mr Willows was doing, and if there was anything I could do to be of assistance.'

Olivia smiled into the phone. Her heart rate slowed. 'That's very kind of you to offer, Detective. Frank is … well, the doctors say he doesn't have long, I'm afraid. Weeks. Maybe days.'

Olivia heard shuffling on the end of the phone. She got the impression the detective was nervous.

'I'm very sorry to hear that. Um, would it be okay if I come and talk to you tomorrow? And Frank too, if that's possible.'

'Frank doesn't really talk much these days, but yes, I suppose ... What's this about, Detective?'

'I'm not sure if you've heard yet, Mrs Willows, but a body has been found, and I'm now running the investigation. It will be announced to the media tomorrow, but I wanted to ... I suppose I wanted to talk to you in person about it first.'

Olivia's heart lurched again. She was beginning to worry the detective could hear her heart thumping through the phone. 'Oh ... I see. I'm not sure what help I could be to the case, but you're welcome to come and ask your questions. Whatever you need.'

'You don't seem too surprised to hear that a body has been found.'

Olivia let out a short laugh. 'I'm afraid you're too late with your news. I've already heard it from the local gossip mill, although God only knows how they heard. To be perfectly honest, I wasn't even sure if the rumour was true.'

Detective Williams snorted at the end of the phone. 'I'll have to come along to one of those coffee mornings. I expect I'd learn a lot.'

'I'm sure you would,' replied Olivia with a chuckle. 'What time can I expect you tomorrow?'

'Is ten o'clock okay for you?'

'Yes, that's fine. I'll make sure Frank is awake.'

'Thank you, I appreciate it. See you tomorrow, Mrs Willows.'

'See you tomorrow, Detective. Goodbye.'

An hour later, Olivia spooned thick chicken casserole into a bowl and made up a tray to take to her husband, complete with a small vase and a single stem of a fern she'd plucked from the garden. It wasn't much, but she'd always been brought up to believe even the smallest detail was worth the effort if it made someone smile. And she longed for her husband to smile again. Other than when she'd been told the news about her daughter expecting a baby, Olivia hadn't genuinely smiled for a very long time either.

She climbed the stairs slowly, so as not to trip, something she'd done several times over the past few months, usually because she was rushing. Her dodgy ankle liked to give out from time to time, catching her off guard, usually at the most unfortunate of moments.

Olivia knocked lightly on the door to her husband's room and entered. The lights were on, and he was propped up with numerous pillows reading a book. His glasses were perched on the edge of his nose, so he took them off when she walked into the room.

'You're reading!' Olivia set the tray on the swivel table by the bed.

'Yes, this book is just getting good, and I don't want to die before I finish it. That would be a tragedy.'

Olivia smirked at her husband's morbid sense of humour. Even in the darkest of times, he found a way to brighten the day. 'What's it about?'

'It's a murder mystery set in the Scottish Highlands.' Frank set the book down and watched while Olivia set up his dinner and swivelled the table, so it was level with his chest. 'I like the fern,' he said, touching it with his delicate, thin fingers. 'Who was that on the phone earlier?'

'Did it wake you?'

'Yes, but I was sort of awake anyway.'

'It was Detective Williams.' Olivia sat down on the comfy chair beside the bed and watched while her husband took his first bite of food.

Frank's eyes turned dark, and he grunted in response. 'What did *he* want?'

'He asked after you.' Another grunt. 'And he asked if we were available tomorrow to answer a few questions.'

'What about?' Frank coughed, set down his spoon and sipped some water from his glass before getting back to his dinner. It was clear he wasn't hungry. Olivia knew he only ate because it made her happy.

'I didn't tell you about it last week because I didn't want to upset you, and I wasn't sure if it was true, but Detective Williams has confirmed it. A body has been found.' Olivia watched as Frank set down his spoon. He sighed heavily and leaned back against his thick pillows.

'Where?' he asked, not making eye contact with her.

'I think you know where.'

Another grunt. 'And why does the detective think we would know anything about it?'

Olivia watched Frank's face again. He was sickly pale, but that could have been due to the illness raging through his body. Or maybe it was something else.

Olivia attempted to lighten her tone. 'I'm not sure. He didn't give details.'

Another grunt.

'You know, Frank, we've been married since we were eighteen. After forty years, I know exactly what that grunt means.'

Frank looked up at his wife and smiled. 'I forgot you're smarter than me, my dear.'

Olivia smiled back. 'Maybe not smarter, just ... observational.' They lapsed into silence while Frank ate a few more spoonfuls, but then he set down his utensil again. Olivia could tell he was struggling. Often, the medication he was on, combined with the sickness, made him lose his appetite. It was a struggle to get anything to stay down at times.

'Do you think the detective will put two and two together?' she asked.

Frank didn't look at her as he replied, 'What are you talking about, Liv? We weren't there, remember?'

'No, of course we weren't ... It's just ... I'm worried, Frank. I'm worried because we're two of the only people left alive who know what happened, and I'm afraid once you're dead and buried

I'll be all alone, and you know I'm not as strong as you and I'm afraid I might … crack.'

Frank pushed his table away, reached out and took her hand. 'My dear, you are the strongest woman I've ever had the pleasure of knowing. You practically single-handedly raised our girls and were there for Brooke every step of the way through her … illness. And now you've been looking after me while I slowly wither and die before your eyes. My dear … you *are* strong, and don't you ever forget it.'

Olivia sniffed as she wiped her eyes with a tissue from her apron pocket. 'Oh, goodness, I forgot to say … Brooke called a few hours ago. She and Jordan are having a baby!'

Frank's face lit up and Olivia saw the glimmer of the happy man he once was. 'Now I can die a happy man.'

# Chapter Seven

## Alex

### *22 January 2024 – 17:30 p.m.*

Alex kicked off his dirty school shoes in the hallway. He then stared at them for a few seconds before picking them up and putting them on the newly purchased shoe rack. He knew it would please his mum that he did that. He liked to keep her happy, especially now he had her undivided attention. The unmistakable smell of her special Thai curry wafted from the kitchen. Smelled like lamb. His favourite. Why was she cooking his favourite meal? It wasn't Saturday. Normally, she cooked his favourite meals at the weekend. Today was Monday …

'Mum?' He stuck his head around the kitchen door. The curry pot simmered on the hob at a low heat, steam rising high to the ceiling, but his mum was nowhere to be seen. A horrible sense of déjà vu passed over him as he remembered getting home several months ago to a similar situation when they lived on Baker Street and he'd found his step-mum, Linda, unconscious and almost dead in the bathtub.

'Mum?' he called again, grabbing hold of the banister and taking a few steps up.

'Alex, I'm up here.'

He let out his breath and jogged upstairs to find his mum on her hands and knees in the middle of her bedroom floor surrounded by small items of clothing. Baby and children's clothes. Pink clothes. His heart sank.

'What are you doing in here?'

'I'm just going through some of Phoebe's clothes.'

He frowned, unsure whether he was witnessing her spiralling down a new dark path, or whether this was a good thing. 'Okay ... why?'

'Dr Allan has given me some homework, and that's to go through all of Phoebe's clothes. I can keep the items I love or that remind me of her, but the rest are going to be donated to the charity shop. I think it's about time. Look at this little pink onesie. Can you believe she fit into this once?'

Alex curled his top lip into a thin smile as his mum held up the item. It was indeed very small. He couldn't remember Phoebe ever wearing it.

'That's ... good?' he said, raising his tone of voice at the end.

His mum smiled at his hesitance. 'Alex, it's fine. You don't have to tread on eggshells around me anymore. I'm doing much better now, thanks to Doctor Allan, and Olivia.'

Alex clenched his jaw and squeezed his fists together behind his back at the mention of their names. What he wouldn't give to hear she was doing better because of him, not them. *Him*. 'That's great, Mum. I'm glad.' If she picked up his forced tone, she didn't let on.

'How was school today?' she asked as she folded a pink jacket and put it on a pile to her left, which was considerably larger than the pile on the right. Alex wasn't sure which pile was the charity pile and which was the keep pile.

'Fine, I guess.'

'And how's Harriet?'

Alex sighed. 'Fine … Look, I know you don't approve of me and her dating, so you don't have to ask how she's doing.'

Emma lowered the yellow t-shirt she was now holding. 'It's not that I don't approve of her, but … well, her mother did burn down our house and …' She stopped and shook her head. 'I'm sorry. I shouldn't hold a grudge against Harriet just because her mother was a conniving cow.'

Alex raised his eyebrows. 'Wow, Mum … you're brutal.'

'Enough cheek from you. Can you go and stir the curry before the bottom catches? I'll be down in a minute. I'll finish this off later.'

'Sure. Mum. Why are we having my favourite curry tonight? It's Monday.'

'I know that, Alex.'

'So, what's the occasion?'

'Do I need an occasion to make my son his favourite meal?'

Alex frowned, unsure whether it was a trick question. 'I guess not.'

'Go. Stir. Now.'

Alex backed out of the room. As he did, he caught a glimpse of his mum bringing a piece of clothing to her face and smelling it.

He stirred the curry, stuck his finger into the mixture and tasted it. It was good. As usual. He wasn't sure what she put into the curry to make it taste so yummy, but she nailed it every time. It was never too spicy either. He didn't like it so hot that he couldn't feel his tongue.

Alex leaned against the side and his mind drifted back to the day he and his friends had found the cave at the bottom of Beaker Ravine.

### 11 January 2024

*Alex pulled a few rocks from the pile, revealing a large, dark hole. It smelled damp and … musty. As he peered into the dark depths beyond, an unmistakable feeling of dread passed through him. Not the type of dread he would often get before a big exam when he knew he hadn't studied properly, but the type that told him something bad was about to happen, despite there being no evidence to suggest it would.*

*Harriet and Alex the First appeared behind him, knocking him out of his strange feeling.*

*'Oh wow,' said Harriet. 'You found it.'*

*'Epic,' said Alex the First.*

*'Are you guys going to stand there or give me a hand?' asked Alex as he dislodged another rock. It fell from the pile he was making and crashed at Harriet's feet. She shrieked and leapt backwards.*

*'I'll let you two boys do the heavy lifting if you don't mind.'*

*Alex rolled his eyes. Why was he even still dating her? Other than being fit, she had nothing else going for her. She was even more of a psycho than he was, especially since she'd admitted she'd bullied and tortured a little girl to tears. Alex had standards. At least, he used to have standards. Now it seemed he was perfectly happy to date a psychopath just because she was pleasant to look at and he couldn't be bothered with the aggravation of breaking up with her.*

*Alex kicked the last of the stones to the side and dusted off his hands on his trousers. He took out his phone and turned on the torch function, holding it aloft as he stepped inside. The cave mouth was barely big enough to fit through, but amazingly, it began to expand the further he walked.*

*'Um, not to bring a downer to this whole thing, but ... isn't this a bit dangerous?' asked Alex the First, sticking his head through the hole. 'This whole thing could collapse at any second or there could be another landslide, which could trap us inside.'*

*'Stop being a pussy and get in here,' snapped Alex as he shuffled awkwardly around to face the cave entrance. Alex the First muttered and swore as he bent down and manoeuvred himself through the small opening. Harriet followed closely behind.*

*Alex's legs shook from the exertion of squatting as he moved forward, trying to avoid hitting his head. His phone torch did an excellent job of lighting the dark hole, but there were still spooky-looking corners and crevices where light couldn't reach. The ground was damp and squelchy, and the walls of the cave* trickled with water. Alex the First was right: it was dangerous to be in here.

Alex reached a spot in the cave where he could stand. He turned and shone his phone back the way he'd come, stretching his back as he did so.

Harriet's and Alex the First's eyes shone yellow as a dark shadow passed across the wall next to them. He watched the shadow grow. The long limbs looked like elongated claws. And the body was shaped like a huge skeleton ...

He shook his head, reminding himself it was merely the light playing tricks. The eerie shadows belonged to them, no one else.

Harriet reached him first and huddled close, clutching his hand as if it were going to save her from a terrible monster attack. 'This place is freaking me out,' she whispered.

Alex the First stood up and copied Alex's movement of stretching his back. 'I wonder how far this goes. Plus ... it smells funky in here.'

Harriet nodded. 'It sort of smells like ...'

'Weed,' finished Alex.

'Yeah. How weird is that?'

'Well, kids did used to come here and smoke joints back in the day before the ravine became a death trap,' said Alex the First.

'Yeah, but how could the smell of weed linger for decades?' asked Alex. He was met with silence. 'Come on, let's go a little deeper and see how far it goes.'

*Harriet let out a small whimper as he pulled his hand out of her grasp. Alex led the way with Harriet in the middle and Alex the First bringing up the rear.*

*'Ouch!' shouted Alex the First.*

*Alex turned at lightning speed. 'What?'*

*'Hit my head.'*

*Alex rolled his eyes and continued.*

*It was slow progress due to the narrow passage and uneven ground. Plus, the darkness seemed thicker down in the cave, almost like it was alive ... The torch still did a good job, but it didn't appear to reach as far into the darkness as it once had at the beginning.*

*A cold tingle crept down Alex's spine. He'd had the sensation before. He recognised it ...*

*'Oh my God, what is that fucking awful smell?' Alex the First gagged.*

*'That's not weed,' replied Harriet, screwing her nose up.*

*Alex silently agreed with his girlfriend. He stopped and scanned his phone light around the area. Nothing but grey rocks and darkness. But he came across a pile of rocks that looked out of place within the cave, as if they'd been piled on top of each other.*

*Alex handed his phone to Harriet. 'Here ... give me some light.'*

*'What are you doing?'*

'Just hold it.' Alex approached the rocks and pulled a few off the top of the pile. They weren't too hard to move. He kept going, removing them one by one and placing them to the side.

He reached some dirt and sticks. He grabbed one of the sticks. It snapped in his hand, so he tossed it aside, going back for more.

Harriet screamed.

The piercing sound reverberated off the walls.

Alex spun around. 'What the fuck?'

Harriet whimpered and pointed a shaky finger at the stick Alex had just discarded. 'W-What is t-that?'

All eyes fell upon the stick.

But it was no stick.

'Holy shit ... That's a bone.'

# Chapter Eight

## Graham

### *22 January 2024 – 18:30 p.m.*

It was earlier than he usually got back from work, so he considered it a small win for the day. After he got off the phone with Mrs Willows, he'd contemplated staying at the office and going over paperwork again, or maybe staring blankly at the murder board until his eyes burned and his head pounded even more, but had decided against it. There was nothing more he could do until his DCs finished questioning some of the townspeople or the DNA profile came back from the lab. Plus, he wasn't due to speak with Mr and Mrs Willows until the morning, so ... with nothing better to do, he went home.

His small country cottage with the badly thatched roof was empty of life upon arrival, the way it always was when he walked through the door, exhausted after a long day of running the small police station in town. The station may have only been small, but recently it sure as hell had a lot of cases open.

Graham had often toyed with the idea of getting a dog or a cat as a companion, but then it wouldn't be fair to the animal because he wasn't home most of the day, which was why he had a couple of goldfish instead: less needy. Fred and Wilma. Two oversized fish who couldn't have cared less if he arrived home late and didn't judge him for eating cold pizza three nights in a row.

He sprinkled a few flakes into the tank and finger-waved at the largest fish (Wilma) who swam out to investigate. How sad his life was that the only creatures he interacted with at home were fish.

Graham left the television off. The only thing on the box at this time of night was either the news, a home improvement show or a game show, none of which appealed to him. He couldn't stand watching the news. He hated it with a passion. Often, he'd arrive at work with no idea of what was going on in the world and his colleagues would tell him various stories of current events. Some people might have called him ignorant, but he didn't care. All he cared about was the small world around him, the one in Cherry Hollow. That was enough drama for him.

He opened the fridge and peered inside, hoping maybe the food fairy had visited him, but she had not. He placed an order from the local takeaway, put some classical music on, poured himself a whiskey and sat down in his leather armchair.

Graham hadn't chosen a life of solitude. When he was a younger man at the start of his career, he'd had a wife and the prospect of starting a family. Christina, however, had other ideas and had grown tired of country living and ran off to the nearest city with a bloke she met on an online dating app. James ... *something*. They'd only been married a year before she took off.

He hadn't bothered trying to form another serious relationship other than with Claire back in the early 2000s, but that had fizzled out as well. The relationship bridge had been well and truly burned. He was too old now; too weathered and worn and tired.

Graham sipped his drink and sighed.

He had friends in town though. There was Phil and Trevor whom he hung out with on a Saturday night at the local pub and played darts or pool until the early hours. But they didn't see each other on any other day.

Then there was …

Graham drained the last of his whiskey.

There were others in town who he'd used to consider friends, but that was a very long time ago. Graham had lived in Cherry Hollow his whole life. Born and raised in the fresh country air. The only time he'd left was to do officer training at the academy, and he'd fought tooth and nail to be able to come back to the town and live out his professional career.

For thirty years he'd been a police officer.

For thirty years, he'd fought on the side of justice and done the right thing.

Or so he thought.

But there was one thing that had plagued him for many years, and it was the one thing that was now rearing its ugly head once again. A black hole from his past had haunted him ever since.

He wished he could turn back time, back forty years to when his life had started to go wrong, when he'd lost all four of his best friends in a single day.

And hadn't, even to this day, known the reason why.

## *26 May 1980*

*His excitement vibrated his insides. Every fibre in his body fizzed. He couldn't wait to see his four best friends and tell them about his holiday on a canal boat. It had been such a fun experience, helping his father with the mechanisms of raising and lowering the water levels to allow the boat through the narrow passages. His mum had spent her days cooking meals in the tiny kitchen or reading on top of the boat while he and his father manned the wheel.*

*But now he just wanted to see his friends and find out what they'd been up to this past week. He decided to visit Mary first because she lived the closest. She lived on Baker Street, number six, and he lived at number twenty.*

*He promised his mum he'd be back within an hour to help her unpack from the trip and then prepare dinner. It was three in the afternoon now. He ran all the way up the road, his floppy hair waving in all directions. By the time he reached the driveway of number six, he was out of breath. He raced up the path and knocked on the door, bouncing up and down on the balls of his feet.*

*He knocked again.*

*'Who is it?'*

*Graham looked up at the voice. Mrs King was sticking her head out of the front bedroom window. 'Hi, Mrs King. Is Mary home?'*

*'No.'*

'Oh ... Is she with the others?'

'I don't know where she is. Please leave.' Mrs King had never been the friendliest of people, but she seemed extra rude today.

Graham frowned as he stepped backwards. 'Will you tell her I dropped by?'

'No. We aren't staying here anymore.'

Graham raised a hand and shielded his eyes from the sun. 'What do you mean, Mrs King?'

'We're moving.'

Graham gasped. 'What? Since when?'

'Since now.'

'Why?'

'Enough of your questions. Mary doesn't want to see you anymore.'

Graham opened his mouth but then closed it. 'I don't understand ... What have I done to make her not want to see me anymore? I've only just got back from a holiday.'

Mrs King tutted loudly. 'Look, I don't have time to explain. Please leave now.'

'Can Mary write to me?'

'What?'

'Please ... She's one of my best friends.'

Mrs King shook her head. 'Graham ... I think it's best you cut ties with Mary. Goodbye.' The bedroom window slammed shut.

'Wait! But—' Graham hung his head, defeated.

*Stepping backwards further, Graham looked up at the house. Mrs King had acted so strangely. Why were the family moving away? What had happened in the past week that would make Mary not want to see or speak to him? He needed to speak to the others, but his mother was expecting him back within the hour, so he'd have to be quick and run.*

# Chapter Nine

## Stephen

### *22 January 2024 – 20:45 p.m.*

The crackling log fire plus the warming whiskey in the thick-bottomed tumbler was finally warming Stephen's bones. The cold and the driving rain all day had been enough to give him a proper chill. The thick darkness of the winter had crept in early, a little after three in the afternoon. He hadn't wanted to be caught out in the dark, so he'd walked back to the hotel from the police station after talking with Detective Williams, had a freezing cold shower, which had made him even colder, and then read through his notes while waiting for dinner.

Now, after a hearty hot meal of lamb chops, mashed potato, green beans and thick gravy, he was settled in the library and bar area next to the fire, which had already been alight when he'd entered. No one else was around yet. He'd seen a few people at dinner, but they had retired to their rooms early. He was alone and that's how he often liked it.

It had never been easy for Stephen to strike up a conversation for general conversation's sake. Probing questions and interviewing he could do in his sleep, but a normal conversation with a stranger was a skill he'd never been able to master, not in his thirty-nine years. The consensus was that people thought him odd. That's what his father had told him. That's what his teachers had told him. And that's what his only ever girlfriend had told him before dumping him on their first anniversary.

But it didn't matter to Stephen. Not anymore. He'd come to accept he was different, and people were always afraid or wary of those who were different. It didn't make him odd. It made him … *him*.

He flicked through his notebook. Before speaking with Detective Williams earlier, he'd been to the local coffee shop, adequately named The Bean Café. He remembered the owner last time being more than welcoming and helpful, so he'd gone to see her again, but this time the young woman had narrowed her eyes at him as he'd entered, giving off a less-than-friendly vibe.

'You again,' she'd said. She'd been in the middle of drying some mugs.

'Hello. Hayley, isn't it?'

'That's right. I'm a little surprised to see you back here.'

Stephen shrugged as he'd approached the counter. He stepped around a customer. 'Yes, well … I couldn't pass up the opportunity of investigating yet another dead body in Cherry Hollow. I'll have a latte please.'

Hayley had squeezed her lips together as she turned and assembled the cup and coffee beans. 'I'll bring it over to your table,' she said, still with her back turned.

Stephen nodded even though she couldn't see him and found an empty table by the window, looking out over the grey street. The last time he'd visited Cherry Hollow was in the height of summer, and it had been a delightful place, but now in the depths of winter, it wasn't quite so welcoming. There was a dark, sad cloud of … *something* in the air. Maybe it had something to do with the discovery of another dead body, or maybe it was just like any normal British town in wintertime, a bit sad, damp and dismal.

Hayley had walked up to his table and set the coffee next to him. 'Enjoy.'

'Do you mind if I ask you a few questions?'

'Are they about the dead body?'

'Yes.'

'Then no.'

'Are you sure?'

Hayley sighed. 'Look, Mr … I'm sorry, I've forgotten your name.'

'Stephen Mallow.'

'Right, Mr Mallow … I'm sorry you've had to come all the way back out here, but the police in this town are investigating the case. We don't need you to come back and stir up more trouble and create more rumours. Cherry Hollow is a nice, pleasant town, which has had its share of tragedy. I just wish people like you would leave us the hell alone.'

Stephen adjusted his bottom on the chair. 'I'm sorry you feel that way, but all I really want to do is find out the truth. People are hiding secrets in this town. It seems someone has been hiding a big one for over forty years.'

'Most of the people from forty years ago have either moved away or are dead.'

'But there are a few still around from that time, yes?'

Hayley rolled her eyes. 'Yes, a couple, I guess.'

'I'm going to need their names.' Stephen poised his pen on his notebook.

'And I'm going to need you to stop asking questions and drink your coffee.'

Stephen locked eyes with Hayley. 'Just one name.'

Hayley shook her head. 'Nope. After what happened last year, I'm done with spreading gossip and saying stuff I shouldn't, especially to nosey journalists like you.'

'Ah, yes. The two building fires on Halloween night. Someone died that night too.' He knew all about that of course because he'd investigated the incidents before he'd come here and had written another brief article which hadn't been published yet. It was still sitting in his outbox, waiting to be sent to Kevin, his boss. There were a lot of holes in the story ... and that's why he was here. Well, that and because someone had sent him an email practically begging him to come. He still had no idea who it could have been.

'Yet another tragic accident,' replied Hayley.

'I highly doubt that. Jordan Evans got stabbed too, didn't he?'

Hayley narrowed her eyes at him. 'The people responsible are now behind bars, awaiting trial.'

'And you're quite sure about that?'

'Yes.'

'Very well. Thank you. That will be all.'

Hayley muttered a few indecent words as she walked back to the counter, leaving Stephen fiddling with his pen, tapping it on the notebook. He wrote a few words, took a sip of his drink, wrote a few more words, and then underlined the name.

*Who looks over fifty years old?*

*<u>Detective Williams.</u>*

*Who else?*

With his tattered notebook resting on his lap, Stephen stared into the flames, going over the conversation he'd had with both Hayley and Detective Williams earlier in the day. Hayley hadn't provided all that much information, other than the fact she hadn't been as forthcoming as before. Why was that? Was it because of the article he'd written a few years ago, or was it because the town was trying to cover up the discovery of the new body? Detective Williams had said himself he wasn't all that happy about announcing it to the world's media.

There was definitely something *off* regarding the way the detective had spoken about the body. To Stephen, it felt like the detective was in denial about what was really going on. Okay, so the man didn't believe in The Creature or how mental health could manifest itself into something so real, but there was no doubt he was freaked out about something.

Thinking about it, Detective Williams would have been a kid back in the mid-to-early-80s, probably a teenager or thereabouts. Maybe even the same age as Jordan, Brooke, Amber and Tyler were when they'd covered up their friend's death ...

No … It wasn't possible, was it?

Surely Detective Williams hadn't known a body was down in the ravine for the past forty-odd years. He was a respected member of the community and a highly renowned police officer who had worked his way up the ranks. Stephen had even read that the disappearance of Kieran Jones had been the first proper case he'd been a part of as a young sergeant. It had made his career, despite having not solved the case until twenty years later.

Stephen decided to give him the benefit of the doubt and not go around accusing the local police chief of his involvement in a forty-year-old murder cover-up. But he could still do with asking him some questions, especially since he was roughly the right age to have been around during that time. If only the detective wasn't such a stubborn, grumpy old git. There was no way in hell Stephen would be able to get a straight answer out of him. He needed a different angle. He needed someone else to question.

Stephen turned to a fresh page of his notebook and wrote a few more notes before getting out his laptop and turning it on.

Once booted, he opened the folder marked 'Cherry Hollow' and clicked on a few newspaper articles, mainly the ones dated around the mid-80s from the area. He had saved quite a few over the last week or so since receiving the email but hadn't had the time to properly go through each one. A few scattered headlines jumped out at him.

*Hottest Summer on Record in the Lake District*
*Tourists Flock to Lake Peace*
*Local Lake a Tourist Hot Spot in the Summer of '81*
*Urgent - New Job Opening in Cherry Hollow for Head Teacher*

Stephen opened the two articles regarding Lake Peace and read them. He'd heard about the lake from a few locals but hadn't visited it the last time he was here. Apparently, it was now the only way a person could gain access to the bottom of Beaker Ravine, as the old path down the side had finally worn away. Therefore, the teenagers who'd found the body must have hiked from the lake and up the riverbed to the hidden cave at the bottom of the ravine. Whether they'd known the cave was there in the first place, he didn't know.

But forty years ago, whoever had been down in the ravine when the person was killed could have gained access from either the lake or down the side of the ravine, depending on whether the path had been there back then.

Stephen wrote down a note.

*Murdered or died?*

Perhaps the person had slipped and fallen to their death and then been dragged into the cave by a wild animal. Stephen didn't know the cause of death yet. Maybe the detective would announce the details tomorrow at the press conference.

However, the anonymous email he'd received regarding the body had made it sound like foul play was involved. Plus, the body had been found buried in a cave. Clearly, it was never supposed to have been found. A wild animal wouldn't have buried it, right?

Stephen clicked on the article regarding the new job opening. It was from the summer of 1980. It was an advert for a new head teacher, but there was a small note at the bottom, which intrigued him.

*Mr Solomon King's sudden departure will be greatly missed. We hope he has a wonderful career wherever he has moved to.*

That was weird.

So, not only did the man leave suddenly, but he also left no forwarding address or told anyone where he was moving to ...

Stephen brought up the local historical title register and typed in Mr King's name, but it came back with no results. He needed to find out where Mr King had lived in Cherry Hollow. Maybe that was a good place to start, but something nagged him in the back of his mind. Something he couldn't quite reach or understand.

There was something odd about this. He knew it, but he just didn't know *how* he knew it.

Stephen had a very particular mind, a unique brain chemistry.

Not only did he have childhood-diagnosed obsessive-compulsive disorder, which lay at one end of the spectrum, but he also had attention-deficit hyperactivity disorder, located at the opposite end. This caused him to not only have overlapping symptoms, but the two conditions often battled against each other, which caused a great deal of aggravation for himself and others. Although, he didn't care if his condition aggravated anyone else.

Sometimes, he struggled to focus on the most normal, everyday task and then he'd become so overly fixated on something, he wouldn't eat or sleep until he'd completed it. He was also restless, forgetful, impulsive and tended to interrupt people, not aware he was being rude. Then there was a strong desire to keep things the same and in the correct order, hence why he hadn't wanted to stay in any other room because he'd stayed in room 11 before, and he knew the layout. Any change in routine often led to him becoming frustrated and anxious, and then his excessive counting and checking of things became so extreme that his daily life was affected.

These conditions were like his own unique superpowers because his brain picked up on things that most people missed. That's why he'd returned to Cherry Hollow, despite promising to never come back. He couldn't let it go after all. There was a mystery here that needed to be solved, and it was an itch he needed to scratch.

He would find out the truth ...

Even if it meant facing his own dark past first.

Stephen leaned back in the chair, finally deciding on the cause of action for tomorrow.

First, there was the press conference, which he'd attend, and then he'd go and visit the school and speak to the head teacher there. Maybe it was the same person who'd taken Mr

King's job. He had no idea if Mr King was connected to anything, but it certainly wouldn't hurt to investigate, even if it was to tick it off the list in his mind.

# Chapter Ten

## Olivia

### *23 January 2024 – 10:10 a.m.*

The butterflies fluttering in her stomach were making her nauseous, along with the three cups of coffee she'd already drunk this morning that were sloshing around. Her body practically trembled from the amount of caffeine it had ingested.

He was late.

Why was he late?

Had he changed his mind?

Had he found something out already?

Was he doing it on purpose to make her squirm?

Olivia paced in front of the door, twisting her floaty top in her fists. She'd taken extra attention to her attire this morning. She wasn't sure why. It wasn't to impress the detective. Maybe it was to set her mind at ease. She always felt better when she made an effort with her appearance. Long gone were the days she'd dye her grey hair blonde though. She'd found ageing gracefully and naturally was enough for her and was perfectly happy with the lines around her eyes; they told a story of her life, not all of which was pleasant.

As she stared at the carpet, her mind raced with an array of probing questions the detective was most likely to ask her. It was his job after all. *Do you know anything about the body that*

*was found? Do you remember anyone going missing around forty
years ago?*

Knock, knock.

Olivia's heart rate doubled. She clutched her chest; even
though she'd been expecting the knock, it had still come out of
nowhere. She plastered a fake smile across her face and opened
the door. Detective Williams stood on her doorstep, a fifty-plus-
year-old man with greying hair and fine lines and wrinkles around
his eyes. He wore a smart suit, but it was obvious he hadn't run
an iron over it. His tie was loose and slightly crooked.

'Hello, Mrs Willows.'

Olivia sighed. 'Oh, Graham, I think we're past the
formalities now, aren't we? Please, call me Olivia.'

Graham nodded. 'Very well … *Olivia*. It's good to see you.'

'And you, Graham. Come in.' She opened the door wider
and stepped aside. He was a tall man, towering over her by at
least a foot and a half. She didn't move in for a hug. It didn't seem
appropriate. 'Would you like a drink?'

'I wouldn't mind a coffee. Didn't sleep well last night.'

'That makes two of us. I've already had my caffeine
intake for the day, but I'll happily make you one. Come into the
kitchen with me, then we'll go and see Frank.' Olivia led the way
through the corridor and into the kitchen at the back of the
house.

'How is he?' asked Graham. 'I'm sorry, I should have
come and seen you both months ago, but … well, I have no valid
excuse.'

Olivia flicked the kettle on. 'You're a busy man, I understand.'

'We haven't spoken properly for a long time, Olivia.'

'Forty-four years,' she replied with a long sigh. 'My goodness, when did we get so old?'

They shared a half-hearted laugh. Olivia caught his eye and promptly looked away, worried he'd see her face redden. Their humour quickly died down and left a strange silence in its place.

'Graham, may I ask you a direct question?'

'Of course.'

Olivia set out a mug for the coffee. 'Do you know who the body belongs to yet?'

'No, not officially.'

Olivia bit her lip and then asked, 'But you have an idea, don't you?'

Graham waited several long seconds before replying, 'Yes.'

Olivia nodded as tears sprung to her ears. 'Milk and sugar?'

'Both, thank you.'

Olivia stirred the mug and handed it to Graham, who took it with a nod of thanks. 'This isn't going to be easy, you understand. I'm a detective and it's my job to solve this case and all the others too.'

Olivia reached out and placed a hand on his arm, steadying his shakiness. 'I understand, *Detective*. Let's go and see Frank and get this over with.'

Olivia tapped on the bedroom door, waited a few seconds then pushed it open. Graham followed her in and closed it. Frank lay in bed, propped up on pillows with an oxygen mask over his nose and mouth. Olivia wasn't alarmed to see him with it on because he sometimes needed it to breathe properly. He relied on it more and more lately.

Graham approached the bed and extended his hand. 'Hello, Franky.'

Frank removed the mask and grinned. 'Hello there, Lee Man.' The men shook hands. Frank gripped Graham's hand in both of his and held on for a few seconds longer than usually deemed normal for a handshake.

Graham let out a laugh. 'Now, there's a nickname I've not heard in a long time. May I?' He nodded at the chair beside the bed.

'Please do,' replied Frank.

Olivia smiled as she sank down into the chair on the other side of the bed and took hold of one of Frank's paper-thin hands. She rubbed her thumb over his delicate skin, trying not to worry about the blue-green veins that crisscrossed over them and up his arm like miniatures rivers. She hadn't heard the name 'Lee Man' since 1980 either, a name Frank and Jack had come up with as a play on Graham's last name Williams. Will + Liams = Lee Man.

How the boys had come up with such a name had always been beyond Olivia, but seeing the two men together now transported her forty-four years into the past.

But it wasn't a comforting journey.

A lot had happened in that time. They weren't the same people anymore.

Frank coughed. He used the hand Olivia wasn't holding to cover his mouth as the cough ricocheted through his body. Once under control, he cleared his throat. 'So, it's taken you forty years to visit me. I must say your timing is impeccable because I'm checking out of here in a few weeks.'

Olivia squeezed his hand tighter.

Graham lowered his head. 'I'm sorry. I have no excuse, as I was saying to Olivia downstairs. I should have come sooner. I was a coward.'

'I think it's safe to say we were all cowards,' replied Frank. 'Liv tells me you're here because of the body found in that cave.'

'Yes, I'm afraid I am.'

Frank looked at his wife and then back to Graham. 'So, out with it ... Ask the question then.'

Olivia held her breath while Graham breathed in deeply. 'Is it who I think it is?' he asked.

'That depends on who you think it is.'

Graham swallowed. 'Mary King.'

Olivia tensed and released the grip on her husband's hand. 'Did you say Mary King?'

'Yes.'

Olivia's heart skipped a beat as she looked at Frank, who was frowning. 'I … No, it's not her, Graham. Why would you think it's Mary?'

Graham opened his mouth, but seemed to rethink what he was about to say, then tried again.

'B-But … her family, they moved away so suddenly. When I got back from my holiday, I went to her house to see her, but she wasn't there. After that day, none of you spoke to me. We weren't friends anymore. I could only assume something had happened while I was away. I never knew what it was, but … all these years later, when the body was found, something in my brain clicked into gear. I thought it was Mary. She's the only one of us I never saw again.' Graham hung his head again and stared at the carpet.

Frank cleared his throat. 'No, Graham, it's not Mary.'

Graham lifted his head. 'The fact you can say that with confidence tells me you know more about the body than you're letting on. I'm a detective now. It's my job to investigate this death.'

Frank grunted. 'If you had your suspicions about who it was then why not announce it to your team?'

'I had to be sure first. I refuse to add to the rumour mill in this town.' Graham stopped and turned to Olivia. 'What the hell happened forty years ago? Why did you stop talking to me? What happened while I was away?'

A silence filled the void. Olivia and Frank swapped glances.

'You don't want to know,' said Frank. His voice dipped and became quieter and weaker. Olivia wasn't sure if it was due to his illness or because of the topic of conversation.

But Graham's voice became sterner. 'Yes, Frank, I do.'

'Is this you asking as an old friend or as a detective whose job it is to uncover the truth?'

Graham rubbed his stubbly chin and sighed. 'A bit of both, I guess.'

'Are you going to arrest us if we don't cooperate?' asked Frank.

'No, of course not, but if you know something and don't tell the police then you're obstructing the course of justice, and I could have you arrested for that.'

Frank laughed, which inevitably caused a small coughing fit. Once he got himself under control, he leaned back against his pillow, exhausted. 'Don't give me that crap, Lee Man.'

Graham sighed. 'Look, I'm sorry to have to do this, but it's been forty-four years. The truth, whatever it is, needs to come out. We all know what happened to Tyler Jenkins and the rest of his friends, including your daughter, Brooke.'

Olivia stiffened as she rose to her feet. 'Please don't bring Brooke into this, Graham.'

'Olivia, I'm sorry, but I know Jordan, Brooke, and Amber were involved in Kieran's death. I've been keeping it quiet for years. I've known for a while. Tyler took the blame for them. I knew it from the start, but I couldn't do anything because there was no proof they were involved.'

'Then it's just a hunch. You don't know anything,' said Frank bluntly.

'Yes, maybe it's just a hunch, but I could have made it difficult for them, but I didn't. And then Amber was killed. The people of Cherry Hollow started to believe they weren't innocent.'

'My Brooke *is* innocent,' said Olivia.

Graham shook his head. 'All I'm saying is ... the truth has a way of catching up with people. It may happen quickly, or it may take years. When the results from the DNA test come back, then I'll know the truth. And if I find out you've been keeping something from me ...' He tailed off and stood up, turning to the door. 'I won't say anything if I can help it. I'll allow you to pass away in peace, Frank, but Olivia ... this could turn bad for you if you don't cooperate, but I'll do my best. However, I can't guarantee your safety once the truth comes out.' Graham glanced at Frank who had turned pale. 'I didn't want it to come to this. I'm sorry.'

'Me too,' said Frank weakly. 'Goodbye, Lee Man.'

'Goodbye, Franky.'

# Chapter Eleven

## Alex

### *23 January 2024 – 10:30 a.m.*

He needed a smoke, but the mid-morning break wasn't long enough to sneak around the back of the school and have one, so Alex leaned against his locker with his arms folded instead, glaring at anyone who walked past and looked at him funny, which most of the kids in the school did. He was still considered the new, weird boy; the one whose mum tried to take her own life and who then burned alive in a house fire. He didn't mind being weird.

It wasn't that he wanted everyone to be afraid of him, but he certainly didn't want people getting too close because that's how things got complicated and how mistakes happened. At least with Harriet and Alex the First, they had their own fucked up issues to deal with, seeing as how both their mums were in prison for arson and manslaughter. They were just as damaged as he was in some ways, but in other ways, he was much worse.

Alex had Maths for his next lesson in ten minutes, and he was seriously considering bailing, but he promised his mum he'd do better at school. He promised he'd work harder and make her proud of him again. She told him she was already proud of him, but whenever she said it, there was something behind her eyes that made him not believe she was telling the truth. He wanted her to be happy and proud of him, and, if doing well in school would make her happy and proud, then that's what he'd do. He'd do anything for his mum. If only she knew that. There had been a time, back before Phoebe had died, he'd been good at Maths. It hadn't been his favourite subject; that had been Geography, but he'd at least been able to complete fractions and decimals with relative ease. Now, it was as if the knowledge had simply vanished, along with common sense, clear thought and practical thinking.

Alex hummed a tune in his head (his sister's favourite) and watched as Mr Peterson, the headmaster, came out of his office a few doors down the corridor. He was talking to someone behind him, and when the man stepped into the corridor, Alex pushed himself away from the locker and straightened up to get a better view. He couldn't hear what they were saying, but Mr Peterson was shaking his head and appeared to be apologising to the other man.

It wasn't that he was surprised to see him here. In fact, it was perfect timing. Alex watched and waited until the men had finished talking and Mr Peterson had retreated into his office before approaching the man, who looked a little anxious.

'Stephen Mallow, right?' asked Alex.

The man whipped his head around to look at him, like a rabbit caught in headlights. Alex hadn't seen a picture of Stephen before, but he had an air about him that told him he was a journalist. The way his eyes seem to scan everything in his vicinity, searching for any titbit of information he could use to his advantage. Journalists were all the same.

'Who wants to know?'

Alex held up his hands, palms facing away from him. 'Relax, man. I don't bite. I'm Alex Smithson.'

Recognition flickered in Stephen's eyes. 'The kid of the woman who was killed in the house fire last year?'

Alex shrugged. 'I mean, she wasn't my *real* mum, but yeah … she was my step-mum, I guess.'

Stephen nodded and looked down as he fiddled with the strap on his laptop bag. He adjusted it on his shoulder. Alex could tell by the way Stephen's left eye was twitching and he was avoiding eye contact that he had no idea how to interact with him properly. He seemed completely out of his comfort zone talking to a teenager. Alex took the hint.

'I read the piece you wrote last year about Cherry Hollow and The Creature.'

Stephen perked his head up and tilted his head to the side. He reminded Alex of a dog awaiting his master's command. 'Oh yeah? What did you think?'

'I think it's a load of bollocks, to tell you the truth, but you did make some good points.'

'Such as?'

'Such as what you said about Beaker Ravine. You were all excited and up for an adventure to figure out the mystery and then you go to the ravine, freak out and leave without a word. What's up with that?'

Stephen paled and swallowed, his eyes darting from side to side. 'I-I'd rather not talk about it.'

'What did you see?'

'Why do you want to know?'

Alex leaned in closer, but Stephen backed away as if Alex smelled bad or if standing too close was going to give him an electric shock. 'Because I saw something there too.'

Stephen nodded. 'Okay, kid, you've sparked my interest.' Stephen reached into his bag and retrieved a notebook and pen. 'What did you see?'

'My younger sister.'

Stephen blew out a breath. 'Not exactly a headliner, kid.'

'She died over two years ago.'

'Okay ... Go on ...' Stephen poised his pen over the paper.

Alex inwardly grinned. 'First, tell me what you saw there.'

Stephen lowered the notebook and glanced over his shoulder. There were a few kids hanging around by the water cooler, but otherwise, they were alone.

'It wasn't so much something I *saw*, but something I *felt*. They say it's what you can't see that scares us the most. Well ... a feeling washed over me that scared me more than I can ever explain. I haven't felt fear like that since ... well, since I was a kid. The only way I can describe it is ... it felt like ... if I didn't get out of there at that exact moment, I was going to die. I even walked towards the fallen tree and ... I looked down and wondered what it'd be like to fall ...'

Alex's insides turned to mush. He knew that feeling. He knew it all too well.

'I've never considered, not even for a moment, taking my own life, but in that instance, standing by the ravine ... it was all I could think about, and that scared me,' said Stephen. He shuddered and glanced around the corridor again. 'Shouldn't you be heading back to class now?'

'Sure, I can do that, but don't you want to know who sent you the anonymous email about the body that was found the other week?'

Stephen frowned. 'How'd you know about that?'

'Because I was the one who sent it to you.'

## 11 January 2024

*Harriet wouldn't stop screaming. Her shrill voice echoed around the cave, sending small cascades of dirt and stones down upon their heads. Her ear-piercing screech plus the confined area made it feel as if the sound was coming from all around him. Dozens and dozens of people screaming all at once, getting louder and louder ...*

*'Will you shut the fuck up!' Alex covered his ears, then brushed dirt off his jacket. 'You'll get us all buried alive down here.'*

*Harriet used Alex's body as a shield against the bones in front of her. 'Why is there a body down here?' Her voice trembled as she pointed a finger at the oddly shaped object.*

*'Relax, it's probably the remains of an animal,' said Alex the First. He bent down and removed a few more rocks. He revealed a dome-shaped rock with a large crack in it.*

*'That doesn't look like an animal to me,' said Alex. 'That's a human skull.'*

*Alex the First jumped away, dropped the skull, and wiped his hands on his trousers' legs. 'Eww, gross!' The skull rolled across the ground and stopped at Alex's feet.*

*'It looks as if it's been down here a while,' said Alex. He shook off Harriet's tight grasp and bent down to inspect it. 'Here … shine the light on it.' Harriet whimpered as she raised the phone. 'I'm no expert, but this skull doesn't look very big. It might have been a kid.'*

*Harriet whimpered again. Alex fought the urge to roll his eyes. Sure, when it came to terrorising a child in a demon costume, she found it hilarious, but when it came to finding the body of a child buried in a cave, she was terrified. I guess everyone had their limits.*

*'Should we head back to town and tell the police?' asked Harriet.*

*'It will take us hours to get back,' said Alex the First. 'We'll have to go back to the lake and then walk to town from there. It's at least five miles and there's no bloody signal around here.'*

*'Not if we go up the side of the ravine,' said Alex.*

*'Um, yeah, genius, remember what I said about the path down the side of the ravine being worn away? It's a death sentence if you attempt to climb up and out that way.'*

*Alex stood and dusted his hands free from dirt. 'Fine. I'll do it then.'*

*'What does it matter if we take a few more hours to inform the police? It's not like this body is going anywhere. It looks as if it's been down here a long time.'*

'*The sooner we tell someone, the sooner you'll be out of here. I expect they'll bring ropes and shit to get down quickly and they can then hoist you guys up.*'

'*But we'll still be questioned. The police will want to know what we were doing down here. The ravine is supposed to be off-limits, remember? We're going to get in trouble, and, I don't know about you, but I get in enough trouble as it is at school. I don't need the police sniffing around me too.*'

'*Why? You got something to hide?*'

*Both the Alexes locked eyes with each other in the gloomy darkness.*

'*No ... you?*' *asked Alex the First.*

*Alex shrugged.* '*Well, we can't just leave it down here and say nothing. This was someone's child.*' *He looked from Harriet to Alex the First and back to Harriet again.* '*I don't believe this. You're suggesting we leave this kid down here and not tell anyone, aren't you?*'

*Harriet nodded.* '*The town doesn't need another body being found.*'

*Alex scoffed.* '*The town? Who cares about the fucking town? This place is messed up and maybe if people stopped killing other people, there wouldn't be so many bodies to find.*' *Alex felt like a hypocrite as he spoke the words.*

*Harriet and Alex the First looked at each other but said nothing.*

'*Wow,*' *said Alex with a laugh,* '*you guys are unbelievable.*' *Alex grabbed his phone from Harriet and took a photo of the skull and bones with the flash on. 'I'm going to climb out of here, find a signal and call the police. If you guys want to stop me, then I suggest you do it now.' Alex waited, half-expecting one of them to run at him with a large stone, but neither of them moved a muscle.*

*'We'll help you,' said Alex the First in a defeated tone. 'But if you slip and fall then I'm going to bury you down here with whoever the fuck this is.' He pointed to the skull.*

*Alex led the way out of the cave, holding his phone aloft. No one said a word until they exited the mouth and were standing in the cold underneath the fallen tree.*

*'Well ... good luck, mate,' said Alex the First. 'I hope you don't die.'*

*'Gee, thanks.'*

*Harriet didn't say a word. She didn't even look at him. Alex couldn't have cared less.*

*Ensuring his phone was secure in his jacket pocket, Alex climbed up the gentle slope to the wall of the ravine where it started to get steeper. The first twenty feet or so weren't too bad. The loose scree and dirt made it a bit precarious, but by using his hands to climb, he was able to stop himself from sliding. It wasn't until he reached the steepest section of the old path that he hit a snag.*

*The path was almost completely eroded.*

*He looked down at his friends. 'Do you guys see another way around this bit from down there?' he called out.*

*Alex the First walked along a few paces, shielding his face against the low sun. 'Not really, man. You're gonna have to jump across the collapsed bit and hope you don't slip and fall. You're not too far up. You might only break a leg if you do fall instead of die.'*

*'Good to know!'*

*'Here to help.'*

*Alex estimated the collapsed portion of the path to be roughly four feet wide. The landing area on the other side of the gap looked sturdy enough to stand on. But Alex the First was right: if he slipped and fell, he would most likely break a bone or two.*

*Alex took out his phone, checking for a signal.*

*Nothing.*

*He needed to climb higher.*

*He took a deep breath ... and jumped.*

*He landed hard on his hands and knees. His left foot slipped backwards, unable to get a grip. Alex threw out his arms, bashing his left elbow against the hard rock wall, but with the other arm, he was able to cling to a rock overhang with just his fingertips.*

*Harriet shrieked below him.*

*'You okay, man?' shouted Alex the First.*

*Alex held his breath as he dragged himself up the slope, unable to summon any sort of response while he was clinging on for his life.*

*He made it ... barely.*

*'I'm good!'*

*'The climb only gets worse from there,'* called out Alex the First.

*Alex sighed. 'You know, I think maybe I'm done with your help for now!'*

# Chapter Twelve

## Graham

### *23 January 2024 – 11:00 a.m.*

As he reached the front door, Olivia placed a hand on his shoulder. Her touch made his heart sink like a stone. He didn't turn to look at her, but dropped his shoulders and sighed as he said, 'I don't know what happened back then, but I know you do. I can't guarantee I can keep you safe, Olivia. I'm afraid of what's going to happen.'

'I'm not asking you to keep me safe, Graham. I don't need to be kept safe. All I'm asking for is time, so I can spend my husband's final days by his side. After that, I don't care what happens to me.'

Graham turned and looked at her. He didn't believe she'd committed the crime, but he knew from experience even the nicest of people could hide dark and hideous secrets. Who was Olivia protecting and why? Was it Frank? It didn't seem fair to bring all this up while he was on his deathbed. Frank had been like a brother to him in his youth. Granted, not anymore, but even seeing him briefly just now had brought all the good old memories back and their days spent running through the fields, climbing trees and attempting to court all the young ladies. But secretly, Frank had only had eyes for Olivia.

'I'll do what I can,' replied Graham.

'You could lose your job.'

'I'm less than a year away from retirement ... I'll survive if it means finding the truth about what happened. I've waited over forty years for one of you to tell me.'

Tears ran down Olivia's cheeks. 'I'm so sorry we let it get this far. We should have told you. We thought we were doing the right thing.'

Graham opened the door and stepped outside. 'I'll be in touch.' His tone was cold and distant. He knew he was doing Olivia a favour by keeping things under wraps, but he didn't want to have to do it. He didn't want to have to lie to his colleagues. He didn't want to have to jeopardise his career. But he had no other choice. He needed to know the truth, no matter the cost.

'I know you will.' Olivia closed the door on him.

Graham stared at the door for several seconds, his brain telling him one thing and his heart another. As a police officer, he had a moral duty to find out the truth about who had put that body down in the cave, but he had a sinking suspicion he wasn't going to like what he found.

As he walked to his car, parked on the curb at the end of the driveway, he glanced at his phone. He had six missed calls from the station and two voicemails. Without listening to the messages, he dialled the number.

'Are they back?' he asked DC Carter as soon as she answered.

'Yes, boss. I tried calling ...'

'On my way.'

Graham broke into a jog and climbed into his car. Now they had the DNA results, they'd have to track down the family before the details could be announced on national television. His press release was in less than an hour. It probably wasn't possible to reach the family in time, so that meant another press conference would have to be scheduled for when the results were finalised and confirmed with the family. This was going to turn into a media frenzy. He could see it happening.

He arrived at the station within ten minutes. Despite the cold temperature outside, he was sweating when he entered the briefing room. DC Baker and DC Carter were waiting for him.

'Tell me,' he said.

DC Carter rose from her chair. 'The DNA has come back with a match. Boss … you're not going to believe who the match is …'

### 28 May 1985

*It had been two days and his friends still hadn't come to see him, despite visiting each of their houses in turn. Their parents had said they were either unwell, not available or it wasn't a good time. Something was going on. Normally, he was allowed to speak with them if they were unwell. He wracked his brains trying to think of what he could have done to upset them or make them angry with him. When he left on holiday a week ago, they'd been on good terms. They hardly ever argued at all, other than silly, childish squabbles.*

*It didn't make sense.*

*Graham was fed up with staying indoors and being alone. He wanted to tell Frank and Jack about the gorgeous girl he spoke to who'd also been holidaying on a canal boat. He wanted to tell Mary he'd seen a kingfisher by the water (her favourite bird) and that it was so blue it practically shone like a diamond. And he wanted to tell Olivia he'd seen some beautiful pink flowers that reminded him of her.*

*But none of them wanted to see him.*

*He'd watched in astonishment as a moving lorry drove away from number six Baker Street late last night. The Kings had moved away ...*

*'Graham, come away from the window, love. Can you give me a hand with the dishes?' asked his mother.*

*'Mum, I don't understand ... Why have Mr and Mrs King moved away so quickly? I haven't seen Mary at all. She didn't even say goodbye.' Graham let the curtains fall across the window and hung his head as he followed his mother into the kitchen. He stood next to her at the sink and dried the plates and bowls as she passed them to him after washing.*

*'I'm sorry, love. I haven't been able to speak to Mr or Mrs King either. No one seems to know what happened. Sometimes people just move away.'*

*'But ... Mr King is the headmaster of the school ...'*

*His mother stared out the window. 'Maybe we'll receive a letter from the school explaining what happened. I'm sure they'll hire a new headmaster soon.'*

'Why haven't my friends come to visit me? They knew I was coming back two days ago.'

'I'm sure when you go back to school on Monday, you'll be able to speak to them then.'

Graham placed a dry bowl on the side. 'I just don't know what I've done for them to stop talking to me.'

'Oh, love, it's not your fault at all. You've done nothing wrong. I can promise you that. Just give them all a little time. They'll come around.' She gave him a hopeful smile, but Graham didn't return it, nor did he feel even remotely hopeful.

Little did he know he'd still be waiting for them to 'come around' more than forty years later.

# Chapter Thirteen

## Stephen

### *23 January 2024 – 10:45 a.m.*

As he stared at the kid in front of him, a cloud of confusion muddled his brain to the point he could barely form words. Had he even heard the kid correctly? Did he say he was the person who had sent him the anonymous email, begging him to come back to Cherry Hollow and investigate the body? It didn't make sense. Why would Alex Smithson do that? He'd never even met him before. Obviously, the boy's plan had worked. He must have known it would work, but the question remained: why?

'Y-You?' Stephen finally managed to splutter.

'Surprised?'

'More like … confused,' said Stephen with a frown. 'I shouldn't even be talking to you. You're just a kid. How old are you? Fifteen? I shouldn't be talking to you without a parent present. I could get in trouble.'

Alex rolled his eyes. 'Relax. And I'm sixteen, man. Nearly seventeen.'

'Fine. Sixteen. I could still get in trouble for talking to a minor.'

'I said relax. I'm not going to accuse you of being a paedophile or whatever.'

Stephen's whole body froze. 'W-What?' The kid was difficult to talk to. He wasn't used to dealing with teenagers. He'd never been able to converse with kids that age even back when he was one. Now, he may as well have been attempting to talk to an alien.

Alex held up his palms towards Stephen. 'Chill, okay? I just want to talk.'

Stephen's shoulders relaxed ever so slightly, but he still took a step backwards. 'Okay ... Why did you send me that email? Why did you want me to come back here, and why didn't you tell me who you were?'

Alex scoffed. 'Would you have come if I'd told you who I was?'

'No. I'd have thought it was just some kid playing a practical joke.'

'Exactly. As I said, I read the article you wrote a couple of years ago when you first came here. I thought you might be interested to know there was another body found here recently.'

'How did you find out about it before anyone else?'

Alex grinned. 'Because I'm the one who found it.'

Stephen sucked in a breath. 'Okay, kid, you've got my attention. What do you want from me?'

'I need help with finding out the truth about this town. I've seen tons of TV shows and films about investigating murders, but it's not like that in real life, is it? Plus, I'm a teenager. No one listens to me or takes me seriously around here. Not even my own mum, so I thought I could bring in the big guns. Someone who knows what to do. Someone who isn't afraid to ask difficult questions.'

'Couldn't you have gone to the police?' As soon as the question left his lips, he wished he could take it back.

Alex laughed. 'Yeah, right. Like the *police* are any help or would take a nearly seventeen-year-old seriously.'

'Okay, okay, I get your point. How did you know I would come?'

Alex shrugged. 'I guess I didn't, but since you're a journalist I assumed you lived for this kind of shit.'

Stephen pursed his lips, unsure how to proceed. 'Fine,' he eventually said. 'I'll help you. I mean, I'm here, aren't I? But I need to know everything you know. I need details. Am I okay to interview you about it? On record?'

'Not without my mum present,' said Alex, folding his arms across his chest.

'What? But you just said—'

'Ah, man, you're too easy.'

'I don't follow.'

'I'm messing with you! What do you want to know?'

Stephen frowned. This teenager was extremely confusing. He'd never been good at normal social interactions, such as understanding jokes or sarcasm. He understood people did those things, but when the joke was on him, he had a hard time grasping the idea.

'Let's not talk here,' said Stephen, lowering his voice. 'Do you know The Cherry Tree?'

'Sure. I'm not coming up to your hotel room if that's what you're asking.'

Stephen shook his head. 'No. That wouldn't be appropriate at all.'

'No shit.'

'They have a bar area where we could conduct the interview. Are you sure you don't want your mother present?'

'I'm sure. She's … still recovering from Linda's death and other stuff. I don't want to drag her into all of this.'

'That's wise. When do you finish school for the day?'

'Whenever I want.'

'When do you *legally* finish school for the day?'

'Half three.'

'Meet me at four at The Cherry Tree.'

Alex nodded. 'Fine. See you at four.'

The kid walked away towards one of the classrooms, leaving Stephen standing in a near-empty hallway. A few kids ran past him and knocked into his shoulder. They didn't apologise. He grumbled as he readjusted his laptop bag and put away his notebook.

Once done, a spark of excitement tingled the back of his neck. He couldn't help but think what Detective Williams would have to say about him interviewing a minor without parental supervision, but he didn't have time to worry about that. He'd deal with the consequences later. If need be, he'd invite that attractive woman in reception to act as a witness to their conversation to avoid any nasty suspicions.

His mind raced with endless possibilities. Had the kid known the body was already there or had it been a lucky break? Not that finding a dead body was considered lucky, but ...

And what about the reason why he'd sent the email? Did the kid have an ulterior motive? Or was what he'd told him true? That he needed help with finding out the truth?

Stephen spun on his heels and walked down the corridor. He put Alex to the back of his mind and instead thought back to his conversation with Mr Peterson, the headmaster, who he'd spoken to before running into Alex. It hadn't gone as he'd hoped. However, two pieces of vital information had come from the chat: Mr Peterson had known Mr King, the previous headmaster, and he had taken over his role when he'd abruptly left in 1980.

And ... something else.

'I'm sorry, Mr Mallow, but I can't divulge personal information about a previous teacher,' he'd said when Stephen had introduced himself and the reason why he was there. He'd explained he wanted to know why Mr King had left town so suddenly, a renowned and respected headmaster of a school.

'You have no idea at all?'

'I didn't say that. I just mean I can't tell you. It isn't ethical.'

'Neither is finding a dead body buried in a cave ...'

'Excuse me? What does that have to do with Mr King leaving?'

Stephen had shrugged. 'I don't know. You tell me.'

'Mr Mallow, are you insinuating that Mr King had something to do with the … *body*?' Mr Peterson had whispered the word as if it were vulgar.

'I didn't say that.' The two men had locked eyes for a moment. 'Mr Peterson, you've been the headmaster here for a long time. You were given the title back in 1980 because there was no one else able to fill the position at such short notice. Is that correct?'

'Yes, but—'

'And you had only been working in this school for a year, correct?'

'Yes, but—'

'And Mr King gave no reason whatsoever for his swift departure and didn't even provide a notice period. Is that right?'

'How the hell do you know all these things?' Mr Peterson had begun to sweat quite considerably at that point and his face had turned red.

Stephen had smiled. 'I do my research.'

'Clearly. Look, yes, you're right. I was a young teacher at the time and the school didn't have enough teachers back then as it was, so I volunteered. Plus, the advert for a new headmaster in the local paper didn't get any responses.'

'So, you saw a position to elevate your professional career and took it.'

Mr Peterson had glared at him over his mahogany desk. 'Are you telling me you're not doing the exact same thing right now?'

'Touché. Can you tell me anything? Anything at all about the circumstances of Mr King's departure from this school?'

Mr Peterson had sighed and slumped down in his high-backed leather chair as if the effort of the conversation was exhausting him. 'All I know is ... Mr King left and never returned. He provided no notice period. No reason why. He didn't tell a soul. He and his whole family just disappeared. No one heard from any of them again. Although ...'

'Yes?'

Mr Peterson had scoffed. 'No, it's ludicrous really. Never mind.'

'No, please. Go on.'

Mr Peterson had frowned as he rubbed his chin. 'Okay ... One day, years later, I could've sworn I saw ... his daughter.'

Stephen's ears had pricked up. 'His daughter?'

'Yes. He had two daughters. I forget the other girl's name. But I do remember Mary. Funny little thing. She went to this school. She was a bit of a troublemaker, but generally had good grades, if I remember correctly.'

'So ... she moved back here when she was an adult?'

Mr Peterson had shaken his head. 'No, that's the thing. It wasn't her, but it sure as hell looked like her ... At least, there was some resemblance there. I think it may have been my over-active imagination.'

Stephen had nodded as he'd jotted down some words in his notebook. 'Thank you for your time, Mr Peterson.' He'd been shown the door and then had run into Alex.

He wasn't sure how exactly, but the pieces of the puzzle were there. It was just going to take time for his brain to fit them together in a logical format.

As Stephen exited the school and headed to his car, he pushed away all thoughts of his visit to Cherry Hollow and looked up to the sky, taking a cleansing breath. Feeling the sun, even in the depths of winter, felt like a luxury at times, especially when there had been a time in his life when he'd seen nothing but darkness, often for days at a time.

Alex had mentioned in his email he thought Stephen had his own darkness to conquer by being here. The kid was right.

The first five words of a familiar song popped into his head.

### February 1995

*Even as a ten-year-old, Stephen loved the song 'The Sound of Silence' by Paul Simon and Art Garfunkel. He knew all the words by heart. But it was the first five words that always resonated with him.*

*The darkness, did indeed, used to be his friend. He would sit and stare at the moon and the twinkly stars for hours at a time, sometimes waking up in the dead of night to look out the window and watch as the world slept.*

*The darkness intrigued him more and more over the years. It made everything look more sinister, even though nothing had physically changed. Trees became creeping claws that twisted and writhed across his windowpane. Every whisper and creak seemed to get louder, more prominent. Even the outline of his stuffed toys in the corner became horrible-looking creatures that looked as if they were truly alive.*

*But none of that scared him.*

*At least it didn't until ...*

*Not since ...*

*Stephen shuddered at the rising cold. It was damp down in the basement of the old house. Damp, dark, and it smelled musty, like earth mixed with something else he couldn't quite work out. He didn't have a blanket, only the clothes on his back. He had shouted himself hoarse hours ago and was now hunched in a corner with his arms wrapped around his body, attempting to keep himself warm ... and awake.*

*The darkness wasn't his friend down here.*

*It had transformed.*

*The darkness seemed to have a whole life of its own now. Those strange shapes and shadows that used to fascinate him now lurked across the floor and walls, creeping ever closer.*

*Stephen saw long limbs and sharp claws reaching towards him, beckoning him closer. He put it down to his over-active imagination and his mind playing tricks on him due to lack of sleep. Because he couldn't sleep.*

*Not down here ... or the darkness would get him. It would drag him under and never let him come up for air. He might never wake up.*

*But would that be such a bad thing?*

*Why had the darkness turned against him?*

*Tears trickled from his eyes as he rocked back and forth.*

*What had he done to deserve this?*

*It had started a few months ago.*

*One day, his father lashed out at him, telling him to stop talking and act properly, like a normal kid. Stephen hadn't understood what that meant. He was normal ... wasn't he? Then, he'd overheard his parents talking about something called ADHD and that it was affecting him and causing him to behave differently.*

*What did that mean?*

*Was he sick?*

*That's what his father had told him once. He'd refused to believe his son was different. So, he'd locked him in the basement for a full twenty-four hours and told him to think about what he'd done.*

*But what had he done?*

*He'd just been himself.*

*Stephen knew there was something different about the way his brain worked. Yes, he was hyperactive, never focussed and was never able to finish one project before starting something else. But that was who he was. He couldn't change his personality to suit his father, could he?*

*Those were the things he thought about down in the darkness.*

*And he'd never been so frightened of the dark before.*

*It was his friend no longer.*

# Chapter Fourteen

## Olivia

### *25 May 1985*

*She wasn't wearing the right shoes for a hike. The ground was uneven and unforgiving. She'd already tripped and scraped her knee and got her pretty dress dirty. Frank helped her over the trickier terrain while Jack and Mary raced ahead. She didn't mind being left behind if Frank was with her. His presence made her feel calmer.*

*'How far upriver are we going?' asked Olivia, stopping to catch her breath. Her eyes watered so badly she was having trouble seeing the path.*

*'I'm not sure. Not much further, I don't think,' replied Frank.*

*'This ravine is very deep, isn't it?'*

*Frank looked up at the steep sides. 'Yeah. It feels like we're in a trench.'*

*Olivia nodded. 'I think maybe we should turn back soon.'*

*'I'll go and talk to Mary and Jack,' said Frank with a smile. He touched her arm, causing goosebumps across her skin. His smile and touch were enough to brighten her whole day. She rubbed her eyes and sneezed as he jogged ahead to speak to the others, who stopped on top of a large boulder and shouted down*

to him as he asked, 'Hey, you guys, I think we should turn back. This terrain is getting dangerous.'

Mary opened her arms wide. 'But it's amazing, isn't it? Look at this place. It's like we're in our own little world.' She reached into the pocket of her dress and pulled out a small sweet; a red Opal Fruit, her favourite, and popped it into her mouth.

Frank sighed. 'If we don't turn back soon, we'll miss our curfew.'

Mary scoffed and then gulped down the half-chewed sweet. 'Who cares? Come on … let's just—'

One second, she was there and the next she was gone.

'Mary!' shouted Jack.

Frank leapt up on the boulder.

Olivia gasped and rushed towards the group. She hadn't even seen Mary fall. She'd just heard her shriek. 'What happened?'

'I don't know. She just slipped and … Mary?' asked Frank.

The sound of laughter echoed through the ravine.

Olivia reached the boulder and moved around the side of it to find Mary on her bottom in the middle of the shallow river. Olivia let out a breath.

The two boys above on the boulder bent over laughing.

'Crikey, I thought you'd … You okay, Mary?' asked Jack.

'Fine. Just a bit wet!' More laughter filled the air.

Olivia waded through the water and extended her hand. Mary grabbed it and Olivia pulled her to her feet. 'Thanks,' said Mary. 'You want a sweet?'

'Don't mention it … and no thanks. You eat a lot of those, you know.'

'So what? They're delicious.'

Olivia had been about to ask if they could turn back, but something caught her eye, and she lost concentration for a moment. Mary, seeing Olivia glancing behind her, looked over her shoulder and saw what Olivia had spotted.

'Oh wow!'

'What?' asked Frank.

'What can you see?' asked Jack, jumping off the boulder and landing next to them in the water.

Olivia pointed to the side of the ravine.

All eyes fell upon a dark cave opening.

'Is that a cave?' asked Jack.

'What does it look like to you, stupid?' replied Frank. He leapt off the boulder and landed on the bank of the river. He walked towards the cave mouth and peered inside.

'Woah.'

Olivia and Mary looked at each other for a split second and then joined the boys by the cave opening. Olivia had forgotten about the urge to return home now.

'Wonder how far back it goes?' asked Mary with her mouth full as she munched on another sweet.

*'Hey ... I've got an idea,' said Jack. He reached into the pocket of his trousers and brought out a cigarette-shaped tube.*

*'Is that what I think it is?' asked Frank.*

*'Yep.'*

*Mary laughed. 'Where on earth did you get pot from?'*

*'Swiped it from my dad.'*

*'I hope you brought some matches or a lighter otherwise it's pretty useless.'*

*Jack reached into his other pocket and held up a small silver lighter. 'Let's smoke it inside.'*

*Olivia took a step back. 'I'll stay out here,' she said.*

*Frank took hold of her hand. 'Come on. It'll be okay. I'll keep you safe.'*

*Olivia looked into his eyes and smiled before following him inside. This time, however, Frank's reassurance didn't settle the butterflies in her stomach. If she'd thought about it for more than a second, she would have decided to wait outside.*

*But she didn't.*

### 23 January 2024 – 12:01 p.m.

Olivia blew out a long breath as she sank into her armchair. She'd been on her feet all morning. After she said goodbye to Graham at the door, she'd been unable to relax and so had distracted herself by hoovering the whole house and rearranging the kitchen cupboards. She'd been meaning to tick that item off her to-do list for a while and now felt elated at finally accomplishing it. Such a shame that only she would appreciate or benefit from the tidy cupboards.

Olivia set her cup of tea and slice of carrot cake on the side table to her right and switched on the television, flicking straight to the local news channel. She didn't *want* to watch the announcement, but she knew she *had* to.

She had to know what was going on regarding the discovery of the body. Frank was asleep upstairs. The talk with Graham had exhausted him and Olivia didn't expect him to wake up for several hours. It was for the best. Frank didn't need to know the details of the investigation. It would cause him too much worry and stress, and she wanted to ensure he spent his remaining days as comfortable as possible.

But that hadn't happened, had it?

No thanks to Graham visiting out of the blue and ripping open old wounds that had closed years ago.

Frank could have been lying in a hospital bed, living out his remaining days being cared for by various nurses and doctors, but he'd refused. He said the doctors had done enough and there was nothing left for them to do, so he'd asked to stay at home. He didn't want to prolong his life. He just wanted to die in his own home in his own bed. Reluctantly, the doctors had agreed. Olivia had been given a list of medication and things she had to do for him each day, but she didn't mind. He'd done more than enough for her over the years, ensuring the family had money for food and heating. He'd worked all hours of the day during Brooke's confinement and had been there at her worst moments too.

Olivia's body tensed as she watched Graham approaching the microphone stand. It appeared he was speaking from some sort of briefing room, quite possibly located within the small police station in Cherry Hollow, but Olivia couldn't be sure because she'd never been inside.

She picked up her cup of tea but left the cake. She didn't quite have the stomach for it now.

Graham cleared his throat and began speaking, looking a little hot and sweaty around the collar. He looked as if he'd rather be anywhere else in the world than that tiny, over-stuffed briefing room. The lights of the cameras highlighted the dark shadows under his eyes.

'Good afternoon, ladies and gentlemen of the press. I'll keep this as short as I can. Please keep all questions until the end.

'On the eleventh of January 2024, a body was discovered in a cave at the bottom of Beaker Ravine. My forensics team have estimated it has been down there between thirty and forty-five years, according to the rate of decomposition. The body itself, however, is that of a child between the ages of eight and ten. DNA has been extracted and processed and a match has been found. However, I am unable to disclose the results at this time until the family have been located and informed. I will now open the floor for questions. But please, only one question at a time.'

The camera spanned to the room where dozens of hands reached into the air.

Olivia's mouth turned dry.

'Yes, you in the second row,' said Graham with a nod.

A woman in her late thirties rose to her feet, a Dictaphone in hand. 'Detective Williams, does this body have anything to do with the other people who have died in Beaker Ravine – Keiran Jones, Tyler Jenkins and Amber Walker?'

Lots of heads nodded and a chorus of murmurs spread across the room.

Graham looked like he was about to vomit as he wiped his forehead with a handkerchief from his pocket. 'I am unable to comment at this time.'

'Does that mean it does?' answered the journalist without a moment's hesitation.

'It means I don't have the answer to that question right now,' replied Graham, a noticeably firm tone to his voice.

The journalist sat down, mumbling something under her breath.

More hands shot into the air.

'Yes, you at the end there,' said Graham.

A man stood and held a pen to his notebook in front of him. 'You say the body is a child between eight and ten. Is it a boy or a girl?'

Graham gulped. 'A girl,' he replied sternly.

'And have you located the family already? Do they still live in Cherry Hollow? Why are there no missing child cases from that time in the area? And how long until you can give us a name?'

Graham blew out a breath. 'That was more than one question, but I'll do my best to answer. For the moment, the family have not been located, but we believe they do not live in

Cherry Hollow anymore. We have had no families coming forward about missing children from that time. I cannot give you a timeline because, until we can locate the family, we cannot release the name.'

'But you do have the name of the child?'

'We believe so, yes.'

'How did the child die? Was she murdered or did she die of natural causes?'

Graham cleared his throat. His eyes kept darting to the side as if he was preparing to make a run for it. 'The cause of death was blunt force trauma to the head. Since there were no further broken bones or injuries to the body, it can be assumed that the girl didn't fall to her death.'

A collective gasp ricocheted around the room.

Olivia held her breath, her cup halfway to her mouth.

Another man stood up and, without raising his hand or waiting for permission to speak, asked, 'Detective Williams, are you saying that this child was murdered?' The camera panned over to the man who Olivia immediately recognised as the journalist who'd visited the town back in 2022.

Graham didn't look amused. 'That is what the evidence points to, yes.'

Stephen Mallow continued without hesitation. 'So, the girl was murdered inside the cave and left there.' Not a question but rather a statement.

Graham nodded. 'Yes.'

'Detective, is it true you were a resident of Cherry Hollow around the time this child was murdered?'

Another collective gasp, yet now a pin drop could have been heard in its aftermath. All eyes swivelled to land on poor Graham who had his mouth open like a codfish. Had the journalist seriously just asked such an abrupt question?

'I … I … Mr Mallow, there are a great many people currently residing in this town who lived here around that time.'

'Not many, according to my research.'

Graham paused for a moment before answering, 'Well, whatever research you may have conducted has no grounds in a murder investigation. I'll ask that you and everyone else please leave the investigation to the police who are more than capable of bringing the killers to justice. Thank you. No further questions.'

Olivia watched as Graham turned off the microphone and exited the stage. The camera panned to the local news broadcaster who began to provide a summary of the announcement.

There was one word that caused Olivia's insides to clench.

Graham had said *killers*, not killer.

Plural.

Had anyone else picked up on his choice of wording?

Olivia placed her untouched cup of tea on the side table. Leaving her cake uneaten too, she pushed herself to her feet and went upstairs to see her husband. She was surprised to find him awake, but tears were flooding his red-rimmed eyes.

'What's wrong?' she asked, rushing to his side.

Frank lifted the book he'd been reading. 'I can't bloody see properly anymore to read this damn book. Now I'll never find out who killed them.'

Olivia smiled as she took the book and sat down in the chair next to his bed. 'Then I shall read it to you.'

'But you hate reading dark thrillers.'

'Yes, but I can't have you leaving this life without finishing this book now, can I?'

Frank smiled as he relaxed against his pillow. 'What happened at the press release, Liv?'

'It doesn't matter. Now ... chapter eighteen, is it?'

'Yes, please. From the top, my dear.'

# Chapter Fifteen

## Alex

### *23 January 2024 – 15:50 p.m.*

He declined the offer to smoke a joint in their usual spot after school. Instead, he said goodbye to Harriet and Alex the First after Biology class, ignoring their questioning stares, and made his way through town towards The Cherry Tree. He stuffed his hands in his pockets and lowered his head against the icy wind. His phone vibrated in his pocket. It was probably Harriet asking why he was blowing her off. He didn't have the inclination or the energy to battle with her and her annoying clinginess. Why was he even with her again? She exhausted him.

Alex had texted his mum earlier to say he was staying late to study in the library, to which she'd replied: *Yeah, right.*

He'd smiled at that. It seemed his mum knew him well after all.

She had then followed up with: *What are you really doing?*

And he'd replied saying he was helping Alex the First with his geography assignment because he was failing miserably and Alex had always been good at geography, having been able to recite the countries of the world in alphabetical order since he was a kid. It was a talent no one knew he could do apart from his mum.

Her reply: *Okay, bring home milk. Thanks x*

Alex frowned at her text. One kiss and no 'I love you'. Okay, something was definitely wrong. She always put at least three kisses and signed off with 'I love you' in her final message. But he didn't have time to worry about what was going on with her now because he'd just arrived at the car park of the hotel.

Alex pushed open the door and stepped inside, stamping his feet on the welcome mat. It had started to rain, so he was glad to be somewhere warm and dry.

'Hello,' said a friendly female voice.

Alex looked up to see an attractive woman in her early thirties behind the reception desk. 'Oh, hi,' he said. 'I'm not checking in or anything. I'm just here to meet Mr Mallow.'

The woman nodded. 'Ah yes, he said you'd be popping by. Alex, is it?'

'That's right.'

'I'm Rachel. He's just through there in the bar area. Can I get you a drink?'

'Vodka tonic?'

'Nice try. I'll get you some water.'

'Thanks.'

Alex's cheeks heated as she winked at him. He then walked into the bar area where he found Stephen Mallow sitting in a high-backed leather chair by the fireplace, which was crackling and giving off a perfect ambient glow.

'Hi, Mr Mallow,' said Alex as he took a seat opposite him in a matching chair. He swivelled his head to look over his shoulder at the array of old books lined up on the shelves on either side of the fireplace. There were none he recognised. Alex wasn't a big reader, having only read a few classics because the school had set them as part of English Literature. The only one he'd vaguely enjoyed had been *Dracula*.

'Ah, Alex, hi. Call me Stephen, please. Good day at school?'

'It was okay.'

'I always enjoyed school myself, although I did struggle with fitting in. I didn't have many friends ... In fact, I don't think I had *any* friends.'

'Sorry to hear that.'

'Do you have friends, Alex?'

Alex shrugged and glanced around the room, taking in the well-stocked bar and array of paintings on the walls. 'Not really. I used to have lots of good friends back before my sister died, but once someone close to you dies then people get all weird and don't know how to act or what to say, and then eventually they give up and stop talking to you completely in case they say the wrong thing. I'm used to it. I have a girlfriend now, but she's ... well, let's just say she's more of an imposition than anything else.'

'So why go out with her?'

'I think she's a psychopath.'

Stephen laughed so hard he had to reach forward and take a sip of water from his glass to calm down.

'What's so funny?'

'I like you, kid. You speak your mind and aren't afraid to tell the truth. That takes guts. You remind me of me.'

Alex wasn't sure how to take that. He squirmed in his chair. 'If you say so,' he replied.

Stephen smiled. 'So ... let's hear it. You sent me that email to get me to come here because you needed my help. What is it exactly you need my help with other than investigating the body you found?'

Alex took a deep breath, held it for a second and then released it. It was something he'd been taught by the school counsellor after Phoebe had died. Sometimes all it took was a deep breath to gather the dark thoughts that swirled around his brain and made him dizzy.

'Last year I tried to help my mum and get to the bottom of why Amber Walker was killed. I had help from Jordan and Brooke, but ... I guess I got a taste for it, for finding the truth and putting everything out in the open. I got a bit wrapped up in the whole conspiracy surrounding The Creature. It's like I'm drawn to it, and I don't know why.'

'What do you think The Creature really is?'

Alex narrowed his eyes. 'Is this a test? Do you already know what it is but just want to see what my theory is?'

'Something like that.'

Another deep breath. 'I don't believe it's real if that's what you're suggesting. It's a creature that's been made up by two kids in this town after Amber Walker talked about seeing it in her dreams. You probably know this already, but she had severe sleep paralysis and insomnia. It was something she made up in her head because of what she and her friends did to Kieran Jones back in 1998.'

Stephen cocked one eyebrow. 'An interesting theory.'

'But you know all this already, don't you?'

'Yes. I like to consider myself an expert on all things relating to Cherry Hollow.'

'Yet you got so freaked out by something you saw or felt at the ravine that you never wanted to visit again ... until I dangled another dead body in front of you ... figuratively speaking.' Alex's face burned.

Stephen held his hand up. 'I get what you mean, don't worry. Can I backpedal a bit? You said you spoke to Jordan and Brooke last year.'

'Yes. They're pretty cool people even though they covered up the murder of their friend. It's a shame they got driven out of town.'

'And that was because of the fire that burned down Jordan's business, right?'

'Yes. And the two women who set the fire also burned down my mum's house and killed my step-mum.'

'Right.' Stephen frowned as he scribbled a few notes down, avoiding his gaze.

'What? You don't believe me?'

Stephen looked up. 'It's not that I don't believe you, but I'm finding it hard to put the pieces together. I can see why those two women burned down Jordan's business. They had issues with the Fated Five and wanted the rest of them gone for good, but what did they have against your mother and stepmother? Nothing. Not from what I can tell. The only person who'd have anything to gain by your stepmother's death ... is you.'

Alex didn't even flinch. 'You're wrong.'

'Perhaps. I've been wrong before. Now ... we're not here to talk about all that anyway. We're here to discuss you finding the body in the cave. Do you mind if I record this?' Stephen reached into his pocket and pulled out his phone.

'I'd rather you didn't. But you can take notes.'

'Fair enough. Would you like someone here as a witness?'

'Na, I'm good.'

As if on cue, Rachel entered carrying a glass of water. She set it down next to Alex. 'Can I get you two anything else?'

'No, we're good. Thanks,' said Alex.

Stephen shook his head. 'No, thank you.'

'I'll be right out there if you need me.'

Alex and Stephen watched as she walked out and then focussed on each other. 'So,' said Stephen, 'let's start with why you were poking around in a dark cave to begin with, shall we?'

By the time Alex finished talking with Stephen and had popped to the corner shop to get milk, it was past six and he was starving. Luckily, the smell of a home-cooked meal wafted from the kitchen as soon as he stepped through the front door.

'Mum, I'm home.' He kicked off his shoes, put them on the rack and hung up his jacket. He carried the milk into the kitchen and put it in the fridge.

His mum took a tray out of the oven and placed it on the countertop. 'How did it go?' she asked, turning to look at him.

'Fine, although Alex the First is really hard to teach.'

'Why's that?'

'He gets distracted all the time.'

'Hardly surprising considering his mother is in prison.'

Alex smirked at his mum's bluntness. 'What's for dinner?'

'Chicken pie.'

'Cool.'

'Did you happen to see the press release today about the body you found?'

Alex paused as he reached for a glass in the cupboard. He and Stephen hadn't discussed the press release at all. It had completely slipped his mind. 'No. Why?'

'The body was that of a little girl.'

Alex set the glass on the side and turned to his mum, knowing how much it would affect her, having lost her own daughter. 'Oh ... jeez ... I didn't know. I knew it was a kid because it was so small but ... Are you okay?'

His mum smiled, but he could tell it was forced. 'Yes, of course. It just ... brought back a lot of memories, you know? I think I'm going to make an emergency appointment with Dr Allan this week.'

Alex fought the urge to roll his eyes. 'You can always talk to me about stuff, Mum.'

'You have enough to worry about, Alex. But I'm fine. Really. Are you sure you don't want me to make an appointment for you too?'

'To see a shrink? No, thanks.'

'Are you sure? It's very helpful and I know I should have seen a therapist years ago, but, well … I just don't want you to struggle as I did, that's all. Your sister dying, then your dad, then Linda … and then finding a dead body … You're only sixteen, Alex. You shouldn't have to deal with that sort of thing.'

'Neither should you, Mum. And I'm nearly seventeen, remember?'

'I remember,' she replied with a smirk. His mum relaxed her shoulders and placed the oven gloves on the side. 'Our family has had its share of loss and heartbreak, that's for sure. I'm glad we're still surviving together. Thank you. You're keeping me strong throughout all of this.' She walked up to him and put her arms around him, squeezing hard. Alex hugged his mum back. 'I love you, Alex.'

'I love you too, Mum.' The animosity he'd felt towards her earlier slipped away as she gripped him tight. He felt her body shaking against his as she wept. He held her, wishing he could tell her the truth about what he'd done for her, but knowing if he did, he might lose her forever. For a moment, he realised he was doing exactly what Linda had done: hiding something from her for his own selfish reasons.

'Mum,' he said quietly. 'Would you still love me even if I'd done something really bad?'

His mum squeezed him harder. 'You could never do anything that would make me stop loving you.' Then she pulled away and looked deep into his eyes. 'Is there something you want to tell me, Alex?'

'No, nothing ... I was just wondering.' He watched as her eyes grew dark and she gave him a weak smile.

'Dinner will be ready in ten minutes.'

'I'll go and have a quick shower.'

Alex raced up the stairs, taking two at a time and took a deep breath at the top.

Did his mum know something? She used to say she knew him better than he knew himself, but for the last two years, she'd hardly taken notice of him at all. And he'd changed a hell of a lot during that time. Not only had he grown from a fourteen-year-old to a nearly seventeen-year-old, developing a deep voice in the process, but he'd changed from a loving and caring young man into someone who could take a life without barely blinking an eye.

His dad.

Linda.

They'd paid the price.

Alex kept thinking about what Jordan had told him last year about The Creature and how it was a manifestation of a person's guilty conscience and that everyone saw it in different forms. Alex still didn't believe in it, not really. He knew his girlfriend and Alex the First had spread the rumour about The

Creature and turned it into some sort of living legend. But he didn't have any other explanation for what he was experiencing and how he felt.

The darkness kept following him.

And he didn't know how to get rid of it other than by trying to do something good to make up for what he'd done wrong. Because he knew it had been wrong to take their lives, but he'd done it to save his mum. He hadn't seen any other way. In his eyes, he'd saved her from those who would only have dragged her down further.

Alex pulled his t-shirt over his head and chucked it across the room onto the floor. He looked at himself in the small mirror perched on his desk. His body was still skinny and weak. As he stripped to his boxers, he caught sight of a book on his shelf, an atlas.

A memory popped into his head of when he'd hidden a scrap of paper inside its pages.

He pulled the book off the shelf, flipped to the middle and lifted the note to the light.

*I'm sorry to do this to you. I love you more than anything and this is the only way I know how to keep you safe. I'm so sorry I wasn't there for you when I should have been. Your dad loves you. You'll be okay, baby. I love you.*

Jordan and Brooke had forgotten about the note after they'd solved Amber's death, but he hadn't. He'd found it under the floorboards in Amber's old house, the house he'd burned to the ground last year. At the time, they'd thought it was a suicide note written by Amber, but that had turned out not to be the case.

It still nagged him. Who had written this note and why? His mum hadn't found it when she'd searched under the floorboards and found the poem about The Creature that Amber's daughter, Bethany, had written. Jordan and Brooke had eventually deduced it could have been written by the previous owner of Amber's house, but neither of them had investigated it any further. They'd had more important things to worry about like Jordan's business burning down and his recovery from getting stabbed in the side and moving to start a new life away from Cherry Hollow and all the drama and grief that came with living there.

But Alex couldn't let it go. He'd get to the bottom of the mystery. Maybe he'd asked Stephen for help. After their conversation earlier, Alex realised that despite Stephen being a bit eccentric, he was a decent person, and deep down, he probably knew the truth about Alex, that he was a little different too.

He set the note down on the side, then headed for the bathroom. The cut on his leg was weeping again, a souvenir from climbing up the side of the ravine after discovering the body. It had almost healed and then he'd gone and picked at the scab because the small stab of pain felt better than nothing at all.

## *11 January 2024*

*The rest of the climb to the top was even harder. With no rope or anything to hold on to for guidance and safety, Alex practically crawled along the crumbling path, clinging to anything he could get a grip on. His palms sweated despite the freezing temperature, and, thanks to the chill factor, they were also numb and refused to work properly.*

*He'd stopped listening to Alex the First's words of wisdom and help ages ago and was now focussed on making the final leap from a rocky ledge to the top of the ravine near where the fallen tree created a bridge.*

*It was at least a five-foot leap. Was it really worth risking his life? Maybe he should have walked back down the river towards the lake and taken the long route after all. Was it too late to turn back? He checked for a signal on his phone one last time.*

*Nothing.*

*Dark clouds hovered overhead, causing the already dull day to feel like nighttime. A cold wind whipped around him, but none of the trees in the wood above appeared to be swaying.*

*It was here.*

*No ... no, it wasn't.*

*The Creature wasn't real. It was just his mind playing tricks on him.*

*Alex took a deep breath and leapt across the gap.*

*A searing heat erupted in his leg.*

*He flung out his right arm and grabbed one of the dangling limbs of the rotten tree. It snapped. He shrieked as his feet slipped from underneath him.*

*'Alex!' His name echoed from down below.*

*His heart felt as if it was about to jump from his chest. His vision swam. He couldn't focus on anything, anything but clinging to the scree on the side of the ravine. He reached up and grabbed another branch of the tree, hauling himself up the side, digging his fingers into the dirt and rocks until he felt a fingernail snap and bleed.*

*He'd made it.*

*Alex collapsed on the ground near the roots of the tree and took a few deep breaths, telling himself he was alive.*

*His leg burned. He checked the damage. A piece of sharp rock had sliced through his jeans and created a deep gash in his left leg, but the blood had already started clotting so he left it and grabbed his phone, holding it up.*

*Nothing.*

*Alex peered over the edge of the ravine and looked down at Harriet and Alex the First. 'I'm going to run back to town and keep trying to get through. Stay there!'*

*'Not like we have anywhere else to go!' shouted Alex the First.*

*Alex began to trek through the thick undergrowth and trees towards Cherry Hollow. He was still a few miles away. It wasn't until he'd made it out the other side of the woods and reached the Danger sign on the fence that a signal appeared on his phone.*

*He called the police.*

*His job was done now.*

*But who did the body belong to?*

*Maybe there was a way he could speed up the investigation.*

# Chapter Sixteen

## Graham

### *23 January 2024 – 13:00 p.m.*

He needed a drink after the press conference. And not coffee. If only he was allowed alcohol at work. His nerves were shot and his whole body ached from his muscles clenching as he'd attempted to not tremble from head to toe. And he called himself a detective chief inspector. Shame and embarrassment washed over him in waves as he'd stepped away from the microphone earlier and battled against the hordes of journalists and made a B-line straight for his office. He'd slammed the door a little too hard, but at least it had signalled to his colleagues that he didn't want to be disturbed.

His head pounded again as if a sledgehammer pummelled upon it, so he popped a couple of painkillers and washed them down with the dregs of cold coffee he'd left in his work mug on his desk. The mug read *I hate my job*. It had been a random gag gift one year during the Secret Santa exchange. He still didn't know who had given him the present. But it was funny … and strangely apt. The main thing he hated about his job, especially now, was giving press releases, particularly when nosey journalists like Stephen Mallow threw a spanner in the works and asked awkward questions.

Yes, he was used to awkward questions in his line of work from the media. He'd rather ask the awkward questions during an interview, but his interviewing days were over, thanks to his promotion to DCI. Now, he was basically a paper pusher and spent most of his time chained to his desk, staring at a screen and ordering people to do their jobs, when he'd much prefer to be the one out there on the ground and getting the job done.

Stephen Mallow's question plagued him. What kind of question was that? *Is it true you were a resident of Cherry Hollow around the time this child was murdered?* He'd known the answer to the question, so why ask it? To make him look bad. To cause him to turn red and look guilty. The man was a lunatic if he thought he had anything to do with it.

He may not have had anything to do with it directly, but he knew who probably had been involved, which was just as bad. But most of them were gone now. All except …

He couldn't do that to them. He couldn't. It wouldn't be right. Not now.

He promised Olivia he'd do everything in his power to stop the truth from coming out until Frank had passed, which was only a matter of weeks, maybe days.

The body.

That little girl.

He knew who she was now.

The DNA matched a person on file. But how was it even possible? He needed to see the results for himself, but bringing up the name was bound to cause his headache to get worse.

Graham slammed his fists down on his desk, took a deep breath and then leaned forward, pulling the computer screen closer. He brought up the case files for Kieran Jones and Tyler Jenkins. He clicked on Tyler's basic information profile and scanned it.

**Name:** Tyler Jenkins

**DOB:** 02 August 1985

**Parents:** Mr and Mrs Jenkins aka Mr and Mrs Warner (changed their names in 2003). Moved away from Cherry Hollow in 2002. Resided in Scotland. Were found in 2019 when Jordan Evans tracked them down and forced them to confess to the abuse of their son. Mrs Warner was sentenced and jailed for life in Ashmore Prison in 2020. Mr Warner was sentenced and jailed for twenty years in Rockwide Prison.

**Died:** 20 July 2018 (death by suicide)

Graham leaned back in his chair. He remembered the case well. Jordan and Amber had come to the station with a recording of Tyler's confession. In it, he admitted to killing Kieran Jones to keep the fact his parents raped and abused him quiet. Kieran had known about it and had threatened to tell his friends.

When the police were unable to locate his parents, Jordan took it upon himself to find them. And find them he had, after almost a year of searching. He'd located them in a remote region of Scotland after they'd changed their names to Mr and Mrs Warner. He wore a wire and they'd confessed everything. Jordan had handed their confession over to Graham and he'd then set the ball rolling and had them sentenced and jailed.

Mr and Mrs Jenkins/Warner were now in prison, but Graham had never actually met them. He'd seen photographs and videos of their court proceedings but hadn't spoken to them personally. Even when they lived in Cherry Hollow with their son, he never conversed with them directly because they'd been well-mannered residents of the community, and he had no reason to suspect that they raped and abused their son at home behind closed doors.

That fact ate away at Graham every day: the fact he'd not seen the evil within Mr and Mrs Jenkins, that he'd not been able to save their son from years of torture and abuse.

The only person he knew who had spoken to them since they'd confessed was Jordan Evans.

He picked up the phone and dialled the number he had on file for him. Jordan had made sure he provided his new home number before he'd moved away at the end of last year.

'Hello, Jordan speaking.'

'Mr Evans, hello. It's Detective Williams.'

'Oh, fuck. What's happened now?'

'Well, I've had better receptions.'

'Sorry, Detective, but it seems whenever you call me it's always with bad news. And, considering the press release you just did an hour ago, I'm assuming this isn't a courtesy call.'

'You watched it then.'

'Yes.'

'Did Brooke watch it?'

'No, because I'm trying to keep her away from stressful situations, especially ones that don't concern her any longer. We're expecting a baby and she's not been too well lately.'

'Ah, congratulations. That's wonderful news.'

'Thank you, Detective. So ... what can I do for you?'

Graham cleared his throat. 'I wanted to ask you about Mr and Mrs Jenkins.'

Jordan paused for five seconds before replying, 'I wasn't expecting you to say that.'

'Back then, I was all about work and didn't take any notice of the local community. Not having any children myself, I wasn't involved with the school or anything, so I barely knew them. But you were best friends with Tyler. You must have spent time over at his house with his parents. What can you tell me about them? When did Tyler first come into your life?'

Jordan blew out a breath. 'Fuck ... That's going back a while now. We became friends with him at about six years old, I think. He was the last to join our friendship group because he hadn't been born here.'

'So, Mr and Mrs Jenkins moved to town in 1991, is that correct?' Graham jotted the information down on a pad of paper.

'Something like that. Don't quote me. It was a long time ago. But yes. As for his parents, well ... As I said in the police report, they were always a bit strange. They kept themselves to themselves mostly, but they got involved with the community. Hell, Mr Jenkins even coached the boys' football team at one point.' Jordan paused for a moment and then said in a quieter voice, 'I hate to say this, but they were just normal parents. No one had any idea what was going on behind closed doors. Tyler was … raped and abused by his parents his whole life. What kind of monsters do you have to be to do that to a person, let alone your own child, your own flesh and blood? What kind of monsters were we that we didn't see it?'

Graham shook his head even though he knew Jordan couldn't see him. 'It's just unthinkable … Tyler … he had no chance of being a normal kid.'

'He hid his bruises and his injuries from us for years, as well as the darkness inside him. He didn't let anyone see he was dead inside. He shone so bright on the outside that none of us could even imagine there was something so dark going on inside. I hate myself every day for never being able to see it, yet I also hate and blame him for never trusting us enough to tell us. Detective … why are you asking me about Tyler's parents? What do they have to do with the body found in the cave?'

Graham sighed. 'I can't tell you details about the case, Jordan.'

'But you can call me up and ask for my help?'

'That's different.'

'Is it? Because I'm not sure if you remember, but I've been involved right from the start. I helped you find Tyler's parents and brought them to justice. If they have something to do with another child's death, then I want to know about it. If that little girl was killed back in the early 80s or whenever it was … then how could it possibly have anything to do with Tyler's parents who only moved to Cherry Hollow in the early 90s?'

Graham closed his eyes. He'd already said too much. Jordan Evans was a smart man. And he was right. He had been there from the start and had brought Tyler's parents to justice and helped put them away. Plus, he'd lost his girlfriend, Amber Walker, because of it all. Because of what had happened to him and his friends twenty-five years ago at the ravine.

That's where he thought this had all started.

But he was wrong.

The darkness had started a long time ago... *before* Keiran's death.

And somehow, it was all connected.

Damn it. It meant Stephen Fucking Mallow was right.

Graham shuffled in his chair. 'Jordan, what I'm about to tell you cannot get out. Do you understand? I could lose my job over this. I most likely will anyway.'

'You can trust me.'

Graham sighed and rubbed his eyes then leaned across his desk on his elbows. 'The little girl's DNA has matching strands to Tyler's.' Graham waited a few seconds to allow the words to sink in.

Jordan coughed. 'What are you saying? How could it match Tyler's DNA? He wasn't alive or even born in the early 80s.'

'No, but his parents were.'

'Are you saying that Tyler's parents – Mr and Mrs Jenkins – had another child?'

'No, the timelines don't fit. They would have been only kids themselves.' Graham sighed again. 'Jordan, I believe the little girl in the cave was the youngest daughter of Mr and Mrs King. You probably won't know who they are, but Mr and Mrs King had two daughters called Mary and Flora. I knew them. Well ... I knew Mary. She was my best friend growing up like you were with Tyler and the rest of the group. Mary, Flora and their parents disappeared in May of 1980. They left the town and never returned. No one ever heard from them again.'

'Okay ... so that timeline seems to fit. So, who was found in the cave? Mary or Flora?'

'It's too young to be Mary. I believe it's Flora.'

'Okay, fine, but ... it still doesn't explain how the DNA matches Tyler's.'

'I believe that Mary King ... one of my best friends growing up ... *is* Tyler's mother. She's Mrs Jenkins, and she came back years later to Cherry Hollow after moving away with her parents. I didn't recognise her because the last time I saw her she was a fifteen-year-old child. Plus, I never actually spoke to Mrs Jenkins. I barely even saw the woman on the street. I think she killed her sister in 1980, covered it up, told her parents, and they moved away.'

There was a long pause on the line. 'Detective, if what you're saying is true ... then the killer is already locked away behind bars. Also ... why would Mary's parents not alert the police to Flora's death? Why was Flora's disappearance not even mentioned?'

Graham covered his eyes with his left hand, the lights of his office making his head pound to the rhythm of his heart. 'Because I think what happened to your friend, Tyler, also was happening to Mary and Flora. I think they were abused by their parents ... and to save themselves, the whole family moved away and disappeared, never telling anyone that one of their daughters was dead.'

Jordan swore under his breath. 'And then Mary continued the vicious circle by growing up to abuse her own son. So, what happens now? How can I help?'

'You can't. You've done enough. You've helped me say it all out loud. I've been trying to deny it for so long. One thing you can do is keep all of this from Brooke. She can't know. No one can know. Not yet. I'm trusting you to not say anything.'

'I agree with you, but why?'

'Because I haven't told you everything. Back when I was a child, I was best friends with not only Mary King but also Brooke's parents, Olivia and Frank, and your father, Jack. I went away on holiday in May of 1980 and, when I returned, none of them spoke to me ever again and Mary and her family moved away. I think all of them were involved in covering up Flora's death ... and I think that sounds very familiar to you, doesn't it?'

Jordan swore again. Loudly, this time.

## *31 May 1980*

*Graham walked through the school gates carrying his bag. It was laden with books, so it should have felt heavy to him, but it was nothing compared to the weight of his sadness that had pressed down upon his shoulders for the past few days. Usually, he'd meet his friends in the far corner of the playground before they all went inside together to their various classes, but not today.*

*Yesterday, none of them had shown up for school at all. Not one of them had been in his normal classes and when he asked one of the teachers where they all were, she'd merely said they must be unwell.*

*Would they show up today? Surely they couldn't afford to miss too much school.*

*Graham's heart leaped as he caught sight of Olivia walking through the gates with her head down. She walked fast, as if she were in a hurry and didn't have time to stop and talk with anyone. As she looked up for a moment, he caught a glimpse of her face: she didn't look like the Olivia he knew. She looked different. Her blonde hair duller, her bright eyes darker and puffy, her pale skin even paler, but in a sickly way. What had happened to her? Was she actually unwell?*

*She saw him and froze, her pupils dilating like a cat's eyes.*

*'Olivia,' he said, walking up to her. She flinched as he reached out his hand. He pulled it back. 'Please,' he begged. 'What's going on? I haven't seen you for days.'*

*Olivia's eyes flooded with tears. 'G-Graham ... I ... I'm sorry.'*

*'I've been trying to talk to you and the others since I got back from my holiday. Mary's left town. Did you know that? What happened? Did you have an argument or something?'*

*Olivia bit her lip. 'Y-Yes.'*

*'About what? Why aren't any of you talking to me? I wasn't even there. What have I done wrong?'*

*Olivia looked over her shoulder and shuddered. 'Y-You've done nothing wrong, Graham.'*

*'Then why are you all avoiding me?'*

*'It's for your own good.'*

*'My own good? What does that mean?'*

*Olivia stamped her foot. 'Graham, just leave it. Mary's gone. We all have to grow up sometime. I'm sorry, but I can't be friends with you anymore. None of us can.'*

*Graham's mouth fell open. His heart pounded. It felt as if it was being ripped from his chest.*

*'B-But ... just tell me why!' He was shouting now and other children in the vicinity were staring at him as well as several of the teachers, but he didn't care. Olivia was being ridiculous. All she had to do was tell him the reason, and then maybe he could begin to understand, but the fact she kept avoiding the answer was infuriating.*

*'I can't tell you why. Trust me, Graham. It's for your own safety.'*

*'My own safety? You're making no sense.'*

*Olivia held her head up high. 'Well, I'm sorry, but you're just going to have to deal with it. None of us ever liked you anyway. Goodbye, Graham.' She stormed past him and into the school building, leaving him standing in the playground by himself.*

*He wished the ground would open and swallow him whole.*

*It was better than the darkness that crept into his soul.*

*It would continue to grow darker over the next forty-four years.*

# Chapter Seventeen
## Stephen
### *23 January 2024 – 18:10 p.m.*

The chat with Alex earlier had been interesting. The boy told him in excruciating detail about finding the body and then climbing up the side of the ravine to call the police. He even explained how his friend and his girlfriend had tried to convince him not to tell anyone. What was it about the residents of this town and covering up deaths? It truly was the murder capital of the Lake District!

He underlined the phrase in his notebook, thinking it would make for a great headline. Alex further explained he wanted to uncover the truth as a way of dealing with his grief over losing his sister, his father and his stepmother. The boy had lost a lot of important people in his life, but as he'd talked about their deaths, it struck Stephen how little emotion came through in his words. The stuff coming out of Alex's mouth was that of some tragic horror movie, yet he barely blinked an eyelid. He didn't sweat or tremble, which made him either an exceptional actor or … something else.

Strange.

He tapped his pen on the paper. He needed a new angle.

Maybe these two kids – Alex Sharp and Harriet Forrester – maybe they had something more to do with it. Then again, it was impossible. They may have been deluded psychopaths who terrorised kids at their school, but they wouldn't have had anything to do with the body down in the ravine and, as far as Stephen knew and what he'd gleaned from Alex, they hadn't murdered anyone.

No. Those two weren't the new angle he needed.

However, Mr King disappearing with his family was certainly an interesting option to investigate. After speaking with Mr Peterson at Alex's school, Stephen realised that Mr King leaving town without a word was a seemingly insignificant event that held more power than anything else.

The only person he knew who had been living here around that time was Detective Graham, but he wasn't going to tell him anything, was he? There was a slim chance he was somehow involved in it … but how?

Stephen couldn't pinpoint the information he needed. There was a piece of the puzzle that was missing, and this was causing him a great deal of suffering, mentally.

The way his brain worked meant that if something wasn't quite finished, or if something was left unresolved, he would torture himself inside over and over. That's why he refused to ever do a secondhand jigsaw puzzle because if a piece was missing, it would destroy him. He couldn't risk it. The only way his brain would allow him to leave something unfinished was if he decided to leave it unfinished. It had to be his choice, no one else's.

His phone buzzed on the table next to his tumbler of whiskey. Yes, it was probably too early in the evening to be on the hard stuff already, but he needed to clear his head of all the noise. And nothing cleared his head better than whiskey.

He picked up his phone and saw it was a text from the kid. He opened it. It was a photo of an old scrap of paper. As soon as he finished reading the scribbled words, another text came through from Alex.

*Thought this might help. I found it last year under the floorboards of my old house, the one Amber Walker used to live in. Think it's from the previous owner, but never found out who it was. Let me know if you find anything.*

Stephen re-read the note.

His brain began to tick again.

Tick ... tick ... tick ...

*BING.*

Stephen grabbed his laptop. Something in his brain had slotted into place.

Amber's house ... He needed to find out who had lived there back in 1980. Somewhere, he'd seen something about that house, but he couldn't remember where.

Unfortunately, an online search led to no results. The information wasn't there electronically. So, who could he ask? Detective Williams was out of the question. Here he was, back searching for people who had lived in the town the longest. Who would know the answer? He could possibly go back and visit Mr Peterson, but he had a feeling he'd already burned that bridge.

Plus, the headmaster would probably give him the excuse of *confidentiality*.

At that moment, Rachel walked in. 'Can I get you another, Mr Mallow?' she asked, nodding at his now empty glass.

Stephen looked up. 'No, thank you. But can I ask you a quick question?'

'Of course.'

'Do you happen to know who lived in Amber Walker's house before she and her husband bought it?'

Rachel's cheeks turned red. 'Um ... I d-didn't really know them, I'm afraid.'

Stephen narrowed his eyes. He wasn't stupid. And she was extremely bad at lying. 'How did you know the Walkers?'

'I j-just told you, I didn't.'

He had no time to be tactful. 'Now you're being defensive, so clearly you did know them. I really need to know. It's important. Please.'

Rachel gulped and stepped closer to him. 'I ... I sort of was seeing her husband for a while.'

Stephen's eyebrows shot to the top of his head. 'You had an affair with Amber's husband?'

'I'm not proud of it, but yes.'

'Is that why they got divorced?'

'It was one of the reasons I suppose but everyone knew they didn't have the perfect marriage. Sean told me stuff about Amber that ... well—'

Stephen raised his hand. 'Look, I'm sorry to interrupt, but I really have no interest in the fact you had an affair with her husband. And I don't care about their marital issues. I need to know who lived in their house before they bought it.'

Rachel sighed. 'How should I know? I think it was empty for a while.'

'How long was it empty for?'

'Look, I really don't know, I'm sorry.'

Stephen squeezed the bridge of his nose, fighting back a snappy retort. He couldn't help it. When the answer was so close, yet so far out of reach, he struggled to contain his emotions.

'Why don't you ask Olivia Willows?'

At the sound of her name, he looked up. 'Brooke's mother?'

'Yes. She's lived here all her life, I think.'

Stephen slapped his forehead. 'Why the hell didn't I think of that? Thank you, Rachel. You've been most helpful. And I promise I won't tell anyone about your affair.'

'Bit late for that. Everyone already knows. It's old news, but I appreciate the gesture. Have a good night, Mr Mallow.'

'Goodnight.'

Stephen glanced at his watch. It was too late to visit Olivia Willows now. The darkness had closed in hours ago, and he never went outside in the dark.

Never.

Not anymore.

The darkness was no longer his friend.

His conversation with Olivia Willows would have to wait until the morning.

Two hours later, after reading several chapters of his book and writing approximately a thousand words of an article he was working on for Kevin, Stephen collected his belongings and decided to call it an early night. As he walked through reception, he caught sight of a door which said *Basement – Staff Only*. He didn't know why the sight of the door stopped him in his tracks, but it did. And it reminded him of a door from his childhood: the basement door of his old home where his father had locked him up.

The darkness swooped closer, dragging a sense of fear over him that was so strong, he felt it tugging him in all directions. His fight or flight response kicked in ...

'Mr Mallow ... are you okay?'

Stephen flinched and bolted up the stairs away from Rachel, unwilling for her to see the tears streaming down his face. He slammed his hotel room door, flicked the light switch on and off seventeen times and collapsed on his bed, breathing heavily.

He knew then the only way to conquer his darkness was to face it. And there was only one thing he was afraid of: the darkness itself. There was a time when he had also been afraid of his father, but several years ago he'd faced that demon and defeated him.

He wasn't sure he could do it again. Not here in Cherry Hollow where fears seemed to take on a life of their own. The darkness seemed thicker and more menacing in this town.

A knock on the door made him sit bolt upright.

'Mr Mallow, I'm sorry to disturb you. I just wanted to make sure you were okay.'

Stephen smiled. It had been a long time since anyone had shown him any sort of kindness or concern. He stood and walked to the door, opening it.

'I'm sorry, Rachel. I'm fine.'

She didn't look as if she bought it. 'Are you sure? You look like you've seen a ghost.'

Stephen smirked at the irony. 'I can assure you I haven't seen a ghost. Can I ask what is down in the basement of this hotel?'

Rachel frowned at his odd question. 'Nothing much. It's where we store some boxes and some of the cleaning equipment and tools. Why?'

'And is the door locked?'

'Yes. Always. There are some steep steps down to the basement and I wouldn't want any hotel guests accidentally falling down them.'

'Thank you.'

Rachel reached out her hand and touched him on his right arm. 'Take care, Mr Mallow. If you need anything, don't hesitate to ask.'

'Thank you.' He paused for a few seconds. 'Actually, there is something I wish to ask you ... Would you care to have a drink with me?'

# Chapter Eighteen
## Olivia
### *24 January 2024 – 08:08 a.m.*

Olivia poured hot water into Frank's favourite mug, allowed the teabag to stew for a minute, then fished it out with a spoon and plopped it into the recycling bin for food waste. She added a straw to the tray. He was barely capable of drinking from a mug now, not without spilling the liquid down his front. A straw was her only option for getting liquids down him. She told him that drinking hot tea through a straw was practically blasphemy, and they'd shared a laugh. If her husband wanted to drink tea through a straw, then she wasn't about to stop him. She'd already dealt with his morning bodily ablutions and given him a quick sponge bath, but he'd barely had the energy to lift his arms or turn his head to the side. His body was failing him quicker each day, almost as if his inevitable death was in a rush to reach its destination.

As Olivia set the tray down on the table by his bed, he opened his eyes. 'Frank, I think it's time to call Brooke and Dorothy,' she said quietly, taking her hand and resting it on his pale arm.

'N-No, I said g-goodbye to Brooke when s-she left. I-I don't want her to come back here. I don't want the girls to remember me like this … t-this skeleton with s-skin on.'

Olivia blinked back the tears. 'Would you like some breakfast or some tea?'

'No, t-thank you. Can you just read to me?'

Olivia picked up the book, leaving his tea and toast to go cold. 'Yes. I feel like it's getting to the good bit,' she said with a smile. She watched as Frank closed his eyes. She couldn't help but wonder if it was going to be for the last time. Her hands trembled as she turned to the correct page. Olivia cleared her throat, fighting against the tears and emotions threatening to overwhelm her, and began to read.

Forty-five minutes later, Olivia gasped as the killer in the story was revealed. 'I was not expecting that, Frank! Were you?' Despite preferring cosy romantic stories, she found herself captivated by the gripping thriller. She looked up from the page and at her husband. His eyes were still closed. He looked so peaceful, so at rest. Smiling, she leaned forward and touched his arm. His chest no longer moved. He was truly, finally, at peace.

Swallowing her grief, she cleared her throat once again and continued reading to her sleeping husband, hoping that, wherever he was, he'd still be able to hear her voice and find out the ending of the story. She read, keeping her tone calm and slow until, two hours later, she finished the final sentence and closed the book.

She stood and set it on the side before leaning over the body of her husband, her childhood crush and constant companion, and kissed him on the forehead. She straightened up and whispered, 'You can take him now.'

A dark shadow emerged from the corner of the room.

It crept quietly and slowly across the space, its long limbs stretching out. But Olivia wasn't afraid because she knew the darkness would come for them all eventually.

Now, it was time to face it for herself.

Olivia left the room and closed the door, allowing the darkness to claim her husband.

Then, and only then, did she call Graham.

### *25 May 1980*

*The cave was dark, damp and cold, despite the warm temperature outside. The light from the day only reached a few feet into the darkness, so they huddled together in a location where they could still see each other. Jack lit the joint and puffed on the end, coughing afterwards.*

*Mary sniggered. 'You're hilarious.'*

*Jack grimaced as he held the joint out for her. 'Here ... Let's see if you do any better.'*

*Mary stuck her tongue out and took the joint, brought it to her lips and inhaled, holding the smoke in her lungs for a few seconds, and then slowly exhaled. Everyone held their breath, waiting for the coughing fit, but it never came.*

*'It's almost as if you've done this before,' said Frank, taking the joint from her.*

*Mary shrugged. 'Once or twice.'*

*As Mary settled on the rock she was perched on, her skirt rode up her leg a little way. Olivia noticed a dark, purplish bruise across her thigh, but it didn't look as if the boys had. Mary caught Olivia staring and adjusted her skirt into position, covering the bruise. Olivia lowered her gaze to the floor, a funny sort of warmth spreading across her chest. She wiped her eyes again, pretending as if she hadn't seen anything.*

*Once Frank stopped coughing his guts up, he held the joint out for Olivia who shook her head. 'No, thanks.'*

*Mary tutted. 'Don't be a wimp, Olivia.'*

*'I'm not a wimp. I just don't want to smoke it.'*

*Frank handed the joint back to Jack. 'It's okay, Liv. You don't have to.'*

*Olivia smiled, dipping her head slightly, hoping the darkness of the cave covered her faint blush.*

*A scuffing sound echoed through the cave from outside.*

*Everyone froze and stared at the entrance.*

*'What was that?' asked Olivia, grasping Frank's arm.*

*'Probably just the wind,' replied Frank.*

*'It sounded like footsteps,' whispered Jack, puffing on the joint again. This time, he only coughed a little. But now everyone's focus was on the approaching noise.*

*'We're miles away from the lake. Did someone follow us here?' asked Mary, keeping her voice low.*

*Frank stood. 'I'll go and check it out.'*

*'Be careful,' said Olivia.*

*All eyes were on Frank as he inched towards the cave entrance. He stuck his head out and looked left and right. 'There's no one out here.' As Frank turned to walk back to the group, the unmistakable sound of footsteps and loose stones rumbled through the cave.*

*Everyone spun around and stared into the darkness.*

*This time, the noise was behind them.*

*There was somebody else in the cave.*

*Or something else …*

# Chapter Nineteen

## Alex

### *24 January 2024 – 08:10 a.m.*

Alex wanted to sneak out of the house early to get to school. Usually, his mum didn't get out of bed till after nine. At least, she had at the start, after Linda had died, but lately, she'd been rising earlier and earlier and when Alex walked into the kitchen to grab himself a slice of toast before school, he found her not only fully showered and dressed, but cleaning the insides of the kitchen cupboards.

'Morning,' she said happily.

Alex popped a slice of bread in the toaster. 'You're up early, Mum.'

'Well, I wanted to tackle some of the jobs I've been neglecting recently. This house needs a decent clean, don't you think?'

'Uh-huh.'

'You know, I was thinking ... I'll talk to Dr Allan first to see if he thinks I'm ready, but how would you feel about me going back to work?'

Alex stopped in his tracks as he was reaching for the jar of peanut butter in the cupboard above the toaster. 'Um ... I guess that would be okay. Do you feel ready to start work again?'

His mum smiled as she nodded. 'I really think I do. My medication is finally working and levelling me out a bit. I feel more … I don't know … stable, I suppose.'

Alex screwed his nose up, turning his face away from her so she didn't see the sadness in his eyes. It wasn't that he didn't *want* her to get a job and start functioning as a normal human being again. He just didn't want her to start work and meet even more people who would probably turn out to be more helpful to her than he was. Maybe he wasn't doing enough for her. Maybe there was something he could do so he could keep an eye on her all the time, even when he was at school. Again, he didn't like that she was cooped up in the house all day, but a job at the school would be a great opportunity for her and for him to remain close by.

'That's great, Mum,' said Alex as he spread a thick dollop of peanut butter on his toast. 'Maybe there's a job going at the school. I could ask around.'

His mum shook her head. 'Oh, no, don't worry about that. I'll pop into the local job centre. I don't think there's one in town, but I'll have a look. Or maybe I can ask Olivia. She's bound to know someone who needs some help. Maybe I could do a cleaning job or something. Start my own business!' She clapped her hands together.

Alex barely recognised the woman in front of him. Had she completely forgotten about her dead daughter, dead ex-husband and dead wife? The idea of her getting better made him sick to his stomach. Was that what he wanted? Was he being selfish by wanting her to stay close to him?

'Alex … what's wrong? Are you okay?' His mum put down the cleaning cloth and approached him.

He flinched away from her and bit into his toast. 'Fine. Yeah. Gotta go.'

'Okay … I might be at Olivia's when you get back from school.'

'Why do you visit her so much?'

'Because she's my friend and her husband only has a few weeks, if not days, to live. She needs a friend right now.'

Alex rolled his eyes. He'd never officially met Mrs Willows in person. She seemed like a needy old woman. Surely she had friends her own age. Why did she have to dig her claws into his mum?

'Fine. Whatever.' He turned and headed out the door before his mum could question him on his moody attitude. He grabbed his keys and jacket, stuffed his feet into his shoes and left the house.

Alex headed straight for the Human Resources department within the school, situated on the top floor at the end of a long corridor. Alex remembered his mum used to work in HR, so he didn't see why she wouldn't be able to pick up where she left off.

He knocked on the door, waited for a reply and then pushed the door open. A middle-aged man with thick black hair looked up from his computer and smiled.

'My, my, you're in early. Can I help you?'

'Do you have any jobs going in the school?' asked Alex.

The man frowned. 'For yourself?'

'No, my mum. She's looking for work and she used to work in HR.'

The man nodded as if that made a lot more sense than Alex asking about a job for himself. 'As luck would have it, I think we do. HR assistant, or there's a job in the school library going. Your mum would have to come in and fill out an application.'

'Do you have the forms? I can print them out on a school computer and take them home for her instead.'

'Yes, of course. I have some printed out already. Here you are.' The man took some sheets of paper from a drawer, stapled them together and handed them to Alex.

'Thanks,' he said with a nod.

Alex stuffed the sheets into his bag and walked back into the corridor. It was too early to head to class, so he decided to go outside for a smoke. As he walked, his phone vibrated in his pocket. He stopped and took note of the caller as he pressed to answer.

'Hello, Mr Mallow.'

'Good morning, Alex. Thanks for that text yesterday regarding the piece of paper you found. It's certainly an interesting piece to the puzzle.'

'Did you find out anything about who could have written it?'

'Not yet, but I believe I know who will be able to answer my questions. Mrs Willows, Brooke's mother, has lived here all her life, so she should be able to help us find out who lived in your old house back in the late 70s and early 80s.'

'I didn't think about that. Good idea. Do you need my help?'

'You've been a great help already, but no, thank you. It's best you stay in school and let me do the digging. It's what you brought me here for, right? I shall keep you updated.'

'Thanks, Mr Mallow. Bye.' He hung up and put his phone back into his pocket.

Alex was finishing his cigarette when the school bell rang.

'Shit,' he muttered. He dropped the cigarette to the floor and stamped on it before putting it in a nearby bin.

He was running late for class, so he broke into a jog as he passed through the double doors, but something stopped him as he went to turn a corner.

Shouting. Feet scuffing on the floor. Crying.

Forgetting his lateness, Alex followed the sounds around another corner and poked his head around the next. What he saw made his blood run cold and the hairs on the back of his neck spring up.

A demon-like dark creature was grasping a child around its neck. The child was choking and silently screaming, making gargling sounds as he frantically kicked his legs.

Alex dropped his bag and sprinted towards the scene.

Upon seeing Alex running at it, The Creature let go of the child who ran off crying.

The Creature turned upon Alex, grabbed hold of its own face and ripped it off. 'Bloody hell, you scared the shit out of me!'

Alex punched Alex the First in the nose with no hesitation, using his body weight behind the attack. 'What the fuck!'

Alex the First yelped.

Harriet appeared from out of nowhere. 'Alex, what are you doing!'

Alex saw red and pointed a stiff finger at each in turn. 'You! You two are still terrorising kids in school with this bullshit?' He picked up the demon mask from the floor and shook it.

Alex the First clutched his nose as blood poured from it, dripping onto the shiny lino floor. 'You broke my nose!'

'Serves you right.'

'We were just having a bit of fun.'

'Like the fun you had with Bethany Walker? What the hell is wrong with both of you?'

Harriet flicked her red hair over her shoulder. 'You're one to talk.'

'What's *that* supposed to mean?'

'You know *exactly* what it means.'

Alex opened his mouth to argue, but loud footsteps echoed down the corridor and then the headmaster appeared. He saw Alex holding the mask and Alex the First holding his bloody nose.

'What is going on here? I've just seen a crying child running past my office. Alex Smithson, what are you doing with that?' Mr Peterson pointed to the mask.

Harriet stepped forward. 'He was scaring that poor kid and then when Alex Sharp tried to stop him, he punched him in the face.'

Alex gritted his teeth and clenched his fists at his sides.

'Is that true?' asked Mr Peterson, turning to Alex.

Again, Alex opened his mouth to argue his case, but then closed it and nodded. 'It was just a joke.'

Mr Peterson sighed as he took the mask from him. 'You'd better come with me, Alex. Harriet, can you take Alex Sharp to the nurse's office, please? Get him checked over. I shall call his mother ...' An awkward silence appeared as Mr Peterson realised his error. 'I mean ... his father. I shall call his father to come and collect him.'

'Yes, Mr Peterson.'

Harriet put her arms around Alex the First's shoulders. Alex glared at them over his own shoulder as he followed the headmaster.

Harriet smirked at him and stuck out her tongue like she was a five-year-old.

At that moment, he swore he would ensure that those two psychopaths would pay for everything they'd done.

It was time to put a stop to their reign of terror once and for all.

# Chapter Twenty

## Graham

### *24 January 2024 – 11:15 a.m.*

His coffee had gone cold ... again. If he drank all the coffee made for him or made himself, then maybe the caffeine would actually give him the energy he needed to get through the long days, but as it was, he barely ingested any caffeine, so what was the point of making the coffee in the first place? He always started drinking it and then something popped up, or the phone rang, or someone called him into a meeting and then it was left.

Today was no different.

He'd already led another short briefing this morning, which hadn't held any new information. His DCs were out in the town questioning people, and he'd already set up a visitation request to see Mrs Warner, aka Mrs Jenkins, at Ashmoore Prison for this afternoon. He needed to speak to her himself. It wasn't that he didn't trust his DCs to do a good job, but there was certain information he didn't want the rest of the team to know yet. Not until he'd got his head around it.

There were some topics of conversation that needed to be handled carefully. Graham had to admit, the prospect of seeing Mary King again filled him with the type of dread that made his stomach twist itself into knots. He'd lain awake last night going over and over it in his mind. Was he actually right? Was Tyler's mother really Mary King, his once-best friend who'd moved away all those years ago and not spoken to him since? Why had she returned to the town and not told anyone? How had no one recognised her? Did her husband know who she really was? All these questions and more spiralled through his mind. He couldn't think about anything else. Even his headache had grown to be an afterthought for the moment.

The phone on his desk sprang to life.

*Here we go again.*

'Detective Williams speaking.' A small sob emanated from the speaker, and he knew exactly who it was and what had happened. 'Has he—'

'He's gone, Graham.'

'Have you called anyone else?'

'No, not yet.'

'Don't. I'll handle it. I'll be there in ten minutes.'

Eight minutes later, Graham knocked on Olivia's door. It opened to reveal a broken woman. The small amount of light she'd had inside her had now flickered out completely, leaving her skin dull, her eyes dark and her overall demeanour crushed.

'I'm so sorry,' said Graham. He wanted to reach out and wrap his arms around her, but it had been a long time since he'd shown anyone affection, so was hesitant in case it was the wrong thing to do, or it felt unnatural. But Olivia didn't seem to care about the forty-four-year friendship gap. She ushered him inside, closed the door and threw her slender arms around him, squeezing as tight as her slight frame would allow.

Graham froze, unsure whether to hug her back, but then the years melted away and it was like hugging his best friend once again.

Olivia sobbed on his shoulder, a damp patch soon forming where she pressed her face into his jacket. How long had this woman kept her emotions in check? How long had she kept the darkness at bay, so she appeared strong on the outside to everyone else?

He wasn't sure how long they held each other, but Olivia eventually lifted her head off his shoulder and fished a tissue from her pocket. She blew her nose.

'Goodness me, I'm so sorry, Graham. Look at the state of your jacket.'

'Forget the jacket. Let me check the ... Let me check him quickly and then I'll call a funeral director to come and take him away and get all the paperwork done. I assume you don't want an autopsy or anything like that?'

Olivia shook her head. 'No, that won't be necessary. Thank you.'

Graham nodded. 'I won't be a minute.'

He left Olivia standing in the hallway and headed up the stairs and to the bedroom he'd visited last time. He took a breath before pushing open the door. His eyes caught sight of the frail man lying in bed. He could have been sleeping. A shadow of darkness hung over the room like a thick blanket.

Graham didn't need to check his pulse to know he was dead, but he did it anyway for no other reason than protocol.

'I'm sorry, Franky,' he whispered. He wanted to say more, wanted to let out his own emotions at the body in front of him, wanted to shout at him for allowing their friendship to break up and for keeping secrets for so long. 'Why couldn't you have just trusted me?'

'We were protecting you,' said a voice from behind.

Graham turned to see Olivia standing in the doorway. 'Mary's alive, isn't she?' he asked.

Olivia nodded. 'Yes, she is.'

'It's Flora. The body.'

Another nod.

'Mary killed her.'

Olivia sniffed in response.

Graham took a step forward, but as he did, the sound of crunching gravel came from outside, followed by a doorbell.

Olivia wiped her eyes. 'That was fast.'

'I haven't called anyone yet.' Olivia turned to walk downstairs, but Graham stopped her. 'I'll go.' He jogged down the stairs and peered through the peephole. 'Son of a—' He wrenched open the door. 'This is quite possibly the worst timing ever, Mr Mallow.'

The man looked positively shocked to see him. 'Detective Williams? What are you doing answering the door to Mrs Willows' house?'

'What are *you* doing ringing her doorbell?'

'I've come to ask her some questions.'

'As I said, it's a bad time. Come back later, or, better yet, come back never.'

'I have every right to be here—'

'Actually, you don't. Now, I suggest you get going before I arrest you.'

Stephen grinned as he shook his head. 'Again, with the arrest threats! Threatening me with getting arrested is not going to work, especially as I'm doing nothing wrong.'

Graham hated that he was right. He clenched his teeth and fists, but Olivia's calming touch on his shoulder made him relax and take a breath. She peered past him.

'I recognise you,' she said.

Stephen stepped forward, ignoring Graham's piercing glare. 'My name is Stephen Mallow, Mrs Willows. I don't think we've met officially. I'm a—'

'Journalist,' she finished.

'Yes.'

'You came to Cherry Hollow a while ago.'

'Yes.'

'And now you're back because there's another body that's been found.'

'Yes.'

Olivia sighed. 'I'm afraid this isn't the best time, Mr Mallow—'

'That's what I was trying to tell him,' added Graham.

Olivia shot him a dark look. 'My husband passed away only this morning.'

Stephen gulped and lowered his head. 'My deepest condolences. I, of course, will come back another time.' He began to back away from the door, keeping his head down.

'Just a moment, Mr Mallow. As long as you do not ask me any questions about my husband's death or the body that was found, then you may come in and ask whatever other questions you have.'

Stephen nodded. 'Of course. Thank you.'

'Very well then.' She stepped aside.

Graham leaned in close to her ear. 'This is a bad idea, Olivia.'

Olivia gave him a small smile. 'I don't doubt that. Will you stay and deal with ... Frank?'

'Yes, I will ... and to keep an eye on ...' He thrust his head at Stephen who was still standing on the doorstep, looking highly amused. Graham wanted nothing more than to wipe the smirk off his face.

Olivia opened the door wider. 'Come in, Mr Mallow.'

'Please, call me Stephen.'

# Chapter Twenty-One
## Stephen
### *24 January 2024 – 11:45 a.m.*

He stamped his feet on the doormat before stepping into the warm house. He instantly felt the itchy compulsion to reach for the nearest light switch and flick it up and down seventeen times. But he didn't. Even he had his boundaries. Doing that sort of thing in front of other people made his insides squirm. He'd let his compulsion take over at the detective's office yesterday on his way out, but he didn't want to do it in front of Mrs Willows.

But what he did do was imagine doing it by closing his eyes. It wasn't perfect, but it was enough to quell the urge.

'Mr Mallow, are you quite well?'

Stephen opened his eyes to see Mrs Willows looking at him with her head tilted to the side.

'Sorry. Yes. Headache.' It was partly true. He did have a headache, thanks to the amount of whiskey he and Rachel had drunk last night in the hotel bar.

Stephen hadn't enjoyed another person's company for a very long time. He and Rachel had sat for hours talking about all sorts. Yes, she was eight or ten years younger than him, but he didn't care, and she didn't seem to mind either. He listened as she told him her story of moving to Cherry Hollow as a young girl with her family, who'd moved there to get out of the hustle and bustle of Birmingham city centre. She told him she had a twin sister called Tina who had moved away several years ago, but she'd decided to stay close to her parents who still lived in the town.

Stephen had regaled her with snippets from his upbringing too. However, he had left out the parts that turned his blood to ice, such as his father locking him in the cold, dark basement, and his mother's sudden death. He didn't mention too much about his parents and luckily, Rachel hadn't pried. Maybe she'd sensed he wasn't comfortable talking about them. He didn't know. But it didn't matter. They'd talked about other things too such as jobs and hobbies, and they'd even discovered they shared a fascination with butterflies.

Then, when the clock above the fireplace in the bar struck midnight, Rachel yawned and said she should probably call it a night as she had to be up early for work. He thanked her for her company, and she gave him a kiss on the cheek as she'd hugged him goodnight.

Stephen smiled as he climbed the stairs to room 11. He hadn't thought about the locked basement in the reception area all night, and as his eyes had fluttered closed, he couldn't help but think how nice it had been to speak to Rachel. She hadn't called him odd. She hadn't mentioned his constant need to move his hands, whether it be fiddling with his whiskey glass or tapping his fingers on the arm of the chair. And, most importantly, she'd said as she put on her coat, 'I'd like to see you again, Stephen, and not just as a guest in the hotel.'

Stephen's heart had practically glowed.

And now, other than the headache, he still felt as if he were floating on a cloud. But he couldn't afford to think about Rachel right now. He had a job to do.

He followed Olivia into the lounge, taking a glance up the stairs as he passed them. Was the body of her husband still up there? He'd died this morning, so did that mean … He shuddered, having never been comfortable with the idea of death. It was so … *final*. He didn't believe in any sort of afterlife, so the thought of death unnerved him. He didn't believe a person had a soul either, at least not one that drifted off to some other plane of existence when they took their last breath. He believed in the here and the now.

But death … like the darkness … frightened him.

The questions he wanted to ask her were practically tripping over themselves in his mind, fighting to be free. But he'd agreed to her terms of being invited inside, so squashed them back down, along with his desire to turn the light switch on and off.

'Please take a seat, Stephen. Would you like a cup of tea?' asked Olivia.

Stephen shook his head. The woman had just lost her husband yet seemed very together and polite. Was that just her way of dealing with her loss? 'No, thank you.'

'Very well.'

Olivia took a seat in the big armchair, which Stephen guessed was her usual place to sit. He glanced over at Detective Williams who leaned against the doorframe. The detective narrowed his eyes at Stephen and then turned and walked upstairs. Stephen could have done with not having the detective breathing down his neck, but, as he'd reminded him earlier, he was doing nothing wrong by asking a few questions. Although, the detective was right in what he'd said earlier: he couldn't have chosen a worse time. But how was he supposed to have known Olivia's husband had died only hours before he'd arrived at her front door?

Stephen lowered himself and his trusty laptop bag onto the sofa and took out his notebook, straightening the pages until he was satisfied. Why was he nervous? It wasn't that he was afraid of speaking to an older woman, but the look in her eyes set him on edge.

He cleared his throat. 'Mrs Willows – sorry, Olivia – how long have you lived in Cherry Hollow?'

'All my life. I was born here.'

'In this house?'

'No, I bought this house with my husband in 1991 so we could raise our family. We married very young, and I fell pregnant with Brooke almost straight away. I was only twenty. I was born in a small house on the outskirts of the town. It's been torn down now, I believe. The council built new larger houses on the grounds several years ago.'

Stephen scribbled away. 'So, it's safe to say you know the town and its residents fairly well.'

Olivia paused before answering. 'Yes, I know almost everyone in town, but a lot has changed over the years. The town isn't what it used to be.'

'Because of what happened in 1998?' Stephen watched Olivia's eyes carefully.

She blinked once but that was all. 'Yes.'

He hoped she'd expand, but she squeezed her lips together instead. Stephen took the hint and moved on. Clearly, bringing up Kieran Jones' disappearance wasn't a topic Olivia wanted to broach, especially as it had been the catalyst to her daughter spending the next twenty years of her life trapped inside her home: this house.

'Is there anyone else who lives in town who has lived here as long as you?' he asked.

Olivia's eyes darkened for a moment. 'Other than old Mrs Price who celebrated her ninety-fifth birthday last week, there's only myself and Graham now that my husband has passed.'

Stephen bowed his head. 'Again, my sincerest condolences. Can you give me Graham's last name?' He already knew it. But he had to be sure.

'Graham Williams, the man who's upstairs tending to my husband.' Her tone told Stephen she wasn't in the mood for pleasantries, which was fair enough.

'I see. Does Mrs Price live alone?'

'Yes. Considering her age, she's still very much capable, but I believe she has a carer who comes to assist her.'

'Was she ever married?'

'Yes, but her husband died some time ago. I'm afraid I don't quite remember when, but it was very sudden. She's been alone ever since.'

'Okay.' Stephen wrote a few notes down. 'Do you happen to know who lived in Amber Walker's house before she and her husband bought it?'

Olivia shifted in her chair. 'It was empty for some time. When Amber and Sean Walker bought the house, they had to do a bit of renovation to bring it up to a decent standard. They did such a fine job on it too. It's such a shame it's gone now.'

'How long was it empty for?'

Olivia scratched the delicate skin on the back of her left hand. 'There was some confusion and delay over the sale due to the previous owners moving out and not selling it, or telling anyone what was to be done with it.'

Stephen's pen was poised, ready for the big reveal. 'So, you do know who owned it before?'

Olivia nodded. 'Yes, it belonged to Mr and Mrs King and their two daughters, Mary and Flora.'

Bingo.

Stephen wrote down the names. The pieces of the puzzle were slotting into place bit by bit. He just needed to push her a little bit further. 'Mr King was the headmaster of the school back in the 1970s, right?'

Olivia raised her eyebrows. 'You seem quite clued up on the history of the town already.'

'I've done some research, yes. Do you know why Mr King and his family left so suddenly in May of 1980? Were you close with his daughters?'

A cough from behind him stopped Olivia from answering. Stephen looked up to see Detective Williams glaring at him with his arms folded.

'The funeral home will be here in twenty minutes to collect ... the body. There will be some forms to sign and things to arrange. I'm happy to stay and help, Olivia, which means it's time for you to leave, Mr Mallow.'

Stephen glanced at Olivia, hoping she'd tell the detective to leave them alone, but it seemed she was also ready for him to leave.

Stephen sighed as he stood up. He didn't want to upset her or cause any trouble. He turned to her. 'Thank you for answering my questions. I just have one more, if it wouldn't be too much trouble.'

Olivia smiled. 'Very well.'

'Did you ever see Mr King or any member of his family again?'

Olivia paused. Stephen saw her bottom lip wobble. 'No, I never saw any of them again.'

Stephen nodded. He had what he needed.

Two and a half hours later, he was sitting in his car, parked down the road from Olivia's house. The detective's car was still parked in her driveway. He'd seen the funeral director's car arrive and watched as they'd wheeled the body bag out on a stretcher and driven away.

It interested him that the detective had used Olivia's first name and she'd done the same with him. It wasn't usual for a police detective, especially a DCI, to deal with the death of someone in the community, so why had he even been there? Did they know each other personally? They must have done, considering Olivia had revealed she and the detective were the only ones who still lived in Cherry Hollow from the 1970s, except for old Mrs Price, who he'd probably be able to discount.

Stephen had a sneaking suspicion something was going on. He didn't know what exactly, but he knew he needed to keep an eye on Olivia and Detective Williams. He had nothing better to do anyway. The fact Mr King had lived in Amber's old house meant it was possible his wife had written the note Alex had found under the floorboards. But why? What was the connection there?

He looked at his watch. It was past lunchtime and his stomach confirmed it by grumbling. He checked the glove compartment. Usually, there was some form of chocolate bar stashed away somewhere, but not this time.

Stephen rubbed his head and decided to say his thoughts out loud to distract himself from his rumbling belly. Sometimes it helped to compartmentalise everything. He ticked items off his fingers as he spoke.

'Mr King was the headmaster of the school back in the 1970s. He had two daughters called Mary and Flora. In May of

1980, he and his family moved out of Cherry Hollow suddenly. He left his house empty. No one seems to know the reason why he moved away. No one has seen or spoken to him since.

'Olivia Willows would have been a teenager in 1980, as would Detective Williams. Maybe around fifteen or sixteen years of age. There's a possibility they were friends back then. The detective has a photo of himself and a group of friends hanging in his office. Maybe Olivia is one of those friends. They possibly would have known Mary and Flora King too.

'Amber Walker and her husband bought Mr King's house and did it up. Then, when Amber died, her husband sold it to Emma and Linda Smithson last year. A note was found under the floorboards by Alex Smithson. That note said ...' Stephen grabbed his phone and scrolled to the photo of the note. '"I'm sorry to do this to you. I love you more than anything and this is the only way I know how to keep you safe. I'm so sorry I wasn't there for you when I should have been. Your dad loves you. You'll be okay, baby. I love you."

'Who wrote this note and why? Was it Mrs King? But why ... why would she have hidden it under the floor? What was the reason for writing this note?' Stephen stopped and tapped his fingers on the steering wheel.

His head ached again, but this time it wasn't due to the hangover. His brain needed answers. What was he missing? What was the connection between Mr King's sudden departure, the body found in the cave and Olivia Willows?

'Could the body be either Mary or Flora King?' he asked himself. 'The timeline fits. Detective Williams hasn't confirmed the identity of the body yet, but it could very well be one of them.'

Movement up ahead caught his eye.

Olivia and Detective Williams were leaving the house together. She had a small bag with her. The detective opened the passenger door of his car, let her get in and then closed it before getting behind the wheel.

Stephen watched the police car reverse out of the driveway.

He put his own car in gear and followed behind, keeping a long stretch of road between them. It wasn't too difficult to follow it around here.

But the car didn't head towards the police station where he'd been expecting it to go.

No, the car was heading out of town.

# Chapter Twenty-Two
## Olivia
### *24 January 2024 – 14:30 p.m.*

Exhaustion threatened to take over her body as she settled into the passenger seat of the police car. It would have been easy to close her eyes and drift off to sleep, but she knew she'd never be able to sleep peacefully until she'd faced the demons of her past. Her dreams would not have been happy or pleasant ones.

Frank was gone.

A piece of her heart was missing: a big piece.

She'd been expecting the inevitable for a long time, ever since he was diagnosed, but it didn't make it any easier. Now he was gone, she felt hollow. She'd been fighting for so long, fighting for her family, her husband, her friends … Now, who was left to fight for, other than herself? Did she even want to continue to fight for herself? Did she care anymore about anything?

All she knew was she needed to face her past.

And that included facing a particular person.

It had to end sometime, especially now she was the only one left … on the outside. It was up to her to either continue to hide the truth from the world or explain what really happened that day in the cave and what Mary had made them all do …

Graham kept strangely quiet during the drive to Ashmoore Prison. He'd never been a huge talker, but now he appeared solemn and far too invested in driving than talking to her. He'd been an absolute lifesaver this morning so she couldn't fault him for that. She'd broken down again in hysterical sobs as her husband's body had been zipped up in the body bag and wheeled out on a stretcher. It didn't feel real. One minute he was there and the next he was gone. She kept replaying his last moments in her mind.

Had he heard her reading out loud as he'd quietly slipped away? Had he been trying to hold on until she'd finished reading the last page? Had he been in pain? Had he been glad to have her by his side or had he wanted to be alone?

What was she supposed to do now? She knew she needed to call her daughters and tell them the devastating news, but there were things she needed to take care of first, things she didn't want Dorothy or Brooke (especially Brooke) to get mixed up in. She'd always known what Brooke had done. There was no proof, but deep down she knew Brooke had been involved in Kieran Jones' death. The darkness followed a pattern ... and she'd started it.

Forty-four years ago.

Now, it was time to end the pattern.

It was time to face the darkness once and for all.

It was time to face Mary King.

### 25 May 1980

*Olivia's skin hummed with anticipation as goosebumps spread across her body. There was someone back there, in the cave. No one had passed them, as they'd been by the entrance the whole time, so whoever it was had been there before they'd arrived. Had they been waiting for them? Or was it an animal and they'd disturbed its den? She was certain there were no bears or wolves in the Lake District.*

*The footsteps got louder. Crunching stones and the shuffling of feet.*

*Olivia took a step back towards the light at the entrance, ready to make a run for her life.*

*'Who's there?' called Frank. He crept towards the back of the cave. Olivia knew he was trying to be brave because the rest of them were frozen to the spot. Even Mary. 'Show yourself!'*

*A few seconds of silence followed as the footsteps stopped.*

*Then, a small dark shadow stepped out from behind a rock.*

*Everyone gasped.*

*'Flora?' Mary's voice was high-pitched and wobbly.*

*'Yes, Mary, it's me. I'm sorry I scared you.'*

*Jack laughed as he clutched his chest. 'You gave us all a fright!'*

*Flora, Mary's younger sister, lowered her head. She looked so small and timid. It wasn't often Olivia saw her. She was only eight years old, so they didn't mix with her age group at school, and Mary never included her in anything. Her light-blue dress was filthy, but what caught Olivia's attention more than her dirty dress and matted hair was the array of bruises on her arms* and legs. They created an odd pattern in the light, all blues and purples and greens, showing that some had been there longer than others. The image made Olivia sick to her stomach.

'What happened?' asked Olivia.

Flora stayed in the shadows. Mary shot Olivia another dark look.

'Did you fall down here?' asked Frank.

Flora nodded, her eyes full of desperation. 'Y-Yes, I climbed down the side of the ravine, and I slipped and fell.'

'What are you even doing down here?' asked Mary, a hint of annoyance in her voice.

'This is where I come to hide.'

'Who are you hiding from?' asked Olivia. As soon as the question left her mouth, she regretted it as Mary spun around and pointed a finger in her face. Aggression flooded Mary's posture as she rounded on Olivia who immediately took a step back.

'Shut up!'

Frank stepped in front of Olivia. 'Hey, there's no need to shout at Liv like that. She was only asking a question.'

'Yeah, well, maybe she should keep her mouth shut and not ask questions when the answers are none of her business. Flora, get out of here. This is our cave now.'

'But—'

'Go home!'

'No. You can't make me. This is my cave!' Flora burst into tears and ran into the darkness, her feet nimbly floating across the uneven stones.

*Mary chased after her, stumbling.*

*'What is going on right now?' asked Jack. 'Should we follow them?'*

*Olivia stared in disbelief as Flora and Mary disappeared into the darkness.*

# Chapter Twenty-Three

## Alex

### *24 January 2024 – 10:10 a.m.*

He knew he was in trouble. It was going to be bad. So bad. A gut-wrenching ache had already started forming in his stomach and his heart was beating too fast for someone who was sat down. He watched and listened, keeping his head bowed as Mr Peterson dialled his mum's number, spoke to her in a solemn tone and explained the situation. He couldn't hear his mum's voice on the other end of the line, but he could imagine how disappointed she must be. It was the last thing he wanted: her to be disappointed in him. And they'd been doing so well lately, or so he'd thought. Had he blown it? Would she believe he was innocent?

His plan of growing closer to her had failed miserably. The whole thing had gone up in smoke thanks to Harriet and Alex the First, who were probably in class howling with laughter that he'd been mistakenly blamed for their prank. Why the hell had they started all that up again? Wasn't once enough?

Mr Peterson placed the offending mask on his desk. The hollow demon eyes stared back at Alex, causing the hairs on the back of his neck to prickle. As Alex stared into the empty depths, his mind created an eerie vision before his eyes.

A huge black creature materialised behind Mr Peterson's chair, forming from nothing but smoke. Alex had never seen anything quite so terrifying. It grew to over eight feet tall, its body huge and disfigured, its head scraping the ceiling, so it had to bend over as if it had a mutilated spine.

The skeleton with skin stretched tight over its bones loomed above him. Its long arms were like branches of a tree, extending into slim claw-like talons at the end. It opened its mouth wide, like a never-ending swirling vortex, as its large fang-like teeth dripped sticky mucus. Alex saw the resemblance to the creature in the *Alien* films.

But its eyes … Those were the worst and most terrifying part about its overall presence. Red and full of fire, they sucked Alex's life from him as he stared … He couldn't look away. He couldn't even blink. There was nothing but the blood-red eyes dragging him closer and closer …

The Creature manoeuvred its huge skeletal body behind Mr Peterson, placed one of its claw hands in front of his throat and sliced straight across as if it were made of butter.

Blood spurted from Mr Peterson's neck and ran in streams down his front, soaking his white shirt. He gargled and his head dropped back …

Alex scrambled to his feet and screamed.

'Alex, what's wrong?' asked Mr Peterson, his throat still oozing blood. His mouth filled with it too and stained his teeth.

'I … I … Go away!'

The Creature disappeared back inside his mind, disintegrating into thin air.

Alex stared at the headmaster who looked normal again, but he did have a frown on his face. 'Are you okay? Do I need to call the nurse?'

'No … I … Nothing, I'm sorry.' Alex slumped down in the chair, sweating. He clutched his chest.

'Very well. Your mother should be here shortly. I'm sorry to say, but after what happened the last time a child was bullied at this school, I have to take this very seriously.'

'You do know it was them who bullied Bethany Walker, right? I wasn't even here when it happened the first time.'

'I'm afraid there's no proof Alex Sharp and Harriet Forrester had anything to do with it.'

Alex laughed. 'You people are so blind.'

Mr Peterson didn't respond.

Alex spent the rest of the time waiting for his mum staring at a random spot on the floor at his feet. He was too afraid to look up in case The Creature came back and sliced Mr Peterson's throat open again. Mr Peterson remained in his chair and carried on with his work. He looked up when there was a knock at the door.

'Come in, Mrs Smithson. Take a seat.'

Alex sensed his mum sitting in the chair next to him. He couldn't look at her. He didn't want to see the look in her eyes. He continued to stare at the floor as Mr Peterson spoke.

'Mrs Smithson, I'm sorry to have to call you in today, but as I said on the phone, there's been an incident at school I feel you need to be made aware of. Your son was seen scaring a younger pupil wearing this mask ...' He placed a hand on top of the item and then removed it. 'Now, I'm not sure if you know, but a similar incident happened last year with Bethany Walker. It all started when she wrote a poem about an evil entity she said was haunting her. Somehow, the poem got leaked to the school and some children were frightened by it.'

At this, Alex looked up, wanting to speak out, but his mum got there first.

'But Alex wasn't even here last year, not until October when we first moved in, and this incident with the poem happened before that. I found it ...' She stopped, probably realising she'd said too much. 'I mean ... I find it hard to believe Alex would frighten anyone.' She looked over to him and he had no choice but to turn and meet her gaze. Her eyes weren't full of anger or disappointment, but something else ... something he hadn't been expecting.

Love.

'Be that as it may, Mrs Smithson, I'm afraid there are two witnesses who saw him today.'

'Have you spoken with the child who was assaulted?'

'Not yet, but—'

'Then how could you know for certain it was Alex?'

'I confessed, Mum,' he said softly.

His mum opened her mouth and then closed it.

Mr Peterson cleared his throat, clearly not at all comfortable with the situation. 'I shall, of course, speak to the child in question, but they ran off before I could speak to them. I will have to inform their parents as well.'

'Who were the witnesses?' asked his mum.

'I'm not at liberty to say.'

His mum nodded; her lips sealed tight. 'I see. What is his punishment?'

Mr Peterson interlaced his fingers and rested his elbows on the desk. 'Considering this is Alex's first offence, I'll go easy on him by giving him two weeks of detention. However, once I've spoken to the child's parents, if they wish to take things further, then I will have to speak to you regarding the outcome.'

'Very well. That seems fair.' His mum stood up. 'I'll take him straight home now if you don't mind.'

'I'll ensure he gets his homework missed from today at school tomorrow,' replied Mr Peterson.

His mum looked down at Alex. 'You're grounded as soon as we get home. No phone. No tablet. No TV.'

Alex stood; his shoulders hunched as he followed her into the corridor without a word. As soon as the door to the headmaster's office closed, she turned to him.

'Can you explain to me why you confessed to something you didn't do?'

Alex's head snapped up. 'What?'

'It was Harriet and Alex, wasn't it?'

'How do you know that?'

'I'm not blind or deaf, young man. Do you think I don't see and hear things? I told you those two were trouble from the start. I never told you this, but I was the one who found the poem Bethany wrote under the floorboards last year. And I know your so-called friend and girlfriend had something to do with bullying her and spreading the rumour about The Creature.'

Alex looked over his shoulder. 'I know it was you who found the poem, Mum.'

Her eyes widened. 'You do? How?'

'Jordan and Brooke told me, but I found something else under there too. It was a note. At first, we thought it was written by Amber before she died, but now we're not so sure.'

'Who's *we*? Jordan and Brooke don't live in town anymore.'

'I'm sort of working with Stephen Mallow, the journalist from London who's in town. I was the one who got him to come back here.'

His mum raised her hand to stop him from explaining anything else. 'Alex, I don't know what the hell is going on with you right now, but standing in the middle of a school corridor is not the place to talk about this.' She placed a hand on his shoulder. 'I don't know why you confessed to scaring a child with a mask on, but whatever you've got planned, I want in. Let's go home and talk about it.'

'Huh?'

'You heard me. We're in this together now.'

'But—'

'But nothing, Alex.'

Alex watched as his mum walked down the corridor towards the exit.

What the fuck had just happened? He'd expected her to arrive at school and explode with rage at him. He hadn't expected her to believe he hadn't committed the bullying act and then offer her help with whatever it was he had planned.

The last thing he wanted was for her to get into trouble, especially as he was hoping to get her a job here, but he couldn't help but feel excited at the prospect of them working together.

Now, it was just him and his mum.

Together again.

Just like he'd always wanted.

Maybe it would all work out after all.

# Chapter Twenty-Four

## Graham

### *24 January 2024 – 16:15 p.m.*

He could tell Olivia needed some time inside her own head, so he didn't press her for conversation during the journey to Ashmoore Prison. The drive gave him time to think. Not that thinking was always a good thing because he had a notorious tendency to overthink and then it would lead to all sorts of dark thoughts that would spiral around his head.

He couldn't get rid of the image of Frank lying dead inside the body bag, nor the image of a dark creature floating above. He hadn't *seen* a creature of any sort of course because that would have been ridiculous. It's not as if the Grim Reaper had come to collect his friend in person. But there had been a ... *presence* inside the bedroom as he'd entered.

A presence that was still making his skin tingle.

His eyes flicked to the rearview mirror several times during the drive. He inwardly smiled.

Graham pulled into a visitor spot in the car park and switched off the engine. 'I think it would be best if I spoke to her first ... alone.'

Olivia continued to stare out of the window, apparently studying the contours of the building in front of her with fascination. 'Yes, you go and do your police thing, Detective.'

Graham sighed. 'This is very difficult for me.'

'I think at this point, Graham, you need to decide whether you're a policeman here on official duty or a friend visiting another friend.'

'I'm not in any way Mary's friend. Not after what she's done.'

'She's not mine either. I don't think she ever really was.'

Graham opened the car door and got out. Olivia followed.

They walked in silence towards the building, checked in and were then scanned for any weapons or sharp objects upon entering the main area. They were then asked a unique question: whether they had eaten any peanuts in the past twenty-four hours or if they had any sort of peanut-containing food on them. Mary King had a fatal allergy to peanuts, something Graham and Olivia had learned the hard way as children when she'd had an anaphylactic shock one day at school when a child on the next table had eaten some. Luckily, it had been a mild attack as she hadn't come into direct contact with the peanuts, but ever since then, nuts of all kinds had been banned in the school. Graham assumed she always carried an EpiPen, or at least the doctor's office at the prison should hold one in case of an emergency.

Graham left Olivia in the waiting area and headed to the secluded visitation room. He'd requested one with no other prisoners or visitors present.

As he walked, his stomach twisted into knots. He hadn't seen Mary in person since they were children before he'd left for his holiday. Now, so many years later, he was about to face her as an adult, but not just that … She was no longer Mary King, but Mary Warner, and before that, Mary Jenkins.

She was the mother who raped and abused her son from a young age until he was a teenager. She was the reason her son had killed Kieran Jones. She was the reason why Cherry Hollow was haunted by a *darkness*. If it hadn't been for Mary King none of this would have happened and the town would have been just another average town in the Lake District, renowned for its beauty and peace rather than as a murder capital. If it had been Mary who'd died that day in the cave rather than Flora … would anything have changed?

Graham opened the door to the visitation room and sucked in a breath. A woman sat in a chair with hands chained in front of her resting on a metal table. She looked nothing like he remembered. He'd seen Mrs Jenkins on television. He'd helped Jordan set her up and she'd confessed everything … almost everything. She'd failed to mention who she truly was. The question remained: why had she confessed to what she'd done to her son? Why not the rest of it? Why not the fact she was actually Mary King and had been masquerading as Mrs Jenkins for years while she lived in Cherry Hollow, her childhood home?

The woman looked up and locked eyes with him. There was nothing there. No flicker of humanity. No friendliness or spark of surprise. The girl called Mary King no longer lived inside the body, the body of an evil woman. She'd been twisted and branded by her own darkness. That's all there was to it. The woman was a psychopath because no normal mother would have done that to her son.

'Hello, Lee Man,' she said, her voice husky as if she'd smoked every day of her adult life.

Graham shut the door and walked to the empty chair at the other end of the table. He was glad there was space between them as well as a barrier. He didn't want to be within touching distance of her, even if her wrists were shackled.

'Hello, Mary.'

She smiled, showing her yellow, stained teeth. Her skin looked leathery and worn, dry even. 'So ... you've finally worked out who I am, after all those years of living in the same town, passing me on the street.'

'You don't exactly look like the young woman I remember.'

'And you don't look like the young man I remember. The years have been kind to you though, Lee Man. The same can't be said for me, I'm afraid.'

At least the woman was honest.

Graham leaned across the table towards her, keeping his palms flat against the cool metal. 'I know what happened now, Mary.'

Mary raised her bushy eyebrows. 'Do you? Are you sure about that?'

'Yes.'

'Why don't you explain what you think happened and I'll tell you if you're right or not.'

'I'd rather hear it from you.'

Mary cackled like a witch. 'You haven't changed a bit, Lee Man. Go on, tell me. I'm dying to hear your thoughts out loud.'

Graham cleared his throat, feeling sick. 'Fine. You killed your sister, Flora, and hid her body in a cave back in 1980. Your family then moved out of town and were never heard from again. Then, unbelievably, you moved back there years later after having plastic surgery to disguise your identity. You were married to Keith Jenkins and had a son, Tyler, who you proceeded to rape and abuse under everyone's noses. He killed his best friend to keep your sick secret in 1998, and then you left town again when he turned eighteen, changed your name and hid away in Scotland, thinking you'd got away with it. But Jordan Evans tracked you down and now you're here … rotting away in a cell for what you did to your son, but keeping the fact you murdered your younger sister when you were a teenager a secret. Does that cover everything, Mary?'

Mary leaned back in her chair, rattling the chains around her wrists. 'That's quite a story, Lee Man, or should I call you *Detective* now?'

'Call me whatever the hell you like, but I know the truth. I'm going to make sure you go down for Flora's murder.'

Mary laughed again, but this time it ended in a coughing fit, which caused her face to turn beetroot red. Graham held his nerve while she composed herself.

'Why bother? I'm already locked up,' she said, sucking in big gulps of air.

'You could still get out for good behaviour one day. It's unlikely, but possible. I can't let that happen. Plus, Flora deserves justice.'

Mary spat on the floor. 'And do you have proof I killed my sister, *Detective*?'

Graham's mouth twitched.

'That's what I thought. Well, Lee Man, it's been great chatting with you now you've finally figured out who I am, but I really must go. I have a busy schedule, you know.' She held up her hand to signal a guard who was no doubt watching through a surveillance camera, but the microphones were off. Graham had explained he didn't want any guards in the room with them or anyone listening.

'I'm not finished, Mary. Your husband is in another prison, is that right?'

Mary shuffled in her seat, pulling her hand back onto her lap. 'Yes. Thank fuck I don't have to see his stupid face ever again. My pathetic husband wasn't strong enough to last inside. I was told he ended his own life in his prison cell a couple of years ago. The darkness took him.'

Graham felt as if he'd been punched in the chest. Hadn't that been what Stephen Mallow had called it? Not The Creature, which was the manifestation of whatever it was that was supposedly haunting everyone involved, but something else that went deeper than merely a scary-looking monster.

'The *what*?' he asked, unable to keep his voice from wobbling.

'The guilt, Lee Man. It finally caught up with him.'

'For what he did to his son?'

'He never did anything to Tyler. He merely kept my secret about what I did to him.'

Graham pushed aside his own thoughts on what the darkness was and pressed further. 'What about you? Why hasn't the darkness taken you yet?'

Mary squeezed her lips together and looked up at the ceiling. Graham followed her line of sight but saw nothing worth staring at. Could she see something up there? Had Stephen Mallow been on to something with his theory of The Creature and the darkness? It made no sense yet ... but Graham was beginning to realise just because he couldn't see something didn't mean it wasn't real.

'Why did you do it, Mary?' he asked. 'Why did you kill Flora, and why did you rape and abuse Tyler, your own son?'

Mary pulled her eyes away from the ceiling and locked them on him like a trained sniper. They were black, empty pits and he didn't like what he saw. Was she truly a psychopath? She didn't appear to have any emotions on the outside. Her body language told him she was calm, controlled and perfectly at ease talking about such a devastating topic. Not a tremor in her voice nor a fluttering of her eyelids gave away her innermost thoughts.

But no one could ever truly know what was going on inside a person's head, could they? Graham would have given anything to see inside Mary's head ... or maybe not. There was a chance that if he did see the horrors inside, he might never recover. The idea of raping your own child not only churned his stomach but made him want to lash out and hurt someone; hurt *her*.

'I've always had the darkness within me, Lee Man, even before everything happened with Flora. But the darkness comes in many forms, so I've realised over the years. We all have a little darkness within us, don't we? Some of us have more than others, but it's our ability to turn on the light which sets us apart from the rest. I just never learned to turn on my light. It was a learned behaviour, you see.'

Graham's breath caught in his throat. 'A-A learned behaviour?'

Mary nodded but made no further comment.

'But ... but you were my friend. Me, Olivia, Franky, Jack and you ... We were best friends.'

Mary smirked, her stained teeth showing again. She licked her lips. 'I was never anyone's *friend*.'

'There has to be a reason ...'

'Why? Why does there have to be a reason why I am the way I am? Just so it makes sense to you in your pathetic little head? Grow up, Lee Man. You only came here today because you can't stand not knowing the truth. Well, you're not going to get it because I take blood oaths very seriously, as you may well remember. My son, of course, decided to break his, and just look at the mess he caused.'

Graham frowned as he leaned forward. 'You took a blood oath? With who?'

Mary stared at him. 'You feel left out, don't you?'

'No.'

Yes, he did. How did she do that? How was she able to see directly into his soul? The truth was, he did feel left out after that day in 1980 when his friends clearly knew something he didn't. It had eaten away at him for many years and still did.

'You said Tyler broke his blood oath. Did you know he'd killed Kieran to keep your family secret safe?'

Mary remained stationary, not even blinking to show she'd heard his question. She looked positively psychotic as she stared back at him with unblinking black eyes. For a moment, he thought she'd gone catatonic, but then she took a deep breath and slowly let it out.

'I'm tired. No more questions.'

Graham stood up. 'I will find evidence you killed your sister, Mary, and I'll make sure you go down for her murder. You're going to rot in here for the rest of your life.'

'I'd like to see you try.'

'You have another visitor by the way.'

Mary cocked one eyebrow. 'Oh? I can't imagine who else would want to see me.'

'Olivia Willows.'

And that was when he finally saw a flicker of panic on Mary's face.

Perhaps she wasn't so good at hiding her emotions after all.

# Chapter Twenty-Five

## Stephen

### *24 January 2024 – 15:55 p.m.*

Stephen slammed his palms against the steering wheel after navigating another tight corner and not seeing any sign of the police car.

'Damn it!'

He pulled over into the next layby and hung his head. Clearly he needed to improve his tailing skills.

Everything had been going well until he'd started driving through the narrower lanes. After that, he'd had to give such a big distance between him and the police car for fear of being spotted that he had lost it completely. They could have taken any number of turnings, off any number of roundabouts and down any number of small roads. He should have known better than to attempt to follow a police car. He wasn't a surveillance specialist, and if Detective Williams was a decent cop, then he probably would have picked up a tail anyway.

Stephen stared out of the windscreen at the countryside. The darkness was almost here. What had he been thinking, following the detective and Olivia so late in the day? For the first time in a long time, he hadn't given any thought to the impending darkness of the late afternoon and now he was stuck in the middle of nowhere, at least an hour from Cherry Hollow, with the darkness creeping closer by the minute.

Stephen closed his eyes and fought against the rising panic in his chest. Every fibre inside him told him to put the car in gear, turn around and drive back to the safety of his hotel. The idea of being stuck out in the pitch-black was enough to set his stomach rolling.

He needed to decide within the next few minutes.

To run away and admit defeat by the darkness, which was going to arrive whether he liked it or not, just like it did at the end of every single day.

Or stay and fight, put his demons behind him and get this case solved.

Stephen opened his eyes and looked through the windscreen. Yes, the darkness was coming, but it wasn't going to hurt him. Not this time. Maybe it could be his friend again.

Maybe …

*I'm staying.*

Stephen took a deep breath, attempting to clear his mind of the negativity that was fighting for freedom.

No. Think. Focus.

He needed to find out where Detective Williams and Olivia had gone. What was around here? Where would they be going? Hopefully, good old Google would provide some answers, so he fished his phone from his jacket pocket, typed in the nearest town and 'what's around here' and crossed his fingers.

The usual things popped up like shops, schools and random things like 'best things to do while visiting'. But otherwise, there wasn't a lot to go on.

Think … think …

He kept scrolling just for something to keep his brain occupied as the darkness settled in around his car. He hated the dark winter evenings. Why couldn't the body have been found in the height of summer when there were more daylight hours?

Then, a thread popped up that rang a bell …

Ashmoore Prison was located ten miles from his location.

Another Google search told him that Mrs Warner, who used to be known as Mrs Jenkins, was locked up there after her court appearance for raping and abusing her son, Tyler. She'd been jailed there since 2019. Her husband had been locked up in a different prison much further away. A newspaper article caught his eye, so he clicked on it and read.

**Prisoner Found Hanging in Cell**
**Date: 28 June 2022**

**The body of Mr Kevin Warner was found hanging inside his cell early on Tuesday morning. He had made rope out of his prison uniform and had attached it to a grate on the ceiling.**

**Mr Warner was arrested and sentenced in 2019, along with his wife, Mary Warner, for raping and abusing their son for over fifteen years while living in Cherry Hollow. Their son, Tyler Jenkins, took his own life in the summer of 2018 after killing young Kieran Jones back in 1998.**

**The case baffled and fascinated many people around the country for two decades.**

**When Mrs Warner, who is currently still locked up in Ashmoore Prison, was told of her husband's passing, she merely smiled. Some say she's a deranged psychopath, incapable of feeling emotion, while others say she's merely a tortured soul.**

**Mr Warner was cremated and buried in a small cemetery on the outskirts of the Lake District. No one attended his funeral.**

Stephen looked up from his phone. There was no way this was a coincidence. They had to have been heading for Ashmoore Prison to speak to Mrs Warner, aka Jenkins, Tyler's mother.

Stephen put the car in gear and pulled out onto the road, following the directions on his phone. The thought of visiting a prison made his stomach clench. He always said he'd never go back to one again. The last time he'd visited a prison was twenty-three years ago.

It had been the most challenging thing he'd ever done, yet had also been the start of his newfound freedom, the first step in facing his childhood fears.

### *April 2001*

*His palms were so sweaty he could barely open the door to the visitation room. He wiped them on his shabby clothes as he scanned the area for a familiar face. Several other prisoners were sitting at tables opposite their loved ones. None of them were wearing cuffs. Maybe they were more trustworthy than the more dangerous ones. He'd rather his father were wearing chains. That way, there was no chance of being hurt.*

*That's when he saw him.*

*He was sitting at a table on the far side of the room. Stephen's stomach lurched. He wished he'd visited the bathroom before walking into the room, but it was too late to turn back now.*

*He'd clocked Stephen already.*

*Feeling as if he was ten years old rather than sixteen, Stephen shuffled across the room and slid into the empty chair opposite his father, who grinned at him.*

*'What'd I tell you, boy? I knew you'd grow up to be a decent-looking young man. Could still do with adding a few pounds of muscle to those chicken-leg arms though.'*

*Stephen had been expecting the first thing to come out of his father's mouth to be an insult, but it still stung, especially when he'd been working hard to bulk up recently, but his adolescent body wasn't ready yet, still clinging on to its boyish charm.*

*'Hi, Dad,' he mumbled.*

*'Still mumbling, I see. Speak up, boy.'*

*Stephen raised his chin and looked at his father. Even after four years, the man still sent shivers down his spine and set off imaginary worms in his stomach. He instinctively touched the side of his face, the last place his father had struck him before finally being arrested and sentenced for child abuse. His mother had died when he was four, so he only had a vague memory of her.*

*She'd been beautiful and kind. He remembered that much. And she'd had long dark hair almost to her waist. He thought he remembered playing with it once or twice. He recalled something else about her too; she'd always had dark patches on her skin. He hadn't known what they were back then, but now he knew they'd been bruises.*

*His father had beaten her daily, but when she died, he'd turned on him instead. Stephen didn't even know how she'd died, only that one day she'd been there, and the next she hadn't, and his father had never provided an explanation.*

*It was why he was here today. Not for himself. But for his mother.*

*'So … how's foster care?' asked his father, crossing his thick arms over his chest. He clearly had a lot of time to work out in prison. His muscles were even larger than Stephen remembered. There was a small cut above his left eye, possibly from a fight. It wouldn't have surprised Stephen in the least.*

*'Better than living with you,' replied Stephen.*

*It was the truth. Yes, he'd been bounced around a few foster homes due to his uniqueness, but at least they didn't beat him every chance they got. He actually thought himself lucky; he'd heard horror stories of kids in the foster system being abused as well. He only had two more years to go and then he was legally an adult and could look after himself. He already knew what he wanted to be: a journalist.*

His father snorted. 'So ... why'd you come to visit your old man, huh? You in trouble?'

'No, I've come to find out the truth about what happened to my mother.'

'Why are you wasting your time with that bitch? She's dead.'

'I want to know how she died.' Maybe it was because he had a questioning mind, or maybe his mother's death had kick-started his fascination with finding out the truth, but whatever the reason, he knew he wanted to make it his career in the future.

'Didn't you read the police report?'

'Yes, but I don't believe it. There are inconsistencies.'

'Oh yeah, like what?'

'Like you telling me you found her dead in the kitchen, but the police report says she was found in the bedroom.'

'Must have gotten mixed up. I wasn't exactly in my right mind after finding my wife dead.'

Stephen pressed on. 'And another thing ... The police report says she died from choking on a piece of food and there was no one around to save her.'

His father narrowed his eyes. 'Yeah, so?'

'She had bruising around her throat.'

'Yeah ... from where she kept grabbing it while she choked to death.' He shifted in his seat, for the first time looking nervous. 'I don't like what you're suggesting here, boy.'

'I'm not suggesting anything. I'm accusing.'

'You think I strangled your mother.'

'Again, I don't think ... I know.'

'You don't have any proof.'

'I don't need any. I just wanted to see the look in your eyes.'

Now his father laughed; a full, throaty laugh, which caused several heads in the room to turn towards him. 'You're sixteen fucking years old. Shouldn't you be out shagging girls and getting drunk?'

'I'm not like you.'

'Ha! You're a virgin. I knew it! Pussy-ass virgin, boy. I'm disappointed in you.'

Stephen rose to his feet, pushing his chair back as he did so, making a loud scraping noise on the hard floor. 'Luckily, I didn't come here for your approval. I just needed to know the truth. And now I do.'

'You know nothing, boy.'

Stephen smiled at his father. 'I know enough.'

# Chapter Twenty-Six

## Olivia

### *24 January 2024 – 17:05 p.m.*

She'd been studying her nails for almost forty minutes, trying to think of anything else other than who she was about to face. Her nails were not in good condition. Chipped, worn and brittle. The last time she'd had her nails painted had been for Dorothy's wedding. Her daughter had chosen a pale pink and cream colour theme, so Olivia had painted her nails to match. It had been a long time since she'd seen Dorothy and her son-in-law, Eric. Plus, her grandson, Patrick, was five now and had started reception last September. It brought tears to Olivia's eyes to think she'd missed his first day of school because she'd been unable to leave Frank. But she'd resigned herself to the fact she would never be in Patrick's life the way she wanted. She would, however, make more of an effort to visit him, especially since Frank … since Frank …

Olivia swallowed the lump in her throat and bit the inside of her mouth. He really was gone now. It still didn't seem real.

She'd been offered a cup of tea about half an hour ago but had opted for water instead. Her mouth was dry, and she had to keep licking her cracked lips to moisten them. Exhaustion and dehydration were the most likely culprits, probably because of crying so much today.

She couldn't wait for the day to be over. But, after this visit, she had to return to an empty house, and she couldn't think of anything worse. She'd no longer have to make her husband meals or give him a sponge bath or help him to the bathroom. Her days would be free to do as she wished, but what would she do? It hadn't crossed her mind until now that she no longer had anyone who was dependent on her for the first time in nearly forty years.

Olivia had only been twenty when Brooke was born, practically still a child herself, and since that day, she'd always had someone else to think about other than herself. She'd always come last. Always.

Olivia looked up at the sound of approaching footsteps to see Graham walking towards her. She could tell by the colour of his face the conversation hadn't gone well. Then again, she hadn't expected it to. She stood up to greet him.

'I'd recommend caution, Olivia ... Mary is ... quite difficult to talk to.'

Olivia smiled. 'You're a detective ... shouldn't you be used to difficult conversations?' She didn't mean to make fun of him and hoped he wouldn't take it the wrong way.

He shook his head. 'I don't think I've ever spoken to someone so ... empty. I don't know how else to explain it. It's like there's nothing inside. She doesn't care about anything. I don't remember her being like that when we were kids, or maybe she was, and I don't remember.'

Olivia took a deep breath. 'Or she was just very good at hiding it. She doesn't have to hide anymore ... Hopefully I won't be long.'

Graham reached out and touched her arm before she took a step. 'Just ... be careful, okay?'

Olivia held his gaze but said nothing before turning and walking down the corridor from where Graham had come seconds earlier. Her heart pounded. Everything around her felt as if she were seeing and hearing it from underwater.

Olivia held her breath as she stepped into the visitation room. She made her way across the silent room, her low heels clicking on the hard floor.

She stopped by the table where Mary was sitting and slowly lowered herself onto the chair. Mary stared at her. Graham was right. There didn't seem to be anything behind her eyes.

Mary looked different from the last time she'd seen her. There was no resemblance to the girl of forty-four years ago. She was gone, destroyed, stripped away. But Olivia had always known who she was, even when Mary had introduced herself as Mrs Jenkins and their children had become best friends. Olivia had always known her true identity. She'd seen past the plastic surgery and the strange accent Mary had adopted. But she'd never said a word. Not a single word. Not even to Frank who'd had no idea the woman he served daily in his shop was his childhood best friend who'd disappeared so long ago. And, when Olivia and Mrs Jenkins had spoken, they'd been polite and civil and normal. But they hadn't been friends and they'd never told each other their secrets.

'Good to see you again, Olivia,' said Mary. Her voice didn't have the same tone it used to. Prison had clearly toughened her emotionally and mentally as well as physically.

'I'm afraid I can't say the same, Mary.'

'How's Frank?'

'He died this morning.'

'Oh.' Olivia waited for some sort of snide remark, but it never came. Mary's face softened for a second. 'I'm sorry. He was a good man. Nothing like *my* husband.'

'Thank you,' said Olivia, not knowing what else to say.

Mary's face turned to stone again. 'So ... you always knew who I was, yet you kept it from everyone.'

'Yes. Your plastic surgery may have changed your facial features, but you could never disguise your heart.'

Mary sneered. 'Let me get this straight ... You knew I was Mary King for all those years we watched our children grow up together, and you never said a word. Did Frank know?'

'No, I don't think he did. I certainly never told him. You were very clever at hiding and keeping yourself closed off from a lot of people. I wanted to ask you all sorts of questions. I wanted to know why you moved back to Cherry Hollow. I don't understand your reasoning.'

'Why does there have to be a reason?'

'There's always a reason.'

Mary tutted. 'Still have an answer for everything, I see.'

'Just tell me why you came back to Cherry Hollow after all that time and never told anyone who you were ... and why you abused your son.'

Mary jabbed a finger towards Olivia. 'Ah ha! That's what this is all about, isn't it? You're feeling guilty because you never figured out what was going on behind closed doors. Just like when we were kids. I know you saw my bruises. And Flora's. But you never said a word, did you? You were a coward then and you're a coward now.'

Olivia squeezed her lips together, determined not to allow Mary to rile her, but it was too late. She already had. It was true. Olivia had never realised one of her daughter's best friends was being abused by his parents, just like she'd never realised Mary and her sister were being abused by theirs. She hated herself for not seeing the signs when they were right in front of her. Maybe the signs hadn't been there for Tyler, as she didn't spend a lot of time with him, but she should have known Mary and Flora were being abused long before she'd found out.

Everything had come full circle.

'Tell me ... When did you first suspect my sister and I were being abused?' asked Mary. She shifted her cuffed hands, jangling the chains against each other.

Olivia shook her head. 'I didn't put two and two together until that day in the cave. I know we didn't see much of Flora, but I'd never seen her covered in that many bruises before. She couldn't have just fallen down the side of the ravine because she'd have had scrapes and cuts too.'

Mary shrugged. 'Normally our dad managed to hit us where the bruises wouldn't be seen. You know, like the chest or sides or the back, but sometimes it was hard to cover them up. Childhood abuse does a lot to a kid, you know. It messes them up.'

'So, it was only your father who hit you?'

'Yes, but our mum knew about it and did nothing so that makes her just as guilty. Just like my husband.'

'Did your father hit her too?'

'Yes.'

'Why did you always give Flora a hard time? You never wanted her to hang out with us or play with us. She had no one.'

Mary gritted her teeth. 'I always hated my sister.'

'But why? What did she ever do to you?'

Mary laughed. The loud cackle made Olivia's stomach churn. 'That's the funny thing about all this. My sister did nothing to me. I just hated her. Maybe it was because my dad hit her more than he hit me. Maybe I had some sick point of view where I thought he loved her more because he paid her more attention. Hell, she got off easy with dying so young. Lucky bitch.'

Olivia sucked in a breath. Hearing Mary talk so atrociously about her own sibling made her want to cry. She still hadn't heard the words she wanted to hear so she pressed on.

'I'm so sorry you had to go through that. No child should ever have to suffer any sort of abuse from either of their parents, but you abused your son, Mary. What's your excuse for that?

What you did to that poor boy was unforgivable, and it makes you no better than your own parents, especially your father.'

Mary rolled her eyes. 'You're only saying that because of what happened with Tyler, your precious Brooke and the rest of their friends.'

Olivia saw red. She clenched her hands into fists. 'My Brooke was housebound for twenty years because of what you did to your son.'

'Oh, so we're playing the blame game now, are we?'

'You don't think this all started because of you? You're the one who wanted to walk along the bottom of the ravine. You're the one who wanted to go into the cave. You're the one who brutally murdered your sister. You're the one who made us all swear a stupid blood oath to cover it up. This all started because of you, Mary. There's no denying that. The darkness that's engulfed our town is all because of you.' Olivia pushed her chair backwards and stood up, leaning over the table towards Mary, jabbing a finger at her. 'You think just because you were abused as a child, it gave you the right to do it to your own. You're a sick, twisted psychopath, and I wish I'd ...' Olivia stopped when she saw the grin spread across Mary's face. She'd said too much. She'd almost slipped up.

Olivia straightened her jacket. 'I'm going to tell Graham everything.'

'Good luck with that,' replied Mary.

'It's time the truth was told.'

Mary narrowed her eyes as she rose to her feet, but because her hands were bound to the table she couldn't fully straighten. Olivia remained where she was, too afraid to get close to Mary for fear of what she might do.

'And what version of the truth will you be telling the detective? Because, from what I gather, you and I have very different versions of what really happened that day in the cave, don't we, *Olivia*?'

### 25 May 1980

*'Mary, wait!' shouted Frank. He lunged after her.*

*Olivia grabbed his arm, digging her nails into his bare skin. 'No, wait. We don't know what's back there.'*

*'Neither do they. We know what Mary's like. She's got a bit of a temper. Poor Flora must be terrified. Come on.'*

*'I have a torch in my bag,' said Jack, reaching into the small backpack he always carried around with him. He flicked it on; the beam was faint but at least it worked.*

*Olivia watched helplessly as Frank and Jack stormed into the darkness of the inner cave. She didn't want to follow them, but the overwhelming stench of smoke now circling the cave entrance was causing her head to swim, and she didn't want to wait outside by herself. Her eyes stung even more now. She rubbed at them fiercely, causing them to stream with tears which blurred her vision.*

*Within a few seconds, a shout pierced the grey darkness. It sounded like Jack's voice. Olivia could barely see to put one foot in front of the other, but the light yellow of the torch ahead kept her heading in the right direction.*

*The brightness from the outside had all but vanished now, leaving only the small torch to illuminate the cave. It made the walls look as if they were crawling with life; dark shadows crept up and over the roof and down the other wall. The sides of the cave squeezed closer with every step until she finally saw Jack and Frank ahead, both crouched on the ground. Frank now held the torch up, making their faces look creepy and shadowy.*

*'What's happened?' she asked.*

*'I was running and tripped over something. I think I've twisted my ankle,' said Jack, clutching his right ankle with his hands and rubbing it.*

*Frank pulled up Jack's trouser leg to inspect it. Olivia sucked in a breath as she saw the swelling and bruising already coming to the surface.*

*'Stay here,' she told the boys. 'I'll go and find Mary and Flora.'*

*'No, you stay. I'll go,' said Frank, standing up.*

*Olivia took the torch from Frank. 'No. I'm perfectly capable, Frank. You get Jack out of the cave. I'm not strong enough to support his weight. It's going to take some time to make our way back. Me, Mary and Flora will catch you up later.'*

*She could tell Frank wasn't keen on the idea; neither was she, but he eventually nodded.*

'Okay. We'll wait outside the mouth of the cave. But if you're not out in fifteen minutes I'm coming to find you.'

'Okay. The cave can't be that deep. Will you be okay without the torch?'

'We'll manage.'

'See you soon.'

Olivia left the boys in darkness. They'd only have to move through the cave a few feet and then the outside brightness would provide enough light to enable them to see themselves out.

It was slow going through the cave. The torch managed to light up her path ahead but did nothing to highlight the rough patches of rock. Where on earth were Mary and Flora and how had they moved through the cave so quickly without a light source?

Olivia rubbed her eyes with her free hand.

'Mary?' she called out. Despite only whispering, her voice rebounded off the walls. She listened as she heard Mary's name bounce back at her.

A scream erupted through the darkness.

A girl's scream.

Fear gripped her insides, almost suffocating her as she increased her pace, ignoring the uneven ground. She went over on her ankle, but it wasn't enough to incapacitate her as it had Jack.

'Flora! Mary!' She rounded the next corner, the torch beam trembling.

A dark shadow loomed in front of her.

She screamed as she dropped the torch.

*Another scream.*

*Whoever was hurt was so close now. But she could barely see anything other than a large black shadow. It towered above a small figure hunched on the ground.*

*Olivia rubbed her eyes again, unable to focus on anything as she gingerly bent down and fumbled her hands over the rough ground searching for the torch she'd dropped.*

*The shadow attacked ...*

*'No!' screamed Olivia.*

*Without thinking, she fell to the ground in search of some sort of weapon. The only thing her free hand found was a large rock, so she scooped it up and approached the dark figure.*

*'Mary, is that you?'*

*'Olivia, stop!'*

*'Where's Flora? I can't see anything.'*

*The shadow was attacking the small figure on the ground. Olivia leapt forward and slammed the rock she was holding down into the darkness.*

*It connected with something hard.*

*Another scream ...*

*Then deadly silence.*

# Chapter Twenty-Seven

## Alex

### *25 January 2024 – 09:00 a.m.*

Alex sat at his desk before class, doodling on a spare piece of paper. He was the first one in the room; the class wasn't due to start for fifteen minutes, but he needed some space to clear his head, and when he arrived at his usual smoking spot this morning and saw Alex the First and Harriet there, he'd made a swift U-turn and come here instead, forgoing his cigarette.

It had been a strange night. Not only had he spent hours talking with his mum, but he'd also realised she knew a hell of a lot more about what was going on in this town than he'd originally thought. How had she come to know so much? There he was assuming she'd been hiding on purpose, keeping as inconspicuous as possible, but what she'd really been doing was gathering evidence on everything that had happened last Halloween … and that was a very, very bad thing for him.

He sat open-mouthed and listened as his mum had rattled off a list of theories about what happened that night. Luckily, she hadn't figured out the truth, but she was convinced about one thing: the fire at their old house on Baker Street hadn't been started by Trisha Sharp and Lucy Forrester, Alex the First's mum and Harriet's mum.

She had also spoken about Jordan Evans and Brooke Willows and their possible involvement in Kieran Jones' murder and how they'd fled the town because they'd known what was coming, but how could they have known a new body would be found? It made no sense. Plus, Alex was aware she was friends with Brooke's mum, Olivia Willows, so was his mum only using her to gather information? How much did Olivia Willows know exactly? Alex had always assumed she was just a doddery elderly woman who had nothing better to do than befriend his mum, but maybe she wasn't as innocent as she made out to be.

Alex knew the truth about Kieran Jones because Jordan and Brooke had told him last year. They'd trusted him because back then they'd been trying to help him. He'd wanted to know why The Creature was haunting the town and they'd revealed that it wasn't real. It was merely a manifestation of people's guilt because of the various tragedies that had happened over the past couple of decades. But now he knew something bad had happened much further back than the late 90s when Kieran died … and he was pretty sure Olivia Willows knew about it. Perhaps Stephen Mallow had already figured all this out. It was his job after all. It was the reason Alex had brought him back here.

Alex stopped drawing and tapped his pencil against the page of his notebook. He'd drawn a strange black shape that looked as if it had claws and fangs. He hadn't heard back from Stephen Mallow regarding the note he'd found under the floorboards, but now he wasn't as concerned with finding out the truth about the body from four decades ago. He had a bigger problem to deal with. Not only was his mum getting too close to the truth about who had killed her wife, but he also needed to get revenge on Alex the First and Harriet. But so did his mum.

She'd seen red when he told her his so-called friends hadn't hesitated when he took the blame and allowed them to get away with terrorising that poor kid. She then started talking about revenge plots and ways to make them squirm.

'Mum,' he'd finally said, 'look, I appreciate you want to help me get back at them, but it's not your place. I know you're my mum and I love you, but I can stand up for myself. Please, just let me handle it.'

She'd stared back at him, barely blinking, and then said in a small whisper, 'Did they burn down our house, Alex? Please, you need to tell me if it was them. I need to know who killed Linda.'

Alex fought the urge to cough as he'd replied, 'No, Mum, it wasn't them. I promise. I don't know who killed Linda.'

'But you'd tell me if you knew, wouldn't you?'

'Y-Yes, of course, I would.' He reached out and squeezed her hand and she'd responded with a weak smile.

'Thank you, Alex. That's all I needed to know.'

'So, you won't go around plotting to get revenge on my friends?'

'I'd hardly call them your friends anymore.'

'Okay, fine, good point. I take it back.'

'But no, I won't. What I would like to talk about though is that note you say you found.'

'What about it?'

'Has Mr Mallow found out who wrote it?'

'No. Not yet.'

His mum nodded and left it at that. He told her about the job at school and handed her the paperwork, which she took with a smile and a promise that she'd apply. Then he explained that tomorrow morning he'd find the boy who'd been bullied and convince him not to say a word about how Alex had swooped him and saved him from the demon in the mask. For his revenge plan to work, Alex the First and Harriet needed to think they'd gotten away with it. He would accept the detention and whatever punishment the boy's parents wanted him to receive.

Alex looked up as the door to the classroom opened. Harriet walked in with a smile on her face, her long red hair cascading in gentle waves across her shoulders. She'd darkened her eyes with make-up and enhanced her lips with red lipstick. She caught sight of Alex sitting by himself.

'Good morning, Alex.' Then she had the audacity to glide across the room and kiss him on the cheek, as if she hadn't thrown him under the bus yesterday.

Alex flinched at her touch. 'Fuck off, Harriet.'

She raised her eyebrows. 'My, my, someone's in a mood today.'

'Are you fucking kidding me?'

'What?'

Alex clenched his jaw. Was she honestly going to stand there and pretend like yesterday hadn't happened? Was she truly that delusional?

Harriet rolled her eyes. 'You're not still sore about what happened yesterday, are you? It's in the past, Alex. Yeesh. No one got hurt.'

'No one apart from some poor kid. He's probably scarred for life just like Bethany.' Alex had spoken to him about twenty minutes ago and, although the kid had been confused about why Alex wanted him to lie, he'd agreed to tell the headmaster Alex's version of the truth.

Harriet scoffed. 'Oh, please. It was just a joke.'

'Well, no one's laughing, are they?'

Harriet took her seat at the desk next to his and leaned across it. 'Why'd you take the blame anyway?'

'Just seemed easier at the time.' He knew he had to be careful. He needed to keep her and Alex the First on his side. He had a plan, so he needed to play along.

Harriet twirled a strand of red hair around her fingers. 'You know, you used to be cool. I thought we could trust you, but every time we try and let you in, you disappoint us.'

Alex doodled on his notebook again, making the claws and fangs longer and meaner. 'Yeah, well ... you're not exactly trustworthy either. Both you and Alex the First are always spending time together without me.'

Harriet cooed. 'Aww, you jealous?'

Alex lifted his head to look at her. The truth was he couldn't care less about the girl in front of him. He'd lost interest in her months ago. At first, he'd been drawn to her because she was cute, but her looks weren't enough to keep his attention. She was crazy, psychotic and mean. But if the whole jealous boyfriend thing would work to keep her on his side, then it was a risk he was willing to take.

'Yes, I'm jealous. I don't want you spending time with him without me anymore.'

Harriet raised her eyebrows. 'You can't tell me who I can or can't hang out with. I've been friends with Alex the First a lot longer than I've known you. We've grown up together in this town. You're just an outsider.'

Ah, crap. It seemed his idea hadn't worked.

Harriet continued, 'And besides, Alex the First gets me, and I get him.'

'What ... because you're both raging psychos who enjoy bullying young kids together?'

Harriet smirked. 'At least we're not *murderers*.'

Alex's heart skipped a beat. 'What do you mean?'

Harriet leaned in close to his ear and whispered, 'I think you know *exactly* what I mean.'

At that moment, the door to the classroom opened and the teacher walked in, followed by several students all talking loudly. Alex stared at Harriet as he asked in a whisper, 'What do you want?'

'Meet us in our spot after school and we'll talk.'

'I can't. I have detention.'

Harriet puffed out a breath. 'That's not my problem, is it?'

The rest of the day passed in a blur. Nothing made sense and whenever the teacher asked him a question, he had to ask for it to be repeated. Alex wanted to try harder at school to make his mum proud, but it was hard when there were so many distractions and unanswered questions.

What the hell had Harriet meant? Did she know he'd killed his dad and his step-mum? Were they trying to get revenge for what had happened to their own mothers, despite them both being guilty of arson?

It was time he put a stop to them once and for all.

Once his last lesson finished, Alex headed for the smoking spot outside of school, knowing full-well he'd be late for his first detention, which would not go down well at all.

When he arrived at the spot, neither of them was there.

'Fuck's sake,' he muttered.

He glanced at his watch, looked up and only managed to catch a glimpse of a large, black creature lunging at him before the back of his head exploded with pain and his world turned dark.

# Chapter Twenty-Eight

## Graham

### *25 January 2024 – 10:15 a.m.*

He couldn't focus. Having spoken to Mary yesterday for the first time in over forty years, he couldn't make heads nor tails of anything. She'd disappeared as his friend, as a young girl, and had appeared all these years later as a stranger, a child abuser, and had been living under his nose the whole time.

Somehow, he made it through the morning briefing to his team without fumbling his words or forgetting anything. Most of the information received, however, floated over his head, merely a jumble of words and phrases, but one piece of information had sunk in, and that was the location of Mr and Mrs King, Mary's parents.

They'd been found ...

It had been unlikely they would still be alive, considering they were in their forties when they'd left town, but he hadn't expected to find out they'd perished in a freak carbon monoxide accident at their home over a decade ago.

They too had changed their last name from King to Truman back in the 80s. No wonder Mary had been able to hide her identity for so long. First, she'd been King, then Truman, then Jenkins and finally, Warner. She'd constantly hidden in the shadows, never drawing attention to herself. Why had she confessed to abusing her son, but not to killing her sister? That was a question that still plagued him.

And why had Mr and Mrs King left town in May of 1980 without informing anyone about their missing daughter, Flora, and then changed their name? What did they have to hide?

Everything came down to that day.

Graham scratched his head, sighing as he did so. There were so many unanswered questions, he didn't know which to focus on first. Years of being in the police force should have prepared him for this moment, but it had the opposite effect. Now, he couldn't get his thoughts in order, so they were jumbled together in one big mess, and his head was pounding because of it.

It didn't help he knew Olivia was still hiding something. Her husband was dead, so why even bother to continue to lie? Who did she think she was protecting?

He dialled her number for two reasons: to ask how she was after returning home alone yesterday evening and to ask her something much more personal.

'Olivia, it's Graham. How are you?'

Her voice trembled slightly, but otherwise, she sounded relatively okay. 'Other than the fact I have nothing to do now, I'm fine, Graham. I'm meeting with the funeral director later today to discuss Frank's funeral plans.'

'Would you like me to be there?'

'No, thank you. I'll manage.'

'Are you going to call your daughters today?'

'It's still not the right time.'

'Olivia, they deserve to know their father is dead. They can come and support you.'

'Not until this is over,' came the abrupt reply.

'*When* will it be over? When *what* is over? There's something you're still not telling me. I need to know. Please … There must be evidence from that day. You must know something. Come to the station and I'll take your statement myself. I'll make it as smooth as possible.'

A long pause appeared on the line, so long Graham checked to ensure the call was still live.

'I'd like to end this on my own terms. I hope you'll respect my wishes.'

'Who are you protecting, Olivia?'

'Goodbye, Graham.'

'Olivia—' But she had already disconnected. 'Fuck,' he muttered, replacing the receiver.

He ran his fingers through his thinning hair. It was time to take drastic action. How was he supposed to protect Olivia, his friend, if she wasn't willing to help him? She'd made it perfectly clear she didn't need his help, other than to deal with the body of her husband, which he'd attended to yesterday. Now she was pushing him away, like she'd done all those years before.

It was time to finish this.

Graham pressed a button on his desk phone. 'DS Carter, a word, please.'

Several seconds later, a knock appeared at the door, followed by a face peering around the frame. 'Yes, sir?'

'Sit, please.' He gestured to the empty chair in front of his desk.

DS Carter promptly took a seat, her eyes wide with excitement. He was aware she was itching for a decent break in the case as much as he was. If she was part of the team to solve this, she'd be credited heavily for her work. He used to be like that back in the day. He remembered his first big case: the disappearance of Kieran Jones and how that had sparked his fascination and devotion to finding out the truth, but as the years had gone by and no new evidence had been found, the case had remained unsolved, and his eagerness had slowly drained.

Until that little blue watch had been found in Beaker Ravine twenty years later, and Jordan Evans and Amber Walker had walked into the station and handed him the evidence he'd needed to solve and close the case for good.

But it had all been a lie, hadn't it?

Because Tyler's confession had been falsified; he was convinced of it. Jordan had all but confirmed it the other day when they'd spoken. He thought very highly of Jordan, despite his sordid past. More than once he'd arrested him for unruly behaviour, but just because a person had a good heart, it didn't mean they always made good choices.

'DS Carter, what do you make of this case so far?' asked Graham, leaning back in his chair.

Her eyes widened even more. 'What do you mean, sir?'

'I'm asking your opinion on this case.'

DS Carter cleared her throat. 'Well, sir, it's certainly a complicated one. Everything appears to be connected somehow.'

'Explain.'

'Well … even though I wasn't around back in 1998 when Kieran Jones disappeared, this case sort of feels like that, doesn't it? I've studied your notes and the files from that case. Everything bad that's happened in this town has started at Beaker Ravine, and now there's been another body found down there, it's making me think all these cases are connected, sir.'

Graham nodded. DS Carter hadn't said anything he wasn't already thinking, but her speech had prompted an idea. 'I agree, DS Carter.'

'Sir, forgive me if this is out of line, but … what Stephen Mallow said about you is correct, is it not? That you lived here back in 1980 when the body was supposedly left in the cave.'

'Yes, I was fifteen at the time.' Graham didn't expand upon the subject despite DS Carter's hopeful expression. 'I'd like you to look into the death of Jack Evans.'

DS Carter frowned at the change in topic. 'Jordan Evans' father? … Why, sir? He died of a heart attack, if I remember correctly, about a year ago.'

'Yes, please just contact the hospital and get his file.'

'Should I contact Jordan Evans too?'

Graham shook his head. 'No, I'd like to leave him out of this as much as possible.'

DS Carter rose to her feet. 'Very well, sir. I'll let you know what I find by the end of the day.'

'Thank you, DS Carter.'

Graham watched as she left the room and closed the door. He stared at the clock on the wall for several seconds, wondering what Mr Mallow was up to now. Probably sticking his nose in where it didn't belong, but if there was one thing he could count on, it was that Mr Mallow had a knack for asking difficult questions.

Maybe he needed his help after all ...

# Chapter Twenty-Nine

## Stephen

### *25 January 2024 – 10:30 a.m.*

Stephen slept better than he'd imagined. After his encounter with Mrs Warner at Ashmoore Prison, he drove back to Cherry Hollow in the pitch black and passed out on his bed fully clothed. He was both elated and petrified to have managed to stay out in the darkness for several hours without having a full-blown panic attack. The last time he tried to stand up to his fears hadn't ended well. It ended with him in the hospital, shouting at the doctors that he was going to die if he went outside at nighttime. Thankfully, he was given the appropriate medication for his delusions, and they'd levelled out his foggy head, but those little pills hadn't cured him. Far from it.

It seemed a trip to this godforsaken town had cured him. The darkness may not have been his best friend anymore, but at least it was a well-known acquaintance he could now tolerate in small doses.

As he sat in his usual chair in the hotel bar, his conversation with Mrs Warner replayed in his head. He had waited until Detective Williams and Olivia left and then entered the prison, checking the log-in book for their names and the prisoner they'd visited: Mrs Warner.

She hadn't been in the best of moods when she'd been dragged back into the visitation room for the third time that day.

'Who the fuck else is there left who wants to visit me?' she shouted as she was forced back into the metal chair. 'Who the fuck are you?' she'd spat at him.

Stephen kept his voice as calm as possible, even though he felt sick at being so close to someone who was a convicted child abuser and rapist. 'Stephen Mallow, a journalist for the *London Times*.'

Mrs Warner had rolled her eyes and snorted. 'Knew it wouldn't take long for the vultures to start circling. Hurry up and ask your questions. I haven't got all day.'

'I'd say you have all the time in the world, Mrs Warner, considering you're in here for life.'

She'd sneered at him. 'Okay, funny guy. What do you want?'

'Why did Detective Williams and Olivia Willows visit you just now?'

'Are you saying you don't know? I thought you were supposed to be a journalist.'

'I am.' Then she'd stared at him with a smirk on her face, quite possibly expecting him to bite back at her, but he didn't. He merely held her gaze and waited for her to answer his question.

She'd eventually sighed. 'Okay, I may as well tell you. I suppose it's all going to come out in the wash eventually. They wanted to blame me for the murder of Flora King.'

Stephen had frowned, not understanding the connection. 'Why would ...' Then a light bulb flicked on inside his mind and the final piece of the puzzle clicked into place. 'Oh my God … You're Mary King, aren't you?'

She had winked at him. 'You got it in one, funny guy.'

'But … How did … What … I don't …' Stephen had closed his eyes and taken a deep breath, attempting to calm the erupting storm of questions. 'I was right. You, Olivia and the detective were all friends when you were young, weren't you?'

'Friends is a strong word to use, but yes, we hung out and spent time together.'

'Who else? Who else was involved?'

'We also knew Jack Evans and Frank Willows.'

Stephen shook his head. 'Of course. How did I not see this before? You're all connected. All of this … The Creature … Beaker Ravine … Your families …' Stephen rose to his feet and pushed away from the table.

'You're leaving already?' she'd asked him, a small hint of hysteria in her voice.

'Yes. Thank you for your time, Mrs Warner.'

'I thought you wanted to know the truth.'

Stephen had stopped in his tracks. He'd adjusted his laptop bag on his shoulder as he turned to her. 'Go on.'

Mrs Warner had grinned, showing him her horrible teeth, but it hadn't been them that had caused his insides to clench or sweat to pour down his face.

It had been the six words she'd uttered next.

He didn't usually drink coffee, but it was the only thing keeping his eyes open as he stared at his laptop. He was attempting to write the biggest and best article of his career. This would, no doubt, catapult him to fame. There was no other journalist who would come to the town. The Creature had spread fear further than this area, yet people were grappling for the next piece of information on his blog. Kevin, his boss, was itching to get his hands on it.

But he couldn't publish it until it was ready. He needed all the answers.

And Mrs Warner had given him the ultimate one yesterday.

There was a possibility she was lying. She was a criminal, possibly a psychopath and a child abuser at the end of the day. She had every reason to lie.

But a nagging feeling in the back of his mind wouldn't go away.

Another piece of the puzzle wanted to be placed but didn't quite fit anywhere ... yet.

Stephen leaned forward to continue typing but was halted by his phone vibrating. When he saw the name on the screen, he couldn't hold back his amusement as he answered.

'You're the last person I expected a call from, Detective. To what do I owe the pleasure?'

'Mr Mallow, as charismatic as ever. I'd like to ask whether your trip to the prison yesterday was enlightening for you.'

'Ah, I take it I'm not as talented at tailing someone as I first thought.'

'Not even a little bit, although I did manage to lose you, so I must say I'm impressed you figured out where to go.'

Stephen leaned back against the high-backed chair. He didn't quite know how to respond to the detective, so a change of topic was in order. 'Detective, why did you call me?'

'I need your help.'

Stephen sat bolt upright. 'I'm sorry, the line must have gone funny. Did you say you need my help?'

'Don't patronise me. I'm sure you've figured out by now who Mrs Warner really is, and I can't seem to get what you said about mental health and The Creature out of my head. My DCs are all busy on the Flora King case, which has basically hit a dead end unless Mary confesses, and I don't see that happening anytime soon. I need someone on the outside who is not involved with this town whatsoever, other than their own morbid fascination about finding the truth.'

'I'm your man, Detective. What do you need me to do?'

'Do you know anything about how Jack Evans died?'

At the mention of the name, Stephen tilted his head. 'Not really, Detective. From what I've gathered, he died of a heart attack during work hours.'

'Hmmm ...'

'I take it you're having second thoughts. Don't tell me someone murdered him too?'

'No, I don't think he was killed. Not by a person anyway.'

'Are you suggesting he was killed by The Creature? So, you do believe me now.'

'I didn't say that. I'm not saying anything.'

Stephen chuckled. 'Okay, fair enough. Mary did mention his name yesterday when I spoke to her. She gave me the impression all of you were involved somehow in Flora's death.'

'Did she say my name?'

'Yes, but only in the context you were all friends at the time.'

The detective grunted. 'Mary's still keeping something from me. Did she tell you anything else you think might be of importance?'

Stephen silently released his breath having been holding it for several seconds. 'Right at the end, as I was about to leave, she did say something which I hadn't taken into consideration before.'

'And that was?'

Stephen hesitated for too long.

'Mr Mallow, might I remind you that withholding important information to a murder investigation is an offence ...'

'You don't need to remind me. I was just giving you time to prepare ... She said she didn't kill her sister. Olivia did.' He expected the detective to react in some way: a gasp or an angry statement. But there was no response. None. 'Detective, did you hear me?'

'I heard you.'

'You knew already, didn't you?'

'I had my suspicions. I didn't want to believe them.'

'It's possible that Mrs Warner … Mary … is merely attempting to confuse us and lay blame elsewhere.'

'It's highly likely that's the case. Mary has never been one to think about anyone other than herself. She's not exactly stable or trustworthy.'

Stephen sighed. 'Yes, but … what could she possibly gain by blaming someone else for her sister's death? She's in prison for life. Telling us Olivia killed her sister wouldn't change her situation. It wouldn't release her from prison because she's in for a different crime.'

'No, but maybe it's not about that anymore. I think they were all involved in Flora's death, or at least in covering it up. The weird thing is that nearly twenty years later, their own kids go and do the same thing with Kieran's death. It's been a vicious circle and I think the only way to end it is for the original people involved to confess. Now, there are only two left, so either Olivia or Mary needs to do it. Who's your money on?'

Stephen stood up and walked to the window. He'd made this snug area of the hotel his own over the past few days. The window by the fireplace looked out over the street, but there was no one out there due to the rain lashing down horizontally.

'I'm afraid I don't know, Detective. You were friends with them. Who's *your* money on?'

'My head says it's Mary. She's the most obvious choice. Why the hell would she have covered for Olivia all these years if Olivia really had done it?'

'People who believe in things with all their hearts are often the most dangerous individuals.'

'What's that supposed to mean?'

Stephen turned away from the window, clutching the phone tighter to his ear. 'Remember what Tyler Jenkins said in his confession tapes. He said his parents, as in Mary King, forced him to make a blood oath to keep their secret. So, by that rationale, Mary believed blood oaths were the only way to keep a secret. Maybe she learned that from her own parents.' He heard the detective move about on the other end of the line. He was possibly pacing his office too.

'Mr Mallow, you might be on to something there.'

'I've been looking into Mr King, Mary's father, who used to be the headmaster of the school here. I think we have to start looking at the reason why he left town without telling the authorities his youngest daughter was missing, and then changed his name.'

'The thought did cross my mind as well, that Mary's father may have been abusing his children and that's why he left and kept his whereabouts a secret.'

'As I said ... it's a vicious circle and it needs to stop now before it starts again with the next generation.'

'Agreed. Thank you, Mr Mallow, for your help. I think I know what to do to make a start with ending all this. Stay alert.'

'I will. Goodbye, Detective.'

'I'll be in touch.'

The rain eventually stopped at around three that afternoon. Stephen finished his article he'd been working on, apart from the final few sentences, which he'd add in later once all this was over.

He couldn't sit still, no matter how hard he tried. He felt as if he should be out there, investigating something ... anything.

The worst thing was he had an overwhelming urge to visit Beaker Ravine, the last place he wanted to go. Last time, he'd almost stepped off the edge for no reason, but now it was as if something was calling him to it.

Stephen checked his phone for a message from Alex, but it remained silent. He fired off a text to him, asking him if he could meet him again, but then realised that sounded a bit creepy, so sent another explaining he needed to ask him some more questions. Both texts remained unread, so Stephen went upstairs, put on his rain jacket in case the heavens decided to open again and headed outside.

His feet took him to the field outside of town, through the long, wet grass, through the rickety old gate and through the overgrown woods. He didn't stop until he reached the edge of the ravine. He couldn't explain it. One minute he'd been at the hotel and the next he was standing by the edge of the cliff, looking out across the expanse.

He froze in horror at what he saw, next to the fallen log.

# Chapter Thirty

## Olivia

### *25 January 2024 – 11:30 a.m.*

She hadn't slept a wink. Instead, she spent the whole night in Frank's old bedroom in the chair beside the bed where he'd died, clutching the book she'd read to him as he took his final breath. It was the only piece of him she had left. His funeral was arranged for three days time. She knew she needed to tell her daughters to give them time to sort work and child arrangements, but the thought of calling and explaining everything filled her with so much dread it almost made her sick.

'What should I do, Frank?' she whispered to the empty room. 'Tell me what to do.'

As she stared at the empty bed, which she'd made up with fresh sheets, a shiver rippled over her body. The house was warm. She hadn't yet lowered the temperature, after having it so high while Frank was alive to keep him comfortable. There were no windows open, so where was the cold draft coming from?

It was then she felt a cold, clammy hand rest on her shoulder. Despite wearing a dress and a cardigan, the touch was so cold it was like an ice cube was touching her bare skin.

*It is time.*

The three words were barely more than a whisper, but the cold breath of whoever had spoken them was close enough to her left ear she could hear them as clear as a bell and feel the warm, musty breath on her cheek.

She didn't flinch. Nor did she turn her head to the side to look at The Creature.

Olivia stood up, clutching the book to her chest, and walked down the stairs, staring straight ahead in a trance. She picked up the phone and dialled Brooke's number. Somehow, the courage to call her beloved daughter filled her body and she needed to do it now before it drained away like water down a plughole.

'Hi, Mum.' Brooke answered after the second ring. She didn't sound right. Her voice was weak and shaky.

'Hello, darling. How are you? What's wrong?'

Brooke paused for a few seconds. 'Let's just say the whole morning sickness thing is a load of crap. I'm basically puking all day long. The doctors have diagnosed me with hyperemesis gravidarum. I had to go into hospital yesterday to be put on a drip. I'm still here now. I can't keep anything down, not even water.'

Olivia's eyes filled with tears. 'Why didn't you call me?'

'I just thought it was normal. Everyone kept telling me being sick was normal in early pregnancy, but as it got worse and worse, I began to realise it wasn't normal. Not as bad as this.'

'Oh, darling, I'm so sorry.'

'It's okay. Jordan's here with me. I know you can't leave Dad. I'll be okay. The doctors say it's likely to improve after the first twelve weeks have passed. Hang on ...' Olivia heard her daughter retch through the phone. 'Sorry ... Are you okay, Mum? Did you call just to check up on me?'

Olivia clutched the book tighter and bit her tongue to stop from exploding into hysterical sobs. 'I ... I ... Yes, I wanted to check in on you, but also ... is it possible to speak to Jordan quickly?'

'Uh ... sure ... he's right here. Hang on.' Olivia heard shuffling at the end of the line.

'Mrs Willows, is everything okay?'

'Honestly, Jordan, I think we're past calling me Mrs Willows now.'

He chuckled. 'Yeah, I guess you're right. What's up?'

Olivia took a deep breath. She knew she needed to remain composed or risk breaking apart completely. 'How is my Brooke ... really?' At that moment her daughter retched again in the background. She heard footsteps. Jordan must have taken the phone outside of the hospital room so Brooke couldn't overhear.

'Honestly ... I've not seen her this sick and weak since ...' His voice wobbled and then cracked.

Olivia's eyes flooded with tears. 'Oh, Jordan ... Tell me. Please.'

Jordan sniffed loudly. 'I feel so helpless, Olivia. I'm standing here watching the woman I love falling to pieces, unable to keep food or water down, unable to barely stand without retching, and I can't do anything to help her. She can't do anything without being sick. As soon as any sort of food touches her lips, she's puking. The doctors have said the baby is perfectly fine, but it's acting like a parasite ... It's sapping everything from her, every ounce of strength. I don't know what to do.'

Olivia took a shaky breath. 'Brooke is strong.'

'I know she is. She's beaten worse before. She spent twenty years locked inside her house.' She heard Jordan take a deep, cleansing breath. 'I'm sorry ... I can't let her see me so shaken, but I'm worried about her and the baby, especially after ... never mind. How's Frank?'

Jordan's change of topic sent a jolt through Olivia's chest. 'He's ... um ... he died yesterday morning.' The words tumbled out of her mouth before she could stop them. She had called to tell Brooke, but then, upon realising she had enough to deal with, had changed her mind. But now the truth was out.

'Olivia ... I'm so sorry. Is anyone there with you now? I would offer to come and—'

'No, no, I don't want you leaving my baby. She needs you more than I do right now. Please, don't tell her.'

'I can't keep this from her. She deserves to know.'

Olivia closed her eyes. 'I just need a couple of days.'

'To do what exactly?'

'To ... to sort some stuff out.'

'Olivia ... what stuff? What's going on? Does this have anything to do with the body that was found? Detective Williams called me.'

Olivia's heart skipped a beat. She'd been secretly hoping word hadn't reached Jordan and Brooke about the body, but she guessed since it was widespread news, it was inevitable he knew.

'I ... I can't talk about it right now,' she whispered.

'Olivia. Stop. This is me you're talking to. Whatever it is you're going through or dealing with it's not worth doing it alone. Trust me. I can help you. Just tell me what's going on.'

Olivia smiled, touched at how thoughtful and caring Jordan was, but she couldn't have him or her daughter and unborn grandchild anywhere near this town. 'You can help me by looking after my daughter and not telling her about her father until I say so.'

'Olivia, I—'

'Goodbye, Jordan.' She hung up.

### 25 May 1980

*The light from the torch dimmed when she dropped it on the damp ground. It flickered and then gradually began to die. Her hands shook so badly she had to drop the heavy rock she'd picked up. It only narrowly missed her foot.*

*What had just happened?*

*She couldn't think straight. Nothing made sense. Was she dreaming? Was that why everything felt fuzzy?*

*The darkness was so thick she couldn't see her hand in front of her puffy eyes. When she struck the attacker, warm spots of liquid had splashed onto her face. She could feel the liquid now trickling down her left cheek. It reached her mouth and her tongue darted out instinctively to taste it.*

*It wasn't rainwater. It was thicker and metallic, slightly sweet.*

*'Mary? What's going on?' she whispered. 'Are you okay?'*

*Olivia trembled as she bent down on the ground and picked up the dying torch, but her hands shook so violently she couldn't keep a grip on it before it slipped through her fingers and clattered to the ground once more.*

*'It's so dark … Where are you?' Olivia reached her hand into the inky darkness and shrieked when her fingertips touched something warm. 'Mary, is that you? Answer me, please.' Her voice was barely above a whisper. The fear inside her was growing too fast for her to bear. She had to get out of there, but first, she had to find Flora and Mary.*

*Their attacker might still be around. She knew she'd hit someone, but she wasn't very strong, so they may have only sustained a superficial wound.*

*Olivia crouched on the ground again and felt around for the torch. Her hands brushed against pebbles and larger rocks and then something sticky and wet: a puddle. She finally found the torch, managing to compose herself enough to hold it steady.*

*The scene that illuminated before her eyes caused her to let out a pain-filled scream; the type of scream that made blood boil and curdle.*

*Flora's small body lay on the ground in front of her, a bloody wound oozing from her head. Her eyes were rolled back, only the whites visible.*

*Mary stood over her, clutching a rock.*

'Mary! What did you do?' shrieked Olivia.

Mary opened her mouth and glared at Olivia. 'I-I didn't do anything. You … you killed her.'

Olivia swallowed back the bile that rose from her stomach. 'N-No! Someone was attacking you … I saw it. I just hit them with a rock to get them to stop.'

'No one was attacking us, Olivia,' said Mary slowly, enunciating every syllable.

Olivia shook her head vigorously. 'No …'

The sound of footsteps echoed through the cave followed by panicked shouts of 'Olivia! Mary! Flora!' from Frank.

Before Olivia knew how to respond, Frank appeared behind her. He must have stumbled and felt his way through the cave, following the flickering light.

Now, three of them stood in the small cave, staring at the body on the floor.

'What the hell happened?' asked Frank. He grabbed Olivia's shoulder and she flinched so suddenly she dropped the torch again.

Olivia's legs turned to jelly, and she had no choice but to sink to her knees. As Frank picked up the torch, she crawled towards Flora's body. She shook her gently, listening as the others spoke above in panicked voices.

'We heard yelling. I've left Jack outside because of his ankle. What happened?'

Mary dropped the rock she was holding to the floor. The sound of it bouncing echoed around the cave. 'Olivia killed Flora.'

'No, I didn't!' cried Olivia. 'Someone was attacking us!'

'What? Who?' asked Frank.

'No one was attacking us, stupid.'

Olivia's eyes flooded with tears. She could barely see straight. The blood from Flora's head spread in a large halo-like puddle. Olivia held her shaking hands out into the dim light. They were covered in Flora's blood. She cried as she wiped them on her dress, smearing it in large streaks.

Frank kneeled next to her. 'Olivia ... it's okay. It was an accident. It's so dark in here. Anyone could have made that mistake.'

'I-I didn't kill her ... Mary did. I just reached out and touched her by accident. That's why my hands are covered in blood.'

'You liar,' said Mary.

Olivia stared at Frank. 'I don't know what happened,' she whispered. 'I can't remember. It all happened so fast. I can barely see anything. My ... My eyes ...'

Frank wrapped his arms around her trembling shoulders. 'It's okay. We'll get through this together.' He looked up at Mary. 'We need someone to go and alert the police.'

Silence filled the cave for several long seconds.

Then both Mary and Olivia spoke at once. 'No.'

Frank squeezed Olivia tighter. 'Liv, we have to tell the police.'

'No,' she said again.

Mary stepped forward. 'No one is saying anything.'

Frank spluttered a laugh like he couldn't quite believe what he was hearing. 'B-But it's the law! We can't cover up a murder!'

'No one murdered anyone,' spat Mary. 'It was an accident ... right, Olivia?'

Olivia nodded. 'Right.'

'And to make sure no one says anything, we'll all going to take a blood oath.'

'A what?' asked Frank.

'I'll explain when we're all together. Go and get Jack.'

'What? Why?'

'Because whether he likes it or not, he's in on this too. We can't exactly keep it a secret from him when we all come out covered in blood and Flora isn't with us, can we?'

Frank rose to his feet, leaving Olivia shaking on the ground. 'Mary ... think about this. This will have repercussions for the rest of our lives. Keeping something as big as this a secret is bound to affect us not only mentally, but physically as well. How are you going to explain Flora's absence to your parents? It's crazy to even think about keeping this a secret.'

'You let me worry about my parents.'

'I won't do it. I won't keep this a secret.'

'Really? Not even if I tell the police it was Olivia who killed Flora? Because it was, you know. No matter what she says, she's lying. She killed her. I saw it happen.'

'If that's true then why don't you want to tell the police? Don't you even care your sister is dead?' Frank's voice had reached hysterical levels.

Mary looked down at her sister on the ground. 'She's in a better place, trust me.'

'You can't be serious!'

'Look at me, Frank. Do I look like I'm kidding?' she screamed.

Olivia covered her ears and squeezed her eyes shut. 'Please, Frank, just go and get Jack.'

'Liv ...'

'Go!'

Frank sighed and shook his head. She saw the disappointment in his eyes as clear as day. It physically hurt her to see him look at her like that, but she had no other choice. Her life was over if she didn't agree to Mary's blood oath.

Frank left the girls with the torch. When he was gone, Olivia turned to Mary.

'What's a blood oath? What does it mean?'

'My parents told me about them. They made me and Flora take one once. It means if you ever tell anyone the truth about what happened today, then you must take your own life because the repercussions will be even worse than death.'

'What did they make you promise?' There was no answer from Mary. 'But surely you don't believe it's true,' she said quietly.

Mary's eyes glistened with tears. 'I'm too afraid to find out.'

# Chapter Thirty-One

## Alex

### *25 January 2024 – 16:30 p.m.*

The first sensation he became aware of was being soaking wet and cold. The back of his head pounded like a drum and his stomach felt as if something had died inside it. He attempted to force his eyes open, but the signals from his brain weren't quite reaching them yet.

Far in the distance, he heard distorted voices. They were familiar, but he couldn't understand what they were saying. He waited for the thick fog in his brain to clear while he took a few deep breaths. In through his nose and out through his mouth.

He was flat on his back; nothing but darkness pierced his eyelids other than a few random flickers of bright light.

'I thought you said you were strong enough to carry him the whole way!' The shrill voice of his girlfriend (or was she an ex-girlfriend now?) exploded in his ears.

'He's heavier than he looks, okay?'

'I knew we should have lured him closer. It was a stupid plan.'

'Yeah, well, you could have come up with a plan of your own if you'd actually used that useless brain of yours.'

'Don't blame me for the fact you're too weak to carry a scrawny boy over your shoulder.'

Alex groaned as he opened his eyes.

'Great. Now he's awake and will be even harder to carry.'

'W-What's going on?' he stuttered. 'Which one of you knocked me out?' He reached round to the back of his head, feeling a cool, sticky substance on his fingers. He slowly sat up and took in his surroundings, but due to the evening darkness, it was difficult to make out anything specific except the two looming shadows above him. He was on the ground among the wet grass and next to him was a gate with a familiar sign. 'Were you taking me to Beaker Ravine?'

Harriet tutted loudly. 'Well, we would have done if bloody Arnold Schwarzenegger here hadn't told me he was strong enough to carry you the whole way and we'd put you in a wheelbarrow like I suggested.'

'Yeah, and I told you there was no way of getting a fucking wheelbarrow through that overgrown wood!' snapped Alex the First.

'Guys, will you stop shouting? I feel like I've got the worst hangover of my life,' moaned Alex as he grabbed the nearby gate and pulled himself to his feet. He wobbled but managed to catch himself in time. 'Why the fuck did you knock me out in the first place?'

'Why'd you think, stupid? We were going to take you to the ravine and throw you off the log,' said Alex the First.

Harriet screamed and stamped her foot like a petulant child. 'Why the hell'd you go and tell him that for? Why are you so stupid, Alex? Now we have to kill him, or he'll go and blab to his mummy.'

Alex groaned again as another wave of nausea and pain washed over him, but he fought against it as he chuckled. 'You two really are the stupidest twats I've ever known.'

Alex the First tensed beside him. 'What did you say?'

'You heard me. You have no idea what you're doing. You think it's funny and cool to terrorise kids and spread rumours, and then think it's a good idea to knock me out, drag me to the ravine and throw me off the log ...' Alex laughed. 'I mean ... you realise your DNA is all over my jacket and stuff, right? Not only that but ...' Alex grinned as he stuck his hand into his jacket pocket and removed his phone, holding it up so they could see the screen.

Harriet shrieked. 'Turn it off now!'

'Bit late for that. I bet the police will be interested to hear what's on here.'

'How long's it been recording for?'

'Since I arrived at the smoking spot, but before that it also recorded our conversation in the classroom.' He winked at Harriet, whose bottom lip began to quiver as tears filled her eyes.

Alex the First took a step forward, holding out his hand while the other was clenched into a fist at his side. 'Give it to me.'

'No, I don't think I will.'

'Give it to me. Now.'

'Fuck off, you psycho.'

Alex the First gritted his teeth. He was in no state to defend himself due to his head wound and possible concussion, but he didn't have any other choice. While the recordings had been planned, he hadn't expected them to knock him out and attempt to kill him.

Harriet whimpered. 'Let's just go. Come on. Maybe it's just a threat.'

Alex the First shook his head, staring at Alex with unblinking eyes of fire. 'It's not a threat. He'll do it. He'll hand it in to the police without a second of hesitation. We must kill him.'

'I'd like to see you try,' replied Alex, sounding more confident than he felt. His body was betraying him with tremors.

'Why don't you just—' Alex the First stopped.

A rustle in the long grass made all three heads turn in that direction.

Then a faint cough emerged from the darkness.

Someone was coming.

'Shit,' muttered Alex the First. 'Who knows we're here?'

Harriet's eyes widened. 'I don't know. Come on. Let's get out of here while we still can.'

Alex the First took a step forward, fists clenched, but then stopped, thinking better of it. 'We're not finished with you yet,' he said as he pointed a finger at Alex, who returned his gesture by holding up his middle finger and shoving it in his face.

He watched as Harriet and Alex the First scurried away like frightened mice, only breathing a sigh of relief when they'd disappeared. He switched off the recording on his phone and pocketed it, turning just in time to see someone emerge through the darkness.

And it was the last person he'd expected to see.

# Chapter Thirty-Two

## Graham

### *25 January 2024 – 16:45 p.m.*

He stretched his arms above his head and cracked his neck side to side, an action that only brought him relief for approximately 0.3 seconds. Now he'd found out Mary's parents were both dead, there didn't appear to be anyone else left related to Flora to inform of her death, apart from Mary, and she, as it turned out, had known all along. It was the strangest case he'd ever encountered.

The poor girl had been down in the dark damp cave for over forty years and had never been reported as missing, so no one had been looking for her. Yet his so-called best friends had known about her whereabouts all this time and not told a soul because of a stupid childish blood oath Mary had learned from her parents.

Now, he needed to tell the world. Another press conference was scheduled for tomorrow at midday. He was writing his statement now, but the words didn't make sense on the page. Nausea roiled in his gut every time he wrote the names Mary or Flora. And when it came to the question of any possible subjects, he paused, unable to write what he was really thinking.

Olivia Willows.

He hadn't told anyone about her possible involvement because, for the moment, that was all he had: a possibility. There was no evidence of her being involved. No DNA had been found inside the cave that didn't already belong to Flora. Unless Olivia came forward and confessed, there was nothing Graham could do. She was going to get away with it.

As far as he was concerned, Mary could rot in jail for the rest of her life for what she did to her son. Olivia … was different. Wasn't she? She wasn't like Mary. She wasn't a horrible selfish person. Had she been framed? Coerced? But what about Frank and Jack? Had they had something to do with it too? It wasn't like he could ask them now.

'Fuck!' he shouted, a little louder than he intended.

A head popped round the door: DS Carter. 'Everything okay in here, boss?'

Graham looked up. 'Yes, just trapped my hand in the drawer.'

'Just sent through those results you wanted.'

'Cheers, DS Carter.' He waited until she'd closed the door before navigating to his emails and clicking open the file on Jack Evans' death.

It was exactly as he'd feared and half-suspected: all normal.

The cause of death was a sudden massive heart attack. Even if he hadn't been alone at the time, there was no way he could have been saved. It had killed him almost instantly. Graham remembered how Jordan had been racked with guilt for not being with him. He'd left to attend to his then-girlfriend, Amber Walker, who'd been having some sort of crisis and left his father to lock up Fix It All by himself. It wasn't unusual for Jack to lock up alone either. It was just one of those unfortunate things.

Graham scrolled down to the section about Jack's previous medical history. He had been in good health overall, having had a full check-up only the month before by the local doctor. No history of any heart conditions. His blood pressure had been a tad on the high side, but he put that down to having some stressful nights at the business. His weight was normal, he ate healthily. He didn't exercise much, but he worked at the shop six days a week. He hadn't been on any type of medication at all; nothing. The man had been in decent shape for his age.

So, why had he dropped dead of a heart attack out of the blue?

Graham clicked on the brief regarding how he'd been found. Jordan had found him. When Jack hadn't returned home from work, his son had driven over to the business and found him dead on the floor behind the reception counter. Jordan had dialled for an ambulance and attempted CPR, but Jack was long gone and had presumably died approximately two hours before he'd been found.

As Graham scanned the screen, a sentence he hadn't picked up on before jumped out at him, causing his breath to catch in his throat.

Jordan had provided the following statement to the officer on the scene: *When I found him on the floor, his eyes were wide and full of terror, almost as if he'd seen something that had terrified him to death. His hands were up, shielding his face.*

Graham read it several times.

His hands were shielding his face …

Shielding his face from what?

Had someone attacked him? But there'd been nothing to suggest anyone else had been there. No defensive wounds or marks. Nothing.

Graham read one word over and over.

Some*thing*?

Not some*one*.

Why had Jordan used that word?

Graham rubbed his chin as he thought about Jack. He had barely spoken to the man in forty years. He knew more about his son, Jordan, than he did about his old friend.

There had been one night, in the local pub, when he found Jack drunk and slurring his speech as he'd draped himself across a table. It had been back in 2003 and his teenage son had been causing havoc in town. Graham had gone to have a quiet drink by himself and had seen his old friend in the corner of the pub, clutching a bottle of whiskey and talking to himself.

Graham had approached the barman. 'Not like Jack to get drunk by himself. What's up with him?'

The barman nodded in Jack's direction. 'His wife's just up and left him. Apparently, she couldn't stand to be around their son any longer.'

'Shit. I knew things were bad, but I didn't realise they were *that* bad.' He ordered a whiskey and sipped at the drink while he watched his friend in the corner. He couldn't leave him like that. So, for the first time since the early 1980s, he approached him.

Graham took his drink and walked up to Jack, who made no move to show he'd heard his footsteps. 'Hi, Jack. Mind if I sit?'

Jack didn't answer, so Graham slid into the booth opposite him.

'I heard about Anne … I'm really sorry.' He kept his voice low so as not to be overheard by the usual Saturday night crowd, but either Jack hadn't heard him or was choosing not to answer. Jack's head was buried in his right arm resting on the table while his other hand twisted the glass round and round causing a watermark.

Graham reached over and placed his hand on Jack's arm.

Jack slowly lifted his head and locked eyes with his former best friend. 'It's my f-fault,' he slurred. Graham watched as tears flooded his eyes, which were red and puffy.

Graham shook his head. 'No, it isn't, Jack. It's not your fault. You can't blame yourself for Jordan's behaviour.'

Jack snorted a laugh, which Graham had found an odd thing to do at the time. 'Can't I?' he'd said before burying his face in his arm again. 'Like you care. You've n-never cared.'

Graham barely heard him over the din of the bar, but those words had hit him deep. The truth was he did care, but Jack, Frank and Olivia had all pushed him away years ago, so it was them who didn't care, according to him.

'Jack … can I do anything to help?' asked Graham.

Jack looked up, his face solemn. 'You can keep the darkness away.'

Graham had frowned, not understanding his meaning. He'd taken it to be merely a drunken statement that made no sense, but now, all these years later, he understood it more. Jack's eyes had been filled with fear, as well as disappointment and grief.

He'd seen him several days later at his business tending to customers the way he always did with a bright smile across his face. Jack nodded at him, acknowledging his presence, but had never talked about what he'd said to him in the bar that night.

Now, Graham would have given anything to have spoken to his best friend again. A gnawing ache started in his chest. He rubbed his hand across his heart and sighed.

He stood up to alleviate the pain also developing in his back, a by-product of sitting down too long and older age rather than nagging guilt. Something in him was itching. Not physically, but a mental itch. He needed to go somewhere and, after speaking with Mr Mallow earlier, he had an idea of where he needed to be and what he needed to do.

He pressed the buzzer on his desk. 'DS Carter, I'm going out for a while. Call me if anything else crops up.'

'Yes, boss.'

Graham shrugged into his jacket and exited the police station. He stopped off at his house and grabbed a large wooden axe from the garden shed before driving as far as the road would take him towards his destination.

The torrential rain had made the ground sodden and by the time he arrived at the edge of the ravine, his boots were caked in mud. He stared at the log across the expanse. The roots on this side were well and truly rotten. It was surprising the tree hadn't collapsed into the void below under its own weight after so many years of erosion.

His mind drifted back to 5 June 1980, the day he'd stood at the edge of the ravine and watched as the tree collapsed into the makeshift bridge he saw now. He'd been there that day. He didn't know why the tree had chosen that exact time to fall, but it had been the start of everything.

And now, Graham wanted to put an end to it.

The fallen tree was a symbol; an evil thing that had been used to take away so many lives. Too many people had jumped from it. Too many people had been drawn to it. He didn't have the power to get rid of the ravine, but he could get rid of the tree.

So, that's what he did.

He swung the axe above his head and brought it crashing down on the weakened roots.

It was then he heard footsteps behind him.

'Detective Williams?'

# Chapter Thirty-Three
## Stephen
### *25 January 2024 – 16:51 p.m.*

Even in the growing darkness, the large dark shape by the fallen tree was unmistakably the detective, but it was the item in his hand that made Stephen's blood turn to ice.

'Detective Williams?'

The man froze just as he was about to bring the axe down upon the roots for the second time. He turned, squinting in his direction.

'What the fuck? Mr Mallow, what are you doing here?'

Stephen stepped out from the cover of the trees, shining his torch directly in the detective's face. 'Shouldn't I be the one asking you that, Detective? Why the hell do you have an axe?'

The detective held his hands up in defence. 'It's not what it looks like.'

'Are you sure? Because it looks as if you're trying to chop down the fallen tree so it falls into the ravine.'

A long pause followed. 'Okay,' replied the detective, 'it's exactly what it looks like.'

'We spoke on the phone less than an hour ago. You said you had an idea as to how to end all this … and this is your idea? Chopping a tree down?'

Detective Williams held his free hand in front of his eyes. 'Will you get that light out of my face?'

Stephen lowered the beam. 'Need any help?' The detective's lips curled into a smirk as Stephen raised what he was holding in his left hand: another axe, but this one a smaller one with a shorter handle.

'Do I want to know where you got that from?'

'I carry a range of items in the back of my car, including a shovel, a can of petrol, an axe, a blanket and bin bags.'

Detective William's face turned to a frown. 'You worry me, Mr Mallow.'

'You can never be too prepared.'

'Uh huh ...'

Stephen chuckled as he made his way through the squelchy mud towards the edge of the ravine. He knew having items like that in the boot of his car seemed odd to most people, but after one unfortunate incident when he'd broken down in the middle of nowhere during a blizzard, he swore to himself he'd always ensure he was prepared during car journeys.

He directed the torch beam down into the depths and whistled. 'Gonna make one almighty bang when it reaches the bottom.'

Detective Williams stepped back up to the roots. 'Yep. Now, move back for a moment. You can take over when my arms get tired.'

'Got it.'

Stephen did as the detective asked and stood aside, fighting against the urge to look over his shoulder at the rustling trees, which formed hideous shadows across the ground.

*The darkness is my friend. The darkness is my friend.*

The tree omitted eerie groans and creaks as Detective Williams chopped at its roots. Each thud of the axe ricocheted around the area where they stood and shook Stephen to his core. He watched as the detective hacked at the tree. The man seemed to have a lot of pent-up anger fizzing through his body as he unleashed it using the only weapon he had at his disposal.

'May I ask you a question?' asked Stephen.

'Shoot,' replied the detective, sounding out of breath.

'Do you truly believe chopping down this tree will end all this ... darkness ... that's been happening in the town for all these years?'

The detective stopped chopping and stood up straight, lowering the head of the axe to the ground with a thud. He turned to Stephen. 'No, I don't believe it will stop it, but I was standing right here when this tree fell back in 1980, and I sure as hell want to be here when it finally collapses and takes with it any weird entity or evil spirit that's been trapped in it for forty years. Whether I believe it or not is irrelevant. I won't have any more of Cherry Hollow's residents taking their own lives from this fucking tree.'

Stephen nodded. 'That's why I'm here too. You and I are a lot alike.'

The detective smirked. 'Don't get too used to it.' He stood aside. 'I'm not as young as I used to be. Please, continue.'

'Thank you,' replied Stephen as he stepped forward with his own axe.

As he lifted it above his head, ready to smash it down, a snap of a twig pierced the darkness like a crash of thunder. Both he and the detective spun around at once, facing the thick trees.

'It sounds like someone else is coming to join the party,' said Stephen.

# Chapter Thirty-Four

## Olivia

### *25 January 2024 – 17:01 p.m.*

As Olivia reached the old gate and sign, she froze, having caught a glimpse of a humanoid shadow ahead. Was someone waiting for her? No one knew she was heading to the ravine. She hadn't told a soul, yet …

Yes, there was certainly someone there and he looked as shocked as she did.

'Alex? What on earth are you doing out here?'

The boy froze.

'Sorry, I don't think we've officially met. I'm Olivia Willows. I'm friends with your mum.'

She watched as recognition flickered across his face. 'Oh, yeah. Sorry, I wasn't expecting anyone to turn up. You may have just saved my life though,' he said with a sigh.

Olivia looked over her shoulder. 'Was someone else here?'

'It's a long story.'

Olivia pulled her jacket tighter around her as she approached him. 'Are you okay? You're not lost, are you?'

'No, I know my way around here.'

Olivia nodded, remembering he had found Flora's body, so he must have known the area around the ravine quite well. 'Of course. Does your mother know you're out here?'

'Not exactly.'

Several beats of silence passed. Olivia wasn't sure whether to press him further on why he was here or send him back to his mother. She barely knew the boy yet felt as if she knew a lot about him, thanks to Emma always speaking so highly of him. She also felt the unmistakable maternal instinct to protect him, despite him not being her own child.

'Why are you out here?' asked Alex, beating her to the punch.

'I'm ... Well, I mean I was ...' She stopped and listened. 'Can you hear that?'

'Hear what?'

'Listen.' Olivia held up her hand to signal his silence.

There it was ...

Thud.

Thud.

Thud.

It was far away, yet the noise reverberated around them, shaking the ground. It reminded Olivia of a steady heartbeat, and she had a horrible image in her head of the ravine or The Creature coming alive ...

'What the hell?' asked Alex. 'It sounds like it's coming from the ravine ...'

'Lead the way, young man.'

'Wait ... you're not going to tell me to go home?'

'Would you listen to me if I did?'

'No.'

'Then I guess I'd better save my breath for the hike to the ravine.'

Alex's mouth twitched into a smile.

Olivia hadn't walked the route in a very long time; decades, even. Yet, it was as if nothing had changed. She could see every blade of grass, every stone, every tree branch as if it were forty-four years ago, despite the darkness creeping ever closer, hiding a lot of the detail in shadows. Olivia and her friends would come this way a lot, usually walking in single file along the narrow path through the thick trees. The trees had been a lot smaller then, thinner, and less foreboding than they were now.

Olivia pushed a large branch out of her way as she followed Alex. She was too old to be traipsing through the woods, but something had been calling to her all day. Granted, she hadn't expected to run into Alex, but now they were on their way to investigate the odd thumping that was still echoing through the trees and getting louder with each forward step.

She'd switched her phone off several hours ago, after Jordan's insistent calling. She knew he meant well, and she regretted telling him about Frank's passing, but it would all be okay soon … She hoped. As long as she could get rid of Alex somehow …

She was on her way to sort everything out and give it what it had wanted from the start.

No more …

It could have her now. She was done hiding and lying and pretending she wasn't the one responsible. Mary was in jail where she belonged. The others were dead. She was the only one left and the darkness wanted her to pay for what she'd done.

Flora deserved the truth.

Everyone did; the entire town deserved to know.

She hadn't brought anything with her, just a warm jacket and a torch. She'd hoped to have reached the ravine by the time the darkness closed in, but it was taking her longer to navigate the uneven path than she imagined, even with Alex as her guide. For the first time in a long time, she cursed her old age. He was patient with her though, which she appreciated.

The thudding was a loud drum in her ears.

A shout echoed from ahead.

Olivia and Alex increased their pace. She silently swore as thorns and branches snagged on her long skirt and scratched at her ankles.

They were so close now ...

Any second, they'd break through the trees and come face to face with the sheer drop.

Then, a loud crack erupted from ahead, piercing the inky darkness and sending a shock wave through the ground.

Several seconds later, the ground trembled as an almighty crash raced towards them. Olivia gasped as her breath left her body at the sheer force of the tremor.

Alex took off at top speed, leaving Olivia trailing behind.

# Chapter Thirty-Five

## Alex

### *25 January 2024 – 17:05 p.m.*

As the crack echoed through the trees towards him, his heart rate doubled. Mrs Willows' footsteps and heavy breathing sounded behind him as he ran, but he didn't stop to wait for her. A horrible sick feeling in his stomach made him run harder and faster until he broke through the trees and came to an abrupt stop at the edge of the ravine.

The sight that awaited him made his heart leap again, but his brain couldn't catch up and comprehend who he was seeing, standing next to the drop, each of them holding an axe.

'What the fuck?' he muttered.

'Mr Smithson … delighted to see you again,' replied Stephen, looking remarkably calm considering the strange situation.

The detective on the other hand didn't look nearly as composed. His hair was sticking up all over the place and, despite the cold temperature and the drizzle of rain, sweat poured down his face. The flickers of torchlight made the whole scene look sinister and out of place.

Several seconds later, Mrs Willows burst through the trees and let out a shriek as she saw who was waiting for her. 'Graham … Stephen … what on earth?' Her breathing was erratic as she gulped in air.

The detective held his hand up. 'I think it's safe to say none of us were expecting company here tonight. All four of us appear to have been drawn to the ravine at the same time and for different reasons.'

'What was the loud crash we just heard?' asked Mrs Willows.

Stephen moved aside and shone the torch at the empty expanse. 'Notice anything different?'

'You guys chopped the tree down?' asked Alex, taking a few steps closer. He wanted to see where it had landed, silently gutted he hadn't witnessed its demise for himself. It must have looked spectacular as it fell. He wondered if it did that thing all large trees did in movies where it lodged itself between the two sides of the crevice as it fell.

He shifted his footing, leaning over the edge.

'I wouldn't do that if I were you—'

'Alex! Watch out!'

Alex had been on several rollercoasters in his life. He loved the thrill, the heart-pumping adrenaline pulsing through his body at the expectation of the sudden drop. Then that moment when his heart stopped as he plummeted to the ground, his stomach leaping upwards to his throat …

This experience was nothing like that.

His heart did stop, and his stomach did leap, but not in the same way. He'd never felt fear like it. It tore apart his insides as he screamed. He only had a split second to react.

He had been too far away for either Stephen or the detective to grab him, so he threw his body towards the side of the ravine, digging his fingers into the muddy earth left behind by the cracked roots.

At the same time, he heard the other three shouting his name somewhere above him, but their voices sounded far away and muffled like he was living in a dream world of his own.

All that mattered now was surviving.

He dug the fingernails of his left hand into the side of the ravine, feeling his nails break and bleed as he scrambled for something – anything – to cling to. But the weight of his body pulled him down.

He tried to find a foothold, but he kept slipping, slipping …

Something hard bashed into the side of the ravine next to him.

Momentarily dazed, he looked up and saw the detective leaning over the edge wielding a long axe. Stephen was stood behind him, holding the detective's jacket, stopping him from sliding down too. Alex knew he only had seconds to respond before he fell and joined the tree at the bottom.

Alex let go of the loose earth and stones with one hand and grabbed the axe handle, his palms wet from sweat and rain, which was now growing heavier by the minute.

The detective grunted as he pulled him up the steep slope to safety. By the time Alex made it to solid ground, everything around him swam in and out of focus. Steady hands shoved him to the ground while he gulped in precious lungfuls of air.

Neither he, Stephen nor the detective spoke as they kneeled on the ground, panting from shock and exertion. But they shared a look and nodded their acknowledgements.

Mrs Willows rushed towards him. 'Alex! Are you okay?' She fussed over him.

'I'm fine. I slipped ...'

'Bloody hell, boy, you gave us all a scare,' said the detective as he stood up and took a deep breath.

'Sorry about that,' muttered Alex. His body continued to shake so much he couldn't make his legs work, so he remained sitting on the ground in the mud, not caring he was drenched.

# Chapter Thirty-Six

## Graham

### *25 January 2024 – 17:10 p.m.*

It felt like hours before his heart rate began to subside. He needed to take control of this situation soon or it was possible one of the three people standing in front of him would leave and refuse to explain why they were there in the first place. He hadn't expected a horde of spectators tonight and, as a detective, he knew they wouldn't be forthcoming with their explanations, especially if it was likely to land them in trouble.

He approached Olivia and placed a hand on her shoulder. 'Are you all right?' he asked her. Her eyes were wide, like a rabbit in headlights, and her whole body was shaking.

She nodded quickly. 'Yes … yes, I'm okay. Just had a bit of a shock. Emma would never have forgiven … Doesn't matter. He's safe. That's all that matters.'

Graham agreed with her. As he'd watched the young lad slip down the ravine, his heart had plummeted through his chest and he'd felt as if he were falling himself. He couldn't let another child fall to their death here. But thankfully, he'd been able to reach Alex in time.

Now his job was to get everyone away from this place unharmed.

But first …

'Right … Now we've all caught our breaths, I think it might be a good idea to explain why we're all here at the same time.' He kept his voice low. 'How about I go first?' He hoped his suggestion would instil some confidence and reassurance in the group.

All three of them nodded, but no one made eye contact. Olivia looked as if she wanted to crawl under the nearest bush and hide. Alex still appeared as white as a sheet and maybe a little green, and Mr Mallow kept shooting glances into the trees as if he was expecting a monster to leap out.

Graham cleared his throat. 'Okay, well, Mr Mallow already knows this, and I also told you all briefly when you first arrived, but I came here tonight with the intention of chopping this tree down and allowing it to fall to the bottom of the ravine. It's taken enough lives and it needed to be destroyed, which is what I've done. I'm not saying I believe it's responsible for all the deaths, but there's something about this ravine I don't like, and this tree seems to be the reason why people keep coming here, although why anyone would want to walk out onto a tree across a ravine is beyond me …' He stopped, aware he was babbling. No one had made any sort of movement or gesture to show they'd heard his speech, but eventually Olivia sighed.

'Thank you, Graham. I-I think it is time the tree went.'

'I never told you this, Olivia, but I was there on the day it fell.'

At this, Olivia perked up. 'You were?'

'It was a week or so after you … after … it happened. I came here by myself to clear my head. There must have been some sort of landslide because it was half hanging off the edge anyway, and I just happened to be there when it fell.'

'I suppose it's poetic you were the one to chop it down then,' answered Mr Mallow.

'Indeed,' replied Graham. 'So … that's my reason for being here. Mr Mallow, how about you go next.'

# Chapter Thirty-Seven

## Stephen

### *25 January 2024 – 17:20 p.m.*

Staring at the detective in the light of the torch combined with the ever-growing moonlight above filled Stephen with the same creeped-out sensation he felt the last time he'd been here. He could have sworn the trees beside him were whispering his name; that the branches were growing longer, twisting and developing long limbs with sharp claws on the end.

But no.

That was impossible because it was just his over-active imagination, wasn't it? Plus, the ravine was renowned for playing tricks on its visitors and now he knew the reason why: because a poor dead girl's soul had been trapped at the bottom for forty-four years. He didn't believe in ghosts or trapped souls, but what other explanation was there?

The detective was waiting for an answer.

Stephen shuddered as another shadow crept across the ground in front of him. 'I ... I ... To be perfectly honest, I've no idea why I'm here, only that for the past few hours it's the only place I could think of going, and every time I tried to ignore the impulse, I felt this overwhelming ... pull, I suppose. I believe it was fate that brought me here tonight, Detective.'

He watched as the detective fought back a laugh. 'Fate?'

'Yes. Fate. Just like it was fate that brought me back to Cherry Hollow.'

'I thought you said someone sent you an anonymous email and convinced you to return?'

Stephen flicked his eyes to Alex, who appeared to be holding his breath. He didn't want to rat the kid out to a cop. 'Yes. Still … that person could have sent the email to any number of journalists. They chose me. Plus, maybe it was fate that made me come here in 2022. I wasn't supposed to come. The guy who was supposed to cover the story called in sick with the flu, so I took his place. See … *fate*.'

The detective held up his hand. 'Okay, enough with this fate crap. Are you telling me you're here for no other reason other than … a *feeling*?'

Stephen shrugged. 'Look, I've already explained on several occasions that The Creature is bigger than just a rumour. I can't explain it. I don't think any of us can explain it, but *something* pulled us all here tonight. *Something* wants us to get to the bottom of all of this, and *something* is not going to let us walk away from here without admitting the truth.'

Stephen saw the detective frown, but he didn't respond. As he glanced at Alex and Olivia, a dark shadow passed overhead and the air around them turned to ice.

Stephen shivered. He blew out a breath and watched as it danced on the light breeze in the torchlight. He continued, attempting to hide the tremble in his voice, 'Whether we like it or not … this ends here … right now … tonight.'

An eerie silence followed his words. The detective swung his torch towards Olivia.

'I think we'd all like to hear from you now.'

# Chapter Thirty-Eight

## Olivia

### *25 January 2024 – 17:25 p.m.*

Her body turned rigid as Graham focussed the torch onto her. He didn't shine it onto her face, which she was grateful for, but at her body.

'What are you doing here tonight?' asked Graham. His voice remained calm, with no aggressive tone, but filled with emotion, nonetheless.

'Graham … please … I don't want to cause any fuss.' She held up her hands, palms facing him, and took one small step backwards. 'None of you were supposed to be here. I ran into young Alex at the old gate. I thought I was coming here alone.'

Graham nodded once. 'Okay … so … *why* did you want to come here alone?'

Olivia opened her mouth, but her voice deserted her. She couldn't say the awful words out loud. Now she was being forced to say them, her idea felt … wrong. She'd been planning to take herself out of the picture entirely. That way, the truth would die with her. But how many of the people she loved would have suffered afterwards?

Olivia hung her head. 'I'm sorry to say but I was going to end my life. I have nothing left, Graham. Frank is gone. My daughters are grown and have families of their own. And I'm trapped in this town because of what … what happened. I don't see another way out. It's like a cloud of darkness is blocking me from seeing anything else.'

Graham's face softened. 'Olivia … I think I speak for everyone here when I say I'm relieved you didn't get the chance to go through with … *that*.' Olivia glanced at Alex and Stephen who nodded their heads solemnly. Graham continued, 'But you must realise you have *everything* to live for. You have a family who loves you, and friends in this town who love and care about you. Ending your life isn't the answer. It's never been the answer. It may seem like the easy option at the time, but this … right here, right now … this is what's supposed to happen. This is how we end this torment. All you need to do is tell the truth … please. Once this is all over, we can begin to rebuild our lives and this town can start to recover from all its trauma. The people of Cherry Hollow have been through enough. *You've* been through enough.'

Olivia's eyes swam with tears. 'But … what if it doesn't work? Brooke is suffering because of everything I've done. She's still suffering. It's all my fault. All of it. I'm sorry. I'm so sorry.' She collapsed to her knees, her body shaking as violent sobs took over. Ever since she'd heard about Brooke suffering through severe sickness during her pregnancy, she'd blamed herself.

Everyone she loved was being punished because of what she'd done.

Several seconds passed before a strong hand touched her shoulder. She looked up as Graham kneeled in front of her, their faces merely inches apart.

'What are you sorry for, Olivia?' He took both her trembling hands and held them in his own, gently squeezing.

She took a deep breath. 'I did it. I killed Flora King. It was all me. Mary never touched her. It was me.'

As soon as the words left her lips, a strong wind whipped across the ravine and knocked them all off balance. Olivia looked up at Stephen who was battling to stay upright, attempting to shield himself using his jacket. Alex tipped over sideways and was lying on the ground, covering his head with his hands. Graham grabbed Olivia as they fell to the ground, covering her with his body.

Heavy, thick storm clouds materialised overhead, and a rumble of thunder echoed in the distance. The wind died back enough for them to right themselves.

Olivia's hair fluttered around her face, sticking to her cheeks which were wet with tears and rain. Graham helped her to her knees.

'What the hell was that?' asked Alex.

Stephen looked up at the clouds. 'I think we'd better make a move soon ... I don't want to be caught out in this storm.'

'In a minute,' said Graham with a stern voice.

Olivia gulped hard and continued, knowing she needed to say more. 'It was an accident. I thought Mary was being attacked by someone. I didn't see ... I couldn't ... My eyes ... I grabbed a rock and ... Mary convinced us all to keep quiet. We took a blood oath. I don't know why, but ... she seemed convinced it was the only way to keep the secret safe.'

Graham nodded and spoke softly. 'Why didn't Mary want anyone to know her sister was dead?'

'Her father abused them. If word got out, he'd have been ruined. She had some sort of strange connection to him. She was glad Flora was dead, so she'd get all her father's attention. She wasn't right, Graham. There was something wrong with her from the start. Didn't you always think there was something she never told us, something she was hiding?'

'Yes. She was being abused by her father.'

'No, not just that. She enjoyed it too. She wanted the attention. Her family left town and disappeared. They never reported their daughter missing and no one apart from us knew what happened to her.'

Graham squeezed her hands tighter. 'When you say *us* ... who are you talking about?'

'I think you already know the answer.'

'I need to hear it from you.'

Olivia sighed and hung her head. 'Frank and Jack.' It pained her to utter their names, but it wasn't as if things would get worse for them now. The only one it could get worse for was her; Mary could rot and die in her cell for all she cared.

Graham reached out and pulled her close. She didn't deserve his hug or his patience and sympathy. 'Thank you.' He whispered the words in her ear. What would have happened had she told him the truth forty-four years ago? Would anything have changed or would he have been swept into their twisted lies too? She'd never planned for any of this to happen.

She hadn't meant for her darkness to engulf everyone she loved and cared about. Her family was never supposed to have suffered for her lies. Her sick, dark legacy was not supposed to have continued. But now she'd spoken the words the darkness had wanted to hear, would they all be set free? Or were they doomed to live in grief, fear and loathing forever?

'Olivia ... I have to take you to the station. Thank you for telling me the truth, but I can't hide this. The truth needs to come out. It's time.'

Olivia smiled weakly. Her energy had been sapped from her body long ago. She no longer had the strength to keep fighting. It would have been easier to end her life and keep everyone safe, but now she'd spoken the truth, the weight of the world seemed less ... punishing, somehow. Olivia felt as if she could stand it now it was no longer her burden to bear alone.

'I know, Graham. I know.'

At this point, Alex cleared his throat. 'Um ... while we're on the topic of truth-telling ... I also have something to say.'

# Chapter Thirty-Nine

## Alex

### *25 January 2024 – 17:35 p.m.*

As he listened to Mrs Willows revealing what happened all those years ago and how she'd lived with the guilt for over forty years, a knot in his stomach made him almost double over. He saw the relief behind her eyes as she uttered the words she'd been keeping locked away in her soul. He'd stumbled against the strong wind as she continued her story. Mr Mallow was attempting to jot down some words in a notebook, which was almost impossible.

It was too much. He couldn't keep it in anymore. He didn't want to turn out like Mrs Willows, Mrs Jenkins, Jordan, or any of those people who'd kept such a devastating secret for so long. He didn't want to live with the growing guilt forever. Because, yes, he killed two members of his family, and at the time he hadn't felt guilty because he'd done it to protect his mum. And he still stood by his choice; but what if that guilt slowly fed on him for years and the whole situation with The Creature started up again?

Maybe the justice system would go easy on him as a minor. He could plead insanity over losing his younger sister ... or maybe ... maybe it just wasn't worth hiding any longer. He knew his sister's death had changed him. Was it too late to change back? Was it too late to start afresh? What about his mum? The truth would destroy her, wouldn't it? He'd spent so long trying to save her, yet now was about to deal the fatal blow.

The detective looked up as he stepped forward.

'What did you say, young man?'

Alex gulped, squeezing his hands into fists at his side. 'I need to confess something too.'

The detective turned to Mrs Willows, ensuring she was okay before rising to his feet and turning the torchlight on Alex. The wind and rain still buffeted around them, the storm growing closer by the second.

'As you're a minor, would you rather wait until you have a parent or guardian present?'

'No, this can't wait.'

'Okay ... if you're sure ...'

'I killed my dad and my step-mum.'

And there it was.

He expected another gust of wind, but there was none. Instead, the evening turned cold, so cold Alex saw his breath dance in front of him as he released it. The detective noticed the change in temperature too because he pulled his jacket tighter and shivered.

'I don't know anything about your dad, but ... are you saying you set fire to your own house last year with your step-mum, Linda, inside?'

'Yes. I did it.'

The detective glanced over at Mr Mallow who was still scribbling as much as he could in his notebook. He frowned, as if he wanted to snap at him for writing, but then seemed to think better of it and turned back to Alex.

'I'm afraid you've got a lot of explaining to do, Mr Smithson.'

'I know.'

'Why did you confess now? Why not earlier?'

Alex looked over at Mrs Willows, still trembling on the ground. 'It seemed like the right time and place to do it. As you said, now all the secrets are out in the open, maybe this town has a chance of recovering and things returning to normal. I don't want to turn out like ...' He gestured at Mrs Willows, who managed to give him a weak smile in return.

'Thank you, Alex, for being braver than I was at your age,' she said.

The detective coughed. 'Right ... well ... I wasn't expecting that. So, why were you heading to the ravine tonight by yourself before you ran into Olivia?'

'The same as Mr Mallow ... I felt an overwhelming pull towards it. Maybe he's right ... maybe we were all drawn here for a reason.'

Stephen clicked his fingers. 'What did I tell you? Fate!'

The detective shot him a dark look. 'Mr Mallow ... care to add any other confessions to the mix while we're at it?'

Stephen flinched as he stopped writing. 'Um ... not unless you care I shoplifted a pen when I was seven.'

'I think you're safe with that one.' Another gust of wind shook the nearby trees, causing a whistle that made Alex's ears ring. 'Well,' said the detective, 'there's no point in all of us standing around here getting colder by the second. That storm looks like a big one. Let's go to the station and sort this mess out, shall we? Alex, I'll be calling your mother en route to meet us there. Olivia … would you like me to call Brooke?'

Alex nodded his agreement even though the thought of his mum finding out the truth made him want to hurl.

'No, please don't. Not yet,' answered Mrs Willows.

'She's going to find out sooner or later.'

'I know, but … just not yet.'

Alex watched while the detective and Mrs Willows conversed. He turned and stared across the expanse to the other side. The darkness had crept even closer now. He felt as if it were smothering him.

Was The Creature truly gone?

Could the town of Cherry Hollow begin to rebuild their lives, or had the mere idea of The Creature done so much damage it was impossible to ever mend?

# Chapter Forty

## Graham

### *25 January 2024 – 18:35 p.m.*

His body was heavy. He wanted to sleep for a whole day, maybe two. But he needed to get Olivia and Alex to the station to get their statements. He couldn't even imagine the size of the shitstorm that was going to hit when all this came out. He was too exhausted for what was to come, but it was almost over. Almost … At least he knew the truth about why his best friends had ghosted him for forty years. Had they made the right decision back then? No. Would he have reacted differently? Probably not, but it was hard to put himself in their shoes because he hadn't been faced with covering up a murder when he was still a child. Not everyone made good decisions, and that's what made them human.

Every step lasted an eternity. Were they walking around in circles? It hadn't felt this far when he'd walked through the woods and the field earlier. Stephen was leading the way, Olivia behind him, then Alex and Graham were at the back. Not that he was expecting either of the middle two to bolt, but he wanted to keep an eye on them, nonetheless.

He didn't know how to feel.

Was he relieved the truth had finally been told? Was he outraged Olivia had killed someone forty years ago and covered it up? Was he devastated his friends had been through such a harrowing experience and left him out of it?

It was impossible to think clearly. His mind was full of clouds and confusion. He wished he didn't have to take Olivia to the station and take her statement, but what other choice did he have? And Alex, granted he didn't know him well, but he was just a kid. But to have murdered his father and step-mum ... and lied about it ...

He'd already phoned ahead and warned DS Carter of their arrival. He'd parked the police car by the edge of the field earlier, so he didn't have to walk far. He opened the car door for Olivia while Alex got into the car from the other side. Stephen climbed into the passenger seat. He turned to Graham as he started the car.

'I'm assuming you'll want me to stay quiet about all this for a while.'

Graham shot him a look that said *Duh!* But then turned his attention back to the road as he pulled away from the layby. 'Just until I've informed the relevant people. I'll be making a statement tomorrow. In fact, I'd like you to do something for me.'

'Oh?'

'Write your story, but make sure it's the truth. Write about The Creature and the mental health side of things you told me about. Write about the darkness and how some people must live in it to survive. Just write the truth. Whatever your version of it is. I trust you.' Graham watched as a grin spread across Stephen's face.

'Now that I can do, Detective. Maybe we can be friends after all.'

'Let's not go that far.' But he shared a smirk with his passenger anyway.


Graham allowed DS Carter to take over once he'd walked Olivia and Alex into the station. She started the paperwork and fingerprints while he entered his office. The first thing his eyes landed on was the picture behind his desk. The one of him and his friends from many years ago, before everything had happened, before the darkness had taken them over, before they'd committed a terrible crime and covered it up. He stared at it for several seconds before removing it from the wall and holding it in his hands. He ran a finger over each of his friends' faces, remembering how they used to laugh and tease each other. When he got to Mary, he stopped, covering her small face with the tip of his finger.

Graham closed his eyes and sighed as he imagined what she and Flora had been through as children. If it weren't for their father, they would have been normal girls and one of them wouldn't be dead and the other wouldn't be a monster. He placed the picture face down on his desk as he lowered himself onto the chair, feeling as if he'd aged a decade in the past hour. He stared at the phone, wondering who he should call first: Jordan or Alex's mother.

He decided on the latter.

While he waited for her to answer, he reached into the desk drawer for the packet of painkillers and silently swore when he found the packet empty. He tossed it in the bin just as she picked up.

'Hello. Emma speaking.'

'Hello, Mrs Smithson. This is Detective Williams.'

'Oh my God, Detective, I can explain everything ...'

'Um ... okay?'

'Alex didn't scare that boy at school. It was those two troublemakers, Harriet Forrester and Alex Sharp. They've been terrorising kids the whole time with a fake demon mask.'

Graham's heart plummeted to his stomach. 'They ... what? What are you talking about?'

'They even bullied poor Bethany Walker. Alex had nothing to do with that.'

Graham leaned forward in his chair. 'Mrs Smithson, before you go any further, I wasn't calling about your son and whether he bullied a child wearing a demon mask. I shall talk to him about it, of course, but ...'

'Y-You weren't? Oh my God, I ... I'm so sorry, but then ... what *were* you calling about?'

Graham inhaled sharply. How was he supposed to explain her son had confessed to killing her ex-husband and recently deceased wife? It was days like these he utterly hated his job.

'Mrs Smithson, I'm afraid Alex has come to me and confessed to a crime.'

He heard a loud gasp through the phone. 'B-But what crime?'

'He … Maybe you should come into the station so I can tell you in person. I'm afraid this isn't the type of news that should be given over the phone.'

'I'm heading out the door now, Detective, but please … just tell me. I can't bear to wait another minute.'

Graham shook his head and covered his eyes with his free hand. The other clutched the phone so tight his fingers turned white. 'He has confessed to two counts of murder, Mrs Smithson. Your ex-husband and your wife, Linda.'

He wasn't sure what reaction he was expecting, but it wasn't silence. And it certainly wasn't her whispering, 'I already know, Detective.'

'You … you know?'

'Well, not for absolute certain, but … I'm afraid I've had my suspicions for a while. And if you're going to ask me why I didn't alert the authorities before then don't bother because if you had a child of your own then you'd know the reason.' Silence lingered for several seconds. 'I'm sorry, I didn't mean anything by that. It's just …'

'I understand you were protecting him.'

'Yes.'

'But now he has confessed, there is no way of protecting him from what's about to happen.'

'What *is* about to happen?'

'How about we discuss that when you arrive? I have another phone call I need to make. I'm very sorry, Mrs Smithson.'

'Thank you, Detective. See you soon.' She hung up.

Graham stared at the receiver as he lowered it. He then picked it up again and was about to begin dialling Jordan's number when the door to his office burst open and Jordan stormed in, his face red and his hair dishevelled. It looked as if he hadn't slept in over a week ... or showered.

'Detective, I need to speak with you.'

Graham rose to his feet. 'Jordan ... I was just about to call you. What are you doing here?'

'Oh yeah? Well, looks like I beat you to it. I can't get hold of Olivia. I'm worried something's happened to her.'

'Did you drive all the way from the New Forest to ask me that?'

Jordan's jaw unclenched ever so slightly. 'No, I came because I was worried she was about to do something stupid. She hung up on me and it freaked me out.'

'And you couldn't have called the station?'

'Brooke practically shoved me out the door and ordered me to drive her here when I told her.'

Graham walked around his desk and stood in front of Jordan. 'Olivia is fine. She's in the back being processed before giving her statement.'

'Her statement?'

'Yes. She's ... she's confessed to the murder of Flora King.'

'She what!' Jordan's face turned beetroot.

Graham held up his hands. 'Okay, before you erupt like you used to do, please believe me when I say I wish it weren't true. But it is. She's confessed.'

'What evidence is there?'

'None.'

Jordan laughed. 'You can't be serious.'

'As hard as it is to believe …'

Jordan lowered his eyes to the floor. 'Fuck,' he muttered.

Graham reached out his hand and placed it on Jordan's shoulder. 'I'm so sorry. Truly, I am.'

'Is it over? I mean … the last time we spoke …' He didn't have to finish the sentence.

Graham sighed. 'As far as I'm concerned, it is over. There's no need to bring up what happened to Kieran.'

Jordan's eyes filled with tears. He blinked and wiped them away with the cuff of his jacket. 'Thank you.'

'Now, Olivia probably won't want you to stay, but you're welcome to. Unless you need to get Brooke back home. How is she, by the way?'

'A little better, but still weak. She's been given some strong anti-nausea medication to stop the sickness. She wouldn't let me come alone back to this place. I'll speak to Olivia first. This isn't going to go down well. I hate to cause her any more stress.'

Graham headed for the door and held it open for Jordan to walk through. 'I'll order us some strong cups of coffee. I think we're going to need it.'

# Chapter Forty-One

## Stephen

### *26 January 2024 – 07:29 a.m.*

He'd stayed at the station until almost midnight drinking copious amounts of strong instant coffee. As he'd heard Olivia's and Alex's confessions by the ravine, he had to provide a statement of his own. He then decided to admit defeat and revealed Alex had been the one to send him an anonymous email about the body, hoping it would make the kid look less ... guilty.

He still couldn't quite get his head around the fact Alex had killed two members of his family. Had the darkness turned him into a killer, or had he already been one? Alex had murdered his father long before he'd arrived in Cherry Hollow, so did that mean the darkness reached further than merely this town? It wasn't just Cherry Hollow, was it?

There was a story there somewhere ...

Stephen sat in his usual armchair by the fireplace at the hotel. The fire was off, but he didn't care about that. Despite going to bed late, he was up early. He had an article to write and finish. And it was going to be the best article he'd ever written. He wanted to do the town justice.

There was no way of knowing if The Creature was truly gone because it was never there to begin with. Justice had been restored, yet it also felt as if something was still missing, some small part that didn't quite fit.

Stephen knew he could rely on his questioning mind. It hadn't steered him wrong before. He leaned back in the chair and thought back to the conversation he'd had with Detective Williams last night, just before he'd left the station. He'd been exhausted, running on nothing but caffeine and the remnants of a bag of Haribo he'd found in his laptop bag.

The detective caught up with him just as he'd been about to walk back to his hotel.

'Mr Mallow, a quick word.'

Stephen's shoulders had sagged. 'Seriously? I've just left the station.'

The detective stood in front of him, turning so his back was to the entrance. 'I'm sorry, but this has to be … off the record.' His voice had lowered.

Stephen barely reacted. 'Off the record, huh?'

'You know I asked you earlier to write the truth and nothing but the truth in your article?'

'Yes.'

The detective leaned a little closer. 'I need you to leave one thing out.'

'What's that?'

'The fact Jordan Evans and Brooke Willows were involved in covering up Kieran's death.'

Stephen raised his eyebrows. 'You're asking me to lie?'

'No, not lie, just … omit a few things.'

'And you're trusting me?'

'You wanted the truth, didn't you? That's what you came here for, and now you've got it.'

'Aren't you afraid that by keeping the truth from everyone the darkness and The Creature will start up again?'

The detective had given him a small smile, barely discernible in the darkness. 'The only people you'd be hurting now are two people who deserve a second chance.'

'Why do they deserve it? Who are they to you?'

'They are the son and daughter of two old friends of mine.'

Stephen had shifted his weight from one foot to the other. 'So, what you're saying is … we now have to carry the guilt of knowing the truth with us for the rest of our lives in order to spare two people more harm.'

The detective had squeezed his lips together, then nodded. 'Everyone has their own darkness to bear, Mr Mallow. Isn't that what you told me once?'

'Indeed.'

Now, sitting in his chair with his laptop perched on the table in front of him, Stephen hovered his fingers over the keyboard.

'Can I get you a refill on your coffee, Stephen?'

He looked up at the sound of Rachel's voice. 'No, thank you, but I'd kill for some freshly squeezed orange juice.'

'Coming right up. How's your article coming along?'

'It's … probably the easiest and hardest piece I've ever had to write.'

Rachel smiled at him. 'Well, I hope you finish it in time before our date tonight.' She winked.

Stephen laughed. 'Don't worry, as soon as I've written it, I'm all yours.'

'I'll leave you in peace to work then.'

Stephen watched her walk away and took a deep breath.

And began to type.

# Chapter Forty-Two

## Olivia

### *26 January 2024 – 10:35 a.m.*

She'd been provided food and water and treated with respect while going through the booking-in process. She was now in a small holding cell awaiting a transfer to the nearest prison, which happened to be the same one Mary was locked up in. It seemed they'd be seeing each other again, after all, and would continue to see each other for the rest of their lives. Olivia couldn't help but smile at the cruel irony of the situation. Maybe in a few years, she could request a transfer. Plus, she'd be seeing her old friends (although to call them friends was a stretch too far) – Lucy and Trisha, who were also locked up there.

She didn't deserve the respect she'd been given. She didn't want to feel anything anymore. But at least the overwhelming flood of guilt no longer drowned her from the inside. Instead, a dark sadness replaced it. What would Frank think of her and how she'd handled it?

Plus, so many "what ifs" were spinning around her head, all jumbling into one incoherent thought. What if she'd told the truth right at the start? What if she left Cherry Hollow as soon as she'd turned eighteen and not married Frank and had two daughters? What if she made more of an effort to search for Mary after she'd left? What if she alerted the authorities about Mary's identity when she'd returned as 'Mrs Jenkins'?

What if … what if … what if …

Olivia looked up at the sound of footsteps and let out a garbled cry when she saw her daughter walking towards her looking almost as pale and thin as she had when she'd been suffering from claustrophobia for all those years.

'Brooke! Darling, what on earth are you doing here? You should be in the hospital. Jordan, why did you let her come here?'

Jordan walked behind Brooke, who immediately turned to her mother. 'Jordan didn't *let* me do anything, Mum. I came because I wanted to. I needed to come, even though I swore I'd never come back here … I really must stop saying that because I always end up returning.' Brooke stopped by the bars, holding onto them for support. 'I want to hear you say it yourself,' she whispered.

Olivia's eyes filled with tears as she hurled herself towards her daughter, grasping her hands through the bars. She was shaking so much she could barely stay upright. 'Darling, I … I only kept the truth for all these years because I thought I was protecting you. Please believe me when I say I had no idea I was causing you so much harm. I didn't know the darkness had come for you too. I didn't know I was the one who was keeping you locked in the house.'

Brooke's eyes narrowed. 'Do you really believe that, Mum? That you were the one who started it all?'

'Yes! I didn't know what the darkness or The Creature or whatever it is people call it … I didn't know what it was, what it was doing to you, to Jordan and Amber. I swear! I didn't put two and two together until Emma moved to town and everything happened last year, and when your father didn't get better when he should have done. Maybe … maybe it had been after us all along.'

Brooke's nostrils flared at the mention of her father.

Olivia couldn't bear to hurt her any further, but she also couldn't cope with lying to her anymore, not to her face. 'Your father died two days ago.'

Brooke made no movement to say she'd heard her. She stared into her mother's eyes and blinked once. Olivia watched as two big tears slid down her daughter's face. 'I know,' she whispered. 'And Jordan didn't tell me. He didn't need to. I just … knew … somehow. That's why I'm here. I knew you needed me. I'm not going to abandon you the way I did all those years ago when you fell down the stairs and broke your ankle and I was too scared to leave my room and help you. The Fear doesn't control me anymore. And as angry as I am at you right now for lying to me and keeping the truth from me … you're still my mum … and I love you.'

Olivia sank to her knees, grasping Brooke's hands through the bars. Brooke knelt with her. 'I love you so much, Brooke.'

'When is the funeral?'

'In two days. I've been told I can attend with a police officer present.'

Brooke hugged her awkwardly through the bars.

'Can someone unlock this bloody cell!' shouted Jordan.

Olivia and Brooke stifled a giggle at the tone of his voice as a police officer came in and unlocked the cell, allowing the women to fully embrace. Olivia was careful not to squeeze her too hard.

'How are you feeling now?' she asked, pulling away and looking down at Brooke's stomach.

'I still feel sick most of the day, but at least I've stopped vomiting every ten minutes. The medication must be finally working.'

'That must have been awful,' replied Olivia, pulling her daughter close again and stroking her back like she used to when she was a child. 'I wish I could be there to watch your son or daughter grow up.'

'You will, Mum. I'll bring them to visit you, I promise.'

Olivia nodded. 'I'd love that. Thank you.'

Olivia knew then she'd be forever indebted to Graham, who had stopped her from doing such a terrible thing. Now, she had so much to look forward to ... But one person still needed to pay for what they'd done.

# Chapter Forty-Three

## Alex

### *26 January 2024 – 10:45 a.m.*

He'd never felt so ashamed of himself in his entire life. Last night had been excruciating and all he'd wanted to do was hide under his duvet and never come out. The disappointment in his mum's eyes had been too much to bear. She stared at him as Detective Williams explained what had happened, and he watched her eyes grow darker and darker as if she were sapping up his bad energy, all his dark demons, and taking them upon herself. He'd done that to her. *Him.*

Alex had given the detective the recording of Alex the First and Harriet in exchange for the promise the head teacher would be told so the two teenagers could receive their just punishment, whatever that would be. The detective said it was doubtful they'd receive jail time, but they'd probably be suspended from school. It was likely their families would move out of the town, but that was all conjecture. Alex was relieved the truth was finally out, and although he was about to face juvenile prison himself, at least they'd no longer get away with bullying innocent victims.

The detective left Alex and his mum alone in the dimly lit room and she hadn't said anything for nearly ten minutes. He felt like a small boy again, when he used to get in trouble, like the time he'd grabbed a tin of paint and smashed it against the wall, then smeared it everywhere. But this was so much worse because he was at risk of losing her forever. However, if she abandoned him, he wouldn't blame her. He deserved it.

Finally, his mum had spoken. 'Tell me why.'

Alex gulped, but an invisible object had become lodged in his throat and his tongue felt like sandpaper. He coughed. 'Mum ... I did it to protect you.'

'Protect me?'

'Yes.'

'From who, Alex?'

He'd never cried before, not properly, not since he was a child. But the tears streamed down his cheeks at that moment. 'From yourself.'

'Explain.'

Every word he wanted to say jostled for position inside his head, but his tongue couldn't keep up. The words spilled from his mouth, most of them barely legible.

'Mum, I did it for you so you wouldn't get hurt. Dad was grieving and he would have brought you down with him. You were having your own issues and struggling so much. I didn't want Dad to make you worse. I saved him. I did it so he wouldn't hurt anymore, but I could never do that to you, Mum. Never. I couldn't. I love you and I just wanted you to feel better. You loved Phoebe so much. We all did, but she was gone, and I didn't know what to do or how to help you. Mum, you have to believe me, I thought I was doing the right thing.'

He stopped and took a breath.

'Linda ... She lied to you from the start. She killed her. She killed Phoebe. She didn't deserve you. I couldn't let her get away with it. She wanted to die. I was doing her a favour. She tried to end things herself, but she didn't do it. I was just helping her out. She was making you feel worse and you would never have got better if I hadn't killed her. I thought I was helping you. You've been doing so well now since she's been gone and it's been amazing having you back again, like the old you before Phoebe died.'

He took another deep breath but found there were no more words left to say without repeating himself. What else could he say? Would she understand his point of view? Was he about to be abandoned by his mum, or would she stand by him because he was the only family she had left?

'Alex,' she said with an exhale, 'I knew it was you.'

He'd expected her to shout and scream at him, maybe stand up and slap him, maybe break down into uncontrollable sobs on the floor, but he hadn't expected her to say that.

'W-What?'

'I didn't know for sure, but I suspected it for a while.'

'B-But ... why didn't you say anything?'

'What would you have wanted me to say?'

Alex shook his head. 'I ... I don't know. Mum ... am I a psychopath?'

'Why would you think that?'

'I don't feel any remorse for what I did. I still believe it was the right thing to do. I don't feel bad or guilty that Dad and Linda are dead.'

His mum smiled. He didn't like the way she looked at him. It wasn't a smile of understanding or of love but of pity. 'There's nothing you could ever do to make me stop loving you. You're my son. A mother's love is a powerful thing.'

'Y-You forgive me?' A glimmer of hope bloomed in his cold heart.

'No, Alex. I will never forgive you for what you did.'

'B-But ...'

'But I'll never stop loving you,' she finished.

The glimmer faded and died. What was going to happen now? Did that mean she was going to support him through his trial and help him?

'Mum ... what happens now?'

She smiled again. 'Now ... we begin to heal ... together.'

# Chapter Forty-Four

## Graham

### *26 January 2024 – 11:45 a.m.*

Somehow, he managed a couple of hours of sleep last night. His body had been too exhausted to put up a fight. After speaking to Stephen outside the station, he got into his car and drove home. He didn't get as far as getting undressed before he'd passed out on his bed with his face buried in the duvet.

When he woke, bleary-eyed and confused, he dragged himself to the shower, stood under the hot jet of water until he felt somewhat more human, then dressed and made himself a strong coffee. He wasn't hungry but had popped a couple of pieces of bread into the toaster, eating it without butter as he made his way out the door and to the station.

Now, here he was, fifteen minutes away from making his final statement about the case. He'd been staring at his computer screen for the last hour, willing the words to flow, but they weren't there. He had no words. Maybe he should have told Mr Mallow to write his statement for him.

'Boss … you almost ready?'

Graham looked up at DS Carter who'd popped her head round the door. 'Nearly.'

It was a lie. Even if he had another day or more to prepare, he'd never be ready to reveal the truth to the world. The truth about Cherry Hollow. What was he supposed to say? He'd asked Stephen to keep a few things secret, and now he was about to do the same.

It was the inevitable vicious circle of impending darkness.

Graham switched off his computer and stood up. He had no notes. Nothing. For the first time in his professional career, he was about to make a statement without having anything prepared.

The small briefing room at the station was packed. Not a single seat was empty, nor was there a lot of standing room down the aisles. It seemed journalists had come from all over the country to hear the news. Everyone wanted a piece of Cherry Hollow, the infamous town that was haunted by a strange creature who lured people to their deaths at an old ravine.

But it wasn't true, was it?

There was no creature and there never had been. All there had ever been were dark, twisted, misunderstood people who had made bad choices. If anything, Cherry Hollow was just like any other town, city or village in the country, and indeed, the world. Because there were dark, twisted and misunderstood people in every walk of life who made bad decisions, who killed people they loved, who lied and cheated and stole.

It just so happened Cherry Hollow was an eerie little town in the Lake District that lent itself to rumour, mystery and mayhem, and Stephen Mallow had made it a tourist attraction with his previous article.

As Graham made his way through the swarms, a cold tingling, like the tickle of small spider legs, climbed up his spine towards the back of his neck. The room stank of bodies: body odour and the stench of desperation.

By the time he reached the podium at the front of the room, he was sweating and cursing himself for adding a jacket to his uniform of dark trousers and a white shirt. He longed to readjust his tie like they did in the movies when people were nervous and hot, but he couldn't show his true feelings. Not to these vultures. They'd eat him alive, and he couldn't afford to show any weakness.

He scanned the crowds, looking for a familiar face. But Stephen Mallow was nowhere to be seen. Graham wasn't sure if that was a good thing or not. Dozens of little red dots on various cameras were scattered around the room. He was live to the whole country.

He cleared his throat and began the hardest statement of his life.

'Good afternoon, ladies and gentlemen. I am Detective Chief Inspector Graham Williams. I see a few new faces and some old ones too. You're all here for one reason and one reason only, and that's for the truth regarding the body that was found in a cave at the bottom of Beaker Ravine fifteen days ago. I will, of course, get to the identity of the body in due course, but first I'd like to tell you a story.' Graham spied a glass of water on the podium, silently thanking whoever it was who'd placed it there:

probably DS Carter. He took a small sip and continued, despite the low hum of activity arising from the horde.

'It's a sad story, but hopefully one that will resonate with you. I can't say whether it's true or not. I'd like to leave that decision up to you.

'There was once a group of children who'd been friends for as long as they could remember. They grew up together through primary school and those early teenage years full of doubt and confusion and strange feelings. They couldn't imagine a life without each other. They loved each other very much. But one of them was a liar. One of them was just pretending to be friends with the others. Why? Because that person didn't know any better. They didn't know they could be loved by others because they hated themselves so much. Their parents didn't love them, and if they did, then they certainly didn't show it.

'One day, there was an accident and one of the friends was tragically killed. The friend who hated themselves told the others to take a blood oath, so they'd never tell the truth about what really happened that day. And because the other friends were scared, they agreed.' A murmur spread around the room, growing louder with every second. Confused faces turned to each other, and a few stray hands rose towards the ceiling. Graham lifted his hand to silence them.

'Please,' he said, 'allow me to finish my story.' The murmur died down. He took the opportunity to sip more water, wondering where the hell he was going with this.

'Many years passed. The children grew into adults. Those adults had children of their own, and the one friend who'd been lying to everyone had fled the area, never to be heard from or seen again. But something had been happening to the friends over the years. Something no one had expected.

'Due to keeping such a dark secret for so long, the friends' mental health took a drastic decline. They saw nothing but darkness surrounding them and with no way out of it. Bad things happened to them. Bad things happened to their children, and they knew if they didn't say something, the bad things would continue to happen long after they were dead. And that's the thing ... the friends started dying, one by one until there were only two left: the one who'd lied, and the one who'd committed the crime in the first place.' Another murmur spread, but this time it was quiet. Graham glanced at DS Carter in the corner who was frowning at him as if he were speaking Chinese.

'One of them had to stop the darkness from spreading before it was too late. So ... one of them did. They told the truth about what happened. But, of course, the darkness didn't stop because people still did bad things. They still lied and killed and tortured and raped. There will always be darkness in the world, but sometimes all it takes is one person to turn on a light ... Maybe if we all did that, the darkness would eventually end and we'd live in a world where our children could be safe.' Graham lowered his gaze to the floor, fighting back the tears brimming in his eyes.

Now there was no hum of noise. Instead, the room was deathly silent as the reporters hung on his every word. Everyone in the room held their breaths, waiting for him to continue, to finish his story.

Graham looked up at the room of confused faces. 'The body at the bottom of the ravine belonged to Flora King. She was the youngest daughter of Solomon King, the headmaster of the school who left town in May of 1980. She was also the younger sister of Mary King who used to live here. Most people in this town may not know her by that name. She lived here as a child and as an adult, but by then was known by a different name ...' He paused, not for dramatic effect, but because he was bracing himself for the bombardment of questions that were about to be thrown at him. '... Mrs Mary Jenkins, the mother of Tyler Jenkins, who killed Kieran Jones twenty-five years ago.'

And then it happened.

The room exploded with noise. People rose from their seats, waving microphones. They shouted questions that were indistinguishable from the roar. Graham waited almost thirty seconds before raising his hand again, signalling silence.

'I'm aware you have many questions. But I am only at liberty to state the facts. I'm sure you're all wondering if we have a suspect in the murder of Flora King. Yes, we do. The person has confessed and will be sentenced and trialled in due course.'

'Is it Mary King?' someone shouted. 'Isn't she already in prison?'

Graham shook his head. 'It is not Mary King. The person who has confessed to killing Flora is Olivia Willows.'

More shouts, gasps and chatter filled the room, but this time Graham didn't ask for silence; he continued regardless of the noise. 'Olivia Willows will be sent to Ashmoore Prison while she awaits sentencing. I will now open the floor to questions ...' As expected, every hand in the room shot towards the ceiling. He nodded at a woman in the front row.

'Yes, please, go ahead.'

The woman sprung from her seat, microphone outstretched. 'Lisa Gardner, Sky News. Who are the other friends in your story? I'm assuming the story is true and there were others involved in Flora's death.'

'What makes you think the story is true?'

The woman half-laughed and half-scoffed. 'Why else would you tell it?'

Graham leaned in close to the microphone. 'What if I'd told the story without the other friends in it? What would have been your question then?'

The woman responded without missing a beat. 'In the story, you talk about the friend who was killed ... Are you talking about Flora King or Kieran Jones? Because the story doesn't quite make sense. Half of it sounds like Kieran Jones' murder and the other half sounds like Flora King's murder ...'

Several heads nodded vigorously in the room.

Graham straightened his back. 'It doesn't matter who I'm talking about.'

'So ... what you're telling us is that the story is basically designed to throw us off track? Or maybe both murders were connected.'

'No, the story was there to make you think. Next question.' The woman slumped down in her chair, muttering under her breath. 'You, two rows back, on the end.'

A man leapt to his feet. 'Yes, thank you. Phil Jessop, BBC News. Where is Mary King now and is she to be charged with anything else relating to this case?'

Graham nodded, happy that a more related question had come up. 'She is still in prison for her crimes against her son. She will continue to serve out the remainder of her sentence.'

'But ... the story ...' Graham raised his eyebrows at the man who turned bright red and cleared his throat. 'Right ... Never mind.' He sat back down.

'Now, without further ado, I shall finish this briefing with an announcement. As of this moment, I am resigning from my position as Detective Chief Inspector and intend to retire at the end of the month. I will no longer be associated with this case. No further questions.'

The roar that erupted from the room was deafening.

Graham saw DS Carter's mouth drop open.

Dozens of hands shot into the air.

Graham stepped down from the podium and made his way through the bustling crowds of journalists. When he reached DS Carter, she let out a long breath.

'Well, boss, no one can ever say you went quietly. By the way, Alex Sharp and Harriet Forrester and their dads are in interrogation room three.'

'Thank you, DS Carter.'

It took several hours before Harriet and Alex were allowed to leave the station with their fathers. Amazingly, both teenagers attempted to blame Alex Smithson, but when he played them the recording, they promptly shut their mouths. Their fathers were in a state of shock and began talking about getting them psychiatric help. Graham hoped it would be enough to stop their own darkness from growing, because he knew, first hand, how dangerous it could become if left untreated.

# Cherry Hollow: The True Story of The Creature ...

## By Stephen Mallow
### Date: 1 February 2024

Back in May of 2022, I visited a quaint town called Cherry Hollow in the Lake District. I was never supposed to go there, but nonetheless, I went, having no idea what it was I was meant to be investigating. I think it's safe to say what I found will haunt me for the rest of my life.

Now, nearly two years later, I finally understand why I went there. It wasn't because my superior chose me because I was the only journalist available at the time to replace the original reporter. It wasn't because I had a secret fascination with all things weird and wonderful and the odd unsolved mystery or two.

It was fate.

That might sound strange. It sounds strange to me too, but I believe it with every fibre of my being.

The town of Cherry Hollow has been subject to a local rumour, an eerie legend, for a long time, and I think it's about time the rumour was set straight. There will be people who will continue to believe whatever they want to believe; that a strange creature was haunting the town and driving the locals to take their own lives.

Everyone thought the start was the disappearance of Kieran Jones back in 1998. The truth is, the darkness swept over the town long before that and will possibly haunt it for eternity.

Back in 1980, a young girl called Flora King was killed in a dark cave at the bottom of Beaker Ravine. Her body lay there for forty-four years before being discovered earlier this year.

Was her death the start of it all?

No.

I don't believe so.

Why?

Because, even before the girl's death, bad things were happening in Cherry Hollow. The headmaster of the school, Solomon King, was abusing his two young daughters. After conducting research, I also discovered the town's oldest resident, Mrs Price, who died only days ago, was manipulating her husband, and eventually killed him by poisoning his food.

So, did that mean that Solomon King and old Mrs Price started it all?

No.

Do you see the pattern here?

The point I'm trying to make is that darkness, in whatever form, is always around. It never leaves. It never stops. And it never will.

Because people do bad things. Humanity is the real darkness, and we all are capable of great and terrible things.

What about The Creature? Was it real, a hoax or a figment of a woman's imagination? Well, I like to think of The

Creature as a symbol; a symbol for our own mistakes, our own dark thoughts. Maybe there's a creature haunting each and every one of us in one way or another ...

The human mind is a wonderful, complicated and dangerous thing. No two minds are the same, which means we all see things in a different light. Trauma, tragedy and guilt affect us in different ways. We react to situations differently. We choose different paths in life.

And that is the point I'm trying to make.

What if, one by one, we start turning on our lights?

What if we start to heal ourselves by being nicer to each other? Helping others. Doing better. Being better.

Then, slowly but surely, each small light will brighten the darkness within this world, making it a better place for future generations to come.

Wouldn't that be a wonderful thing?

Wouldn't that be the ultimate goal?

Maybe The Creature isn't so bad after all ... if it can make us see the darkness within ourselves.

# Epilogue

Olivia readjusted her prison uniform, squeezing the small item in her pocket with her left hand. She'd adapted surprisingly well to prison life. She'd made friends with many of the other prisoners but had stayed clear of Lucy and Trisha even though the first time they saw her they'd rushed over, demanding to know why she was there. It seemed old habits didn't die hard after all, even in lock up. They were still a couple of nosey neighbours, and they would eventually be injured or killed inside the prison walls if they weren't careful.

No, it wasn't the end she'd envisioned for herself, but she knew she deserved it, so was happy to pay her dues. She'd started up a book club and had come to be known as the grandmother of the prison, which she found highly amusing, considering there were several prisoners who had at least two decades on her: they were in for life. She'd been told her sentence was fifteen years, ten with good behaviour, so there was a chance she'd live to see the outside world again, and that filled her with more hope and determination than anything.

Brooke and Jordan had already been to visit several times. She hated putting them out. It was a long way to travel for Brooke, who was now six months pregnant and growing bigger by the day. Her severe sickness had subsided, and she was finally enjoying her pregnancy and beginning to put on weight, after having lost so much during her hospitalisation. At least there was a chance Olivia would be able to see her grandchild outside of these walls one day.

Mary kept herself distant from Olivia. A lot of the prisoners kept their distance from Mary. She wasn't a well-liked woman, and the guards often gave her a hard time.

Mary's cell was where Olivia was heading now. She'd never visited Mary before, but she knew where her cell was located. Mary very rarely left it, other than to attend meals and walk around the yard. Olivia was told she preferred to spend time by herself rather than face the other female prisoners and guards.

Olivia clutched the item tighter in her hand as she rounded the corner. She peered her head round the open door, knocking on it.

Mary looked up from reading her book and smiled when she saw Olivia. 'Well, well … aren't you a sight for sore eyes. I wondered how long it would take for you to come and visit me.'

'Hello, Mary.'

'You've been inside a few months now, right? How are you finding it?'

Olivia stepped further into the cell. 'Really, Mary, you want to make small talk?'

'Isn't that why you're here? It's not like there's much else to do.'

Olivia smiled. 'No, I'm not here to make small talk.'

'Then why are you here?'

'To make peace.'

Mary frowned as she placed her book on her bed and rose to her feet, never once breaking eye contact with Olivia. 'Make ... peace,' she echoed slowly.

'That's right. And I come bearing a gift. One of the other women gave it to me, but I'm afraid I don't care for the taste, and I remember how much you loved this particular flavour as a child.' Olivia pulled her left hand out of her pocket and held out a small, square sweet.

It was a Starburst, the red one.

Mary smiled. 'Weren't they called Opal Fruits back in our day?'

'Indeed, they were,' replied Olivia.

'The red ones were always my favourite,' said Mary.

Olivia kept her palm open, her hand outstretched to Mary. 'I remember.'

Mary took the sweet and unwrapped it. It wasn't often the prisoners had sweets and treats, only if family or friends brought them in, and Mary had neither. 'Why do you want to make peace now? What's the catch?' she asked.

'There's no catch, Mary. We are both going to be in here for a while. You for the rest of your life, and me for ... Well, hopefully, I can make it out of here with good behaviour. Despite our pasts, I'd like to put aside our differences and at least be civil, so we don't fear running into each other in the halls. They are quite small, after all.'

Mary smirked. 'I'm not afraid of you, Olivia.'

'Nor I of you.'

Mary popped the sweet into her mouth and bit down, smiling. 'Just as delicious as I remember. Takes me take to my childhood, not that it's a time I like to recall very often. But, for what it's worth ... thank you.'

Olivia nodded.

Mary smiled back.

Then she coughed and Olivia watched as her face froze. Terror swam behind her eyes as she grasped her throat. She reached out to Olivia for help, but Olivia stepped backwards, allowing Mary to collapse to the ground where she began convulsing, jerking and frothing at the mouth.

It didn't take long.

Olivia watched as Mary took her last breath.

She left the room.

Peanut oil had been tricky to get into the prison, but thankfully Graham had offered a helping hand with that. It had been easier than she'd expected to inject the oil into Mary's favourite sweet.

Finally, her conscience was clear, and she'd done it for no other reason than to be at peace within herself. Mary could never hurt another child ever again.

*******************************

Want to be kept up to date with my next book release?
Sign up to my newsletter via my website.
www.jessicahuntleyauthor.com
*******************************

Order my next psychological thriller today!

Perfect for readers who enjoy female revenge stories, twists, and humour.

Out on 1st April 2024!

# Did you like this book?

I really hope you enjoyed reading The Darkness That Came Before, the third and final novel in "The Darkness" series.

If you have, please consider leaving me a review on Amazon and Goodreads, share a review on your social media pages and tag me, share my book to any book clubs you may be a part of or recommend my book to friends and family.

Reviews are massively important, especially to self-published authors. They help find other readers who may enjoy the book and spread the word to a wider audience.

**For a FREE Novella – My Bad Self, sign up for my monthly newsletter at:**

www.jessicahuntleyauthor.com

# Connect with Jessica

Find and connect with me online via the following platforms.

Sign up to my email list via my website to be notified of future books and receive my monthly author newsletter:

www.jessicahuntleyauthor.com

Follow me on Facebook: Jessica Huntley - Author - @jessica.reading.writing

Follow me on Instagram: @jessica_reading_writing

Follow me on Twitter: @jess_read_write

Follow me on TikTok: @jessica_reading_writing

Follow me on Goodreads: jessica_reading_writing

Follow me on my Amazon Author Page - Jessica Huntley

www.ingramcontent.com/pod-product-compliance
Lightning Source LLC
Chambersburg PA
CBHW011601210726
48287CB00012BC/2674